I0527673

Debatable Decisions

BY

HERBERT JAXON

Grosvenor House
Publishing Limited

All rights reserved
Copyright © Herbert Jaxon, 2025

The right of Herbert Jaxon to be identified as the author of this
work has been asserted in accordance with Section 78
of the Copyright, Designs and Patents Act 1988

The book cover is copyright to Herbert Jaxon

This book is published by
Grosvenor House Publishing Ltd
Link House
140 The Broadway, Tolworth, Surrey, KT6 7HT.
www.grosvenorhousepublishing.co.uk

This book is sold subject to the conditions that it shall not, by way of
trade or otherwise, be lent, resold, hired out or otherwise circulated
without the author's or publisher's prior consent in any form of
binding or cover other than that in which it is published and
without a similar condition including this condition being
imposed on the subsequent purchaser.

A CIP record for this book
is available from the British Library

Paperback ISBN 978-1-83615-327-6

For Jen

BY THE SAME AUTHOR

Secondhand Worms, Grosvenor House Publishing, 2024

WHAT THEY SAID ABOUT MR JAXON'S WORK.....

My wife actually *laughed* at one of your poems! *(A man in a pub.)*

That poem you sent me was in bloody French! You *poseur*! *(A friend of Mr Jaxon, thanking him for his Christmas card.)*

Hey! There was no poem in my card this year! *(This same friend, the following Christmas, having discovered that Mr Jaxon had considerately deleted him from the jaxonian 'poetry' distribution list.)*

You write surprisingly stilted English…. *(A tutor at Durham University, engaging in the often thankless task of trying to educate Mr Jaxon.)*

I think your rhyme schemes are belaboured rather than contrived – but they are contrived as well. *(An imaginary friend[1] of Mr Jaxon, offering encouragement.)*

If you had cut out all the poems that ought to have been cut out there would have been none left in your book! *(The same lady, perhaps offering her services as editrix.)*

When you revise your poems, they don't get better; they just become different. *(Her again. Bless her.)*

Your most debatable decision was to include some of those poems! *(All right. We've got the idea. Thank you.)*

Some of Herbert's poems are *quite* good. *(A different man in a different pub.)*

---

1 The lady is real. It is their friendship that is imaginary.

Pas mal pour un Anglais… *(A French friend of a French friend of Mr Jaxon.)*

That last poem you sent me did go on a bit…. *(Yet another friend of Mr Jaxon.)*

Hey! There was no poem in the last card you sent me! *(This same friend a few weeks later, on receipt of her birthday card, indicating that it is impossible to please any of the people any of the time.)*

Rimbaud stopped writing poetry when he was aged 19. So did I. Unfortunately, I wrote *Secondhand Worms* after I was 19. *(Herbert Jaxon.)*

CONTENTS

INTRODUCTION

This is a work of fiction, masquerading as an autobiography. Everything herein, including this statement, is a lie[2].

---

2 The Liar Paradox. Quoted often, since ancient times.

x i

CHAPTER 0 : NAUGHTY[3]!

I was up in town on Sunday, but it wasn't until Monday
That I felt I was recovering from the shock
Of an incident that galled me – well, in truth, it quite appalled me,
And my faith in human nature took a knock.

I'm not normally umbrageous but I witnessed some outrageous
Bad behaviour that reduced a girl to tears;
I could never have conceived it, and I'd scarcely have believed it
If I hadn't seen it all, with my own ears.

I was browsing in a bookshop – that one just behind the cook shop –
And was leafing through the dirty books on show,
When the girl behind the counter chanced to suffer an encounter
With a proper cad – a nasty so and so…

Early doors the guy in question offered no outward suggestion
Of the dirty trick he was about to pull;
His demeanour was quite charming, and his mien wholly disarming,
While his weasel words were wrapped in cotton wool.

He was erudite and pensive, and I deemed him inoffensive,
As he greeted the young lady with a smile;
It was easy overhearing what he said, without appearing
To be listening in on his Lothario style.

After touching on the beauty of that lovely little cutie,
He informed her he 'would like to make her day'.
At his words she reddened slightly, but she listened on politely,
And she didn't tell the rat to go away.

---

3 Wouldn't it be awful, Reader, if the scene that follows were to be repeated in
every book shop throughout the land? Please don't ever consider doing anything
similar.

I was waiting for crescendo to his blatant innuendo,
But instead he told her that he was on course
To create a book collection that would be, without exception,
Quite the finest of its kind in Gerrards Cross.

He proceeded next to docket, from a file pulled from his pocket,
All the books he thought he needed as a start;
There was literature and science, mindfulness and self-reliance,
Origami, culture, history, sport and art.

He went on to cite in detail all the titles she could retail,
Stressing just how much commission she would earn;
What to me seemed rather rash was that he offered to pay in cash, as
If to flaunt the fact that he had cash to burn.

While that reprobate was rapping our poor dollybird was flapping,
Tripping back and forth, with books in either arm,
Which she stacked up on the counter, and on surfaces around her,
In unsteady piles, that caused her some alarm.

Let me try to give a flavour of the sort of spiel he gave her,
While describing all the books he said he'd buy;
But it won't be word for word because, although I saw and heard, he
Spoke too fast for me to make notes on the sly.

"Give me first *Great Expectation*s; Isaac Asimov's *Foundations*;
"And the hardbacks of *Tom Jones*, and *William Tell*;
"And a volume of *The Howling*, all the *Potters*, J K Rowling,
"And a copy of *The Crucible* as well.

"I want everything by Hardy, Harold Pinter's *Birthday Party*,
"Crusoe (Robinson), by Daniel Defoe;
"I need something by Anne Brontë; a critique of Carlo Ponti;
"Plus the omnibus of Edgar Allan Poe.

"After that I want a Bible; and a tome on criminal libel;
"And a copy of *The Catcher in the Rye*;
"Next I'll go for *War and Peace*, and then for *Beauty and the
          Beast*, and
"Pickwick Papers, Madame Bovary, and *The Fly*...

"Jean-Paul Sartre, and Camus... *À la recherche du temps perdu*...
"Pride and Prejudice, David Copperfield, and more;
"Becketts's thing on *Pricks and Kicks*; *Don Quixote, Moby Dick*;
"Sons and Lovers... *Tartuffe*... *Nineteen Eighty-Four*...

"Then *The Taming of the Shrew*, and all the plays of Chekhov,
          too, and
"All the *Fables* by Monsieur de La Fontaine;
"Give me, please, *The Ipcress File*, and then (of course) *Death on
          the Nile,* and
"Then the one that Steinbeck called *Of Mice and Men*.

"Next, a guidebook on Sumatra; and then the lyrics of Sinatra;
"And some books with pretty pictures on the cover!
"Then a book on Crete's topography, and a book of soft pornography,
"And that thing about old *Lady Thingy's Lover*.

"Have you something on theosophy? I want several on philosophy:
"Bertrand Russell, Friedrich Nietzsche, and Karl Marx;
"Modern Russians? Boris Blinkov? Any others you can think of?
"Then some books on quantum physics – quarks[4] and quarks[5].

"Desmond Morris' *Human Zoo*; Heller's gem, *Catch Twenty-two*;
"And a copy of *Rebecca*, and *Jane Eyre*;
"And a book of *Aesop's Fables*, and then *Annie of Green Gables*,
"And then Alistair MacLean's *Where Eagles Dare*!

---

4 Pronounced to rhyme with 'forks'.

5 Pronounced to rhyme with 'parks'.

"I want all the works of Tennyson; *Subtle ways of cooking Venison*;
"*Peter Pan*; and William Shakespeare's *Winter's Tale*;
"Then a guidebook on New Delhi; all the poems of Percy Shelley;
"And a book on how to brew your own real ale!"

Still the scoundrel wasn't done, he asked for *How The West Was Won*; he
Also wanted *Robin Hood*, and *Westward Ho!*,
And a copy of *Othello*; and of *How to play the 'Cello*;
Frankenstein, and *Ulysses*, and *Ivanhoe*.

Then he said: "I think I'd better take a copy of that *Letter
"From America* – Ally Cook – if that's still out;
"Give me *Teach Yourself Swahili*; and *The Wit of Denis Healey*;
"And a copy of the Beatles' book called *Shout!*"

Then: "I need *Lord of the Flies*, and, in addition, *Bridge of Spies*, and
"Then the one about that cabin, and Uncle Tom;
"And *The Count of Monte Cristo*; and a *Guide to San Francisco*;
"Dr Strangelove – How I grew to love the bomb!

"I'll take *Huckleberry Finn*, and P D James' *Original Sin*, and
"Koestler's novel called *Arrival and Departure*;
"*Peaky Blinders*, and *The Scream*, and then *A Midsummer Night's
        Dream*,
"And (if I must) I'll take just one by Jeffrey Archer.

"Lewis Carroll; *Christmas Carol*; have you *Three Men and a Barrel*?
"Or that one about the hunchback, and the bells?
"Then some comedy by The Goons? One on how to play the spoons?
"Then a nicely bound collection of H G Wells?

"I want one on mathematics; one on treatments for rheumatics;
"And an omnibus compendium of Zola;
"One on animals at the zoo; and one on trees – and flowers, too; and
"One on cheeses – camembert to gorgonzola!

"Got a good encyclopaedia? Or a book on social media?
"Or some heavy sh*t on quasars, and black holes?
"One with paintings by Picasso? One on sculpture? Michelangelo?
"One with photos of Jeff Astle scoring goals?

"Have you got *Dennis the Menace*? Or *The Greats of Modern
        Tennis*?
"Or that one that tells you how to win at darts?
"Half a dozen books on chess and, well (as if you couldn't guess) I
"Need a book on each of all the martial arts.

"Did I mention *Captain Hook*? I'll take a cryptic crossword book; I
"Also need both *Little Women* and *Little Men*;
"Then *The Life of George the Third*; and next, *To Kill a
        Mockingbird*; and
"I want all the verse that flowed from Byron's pen.

"That new novel, *Wednesday's Child*; and all the works of Oscar
        Wilde; and
"*Coral Island*, *Grapes of Wrath,* and *Mansfield Park*;
"Then I'll take *Whisky Galore* (or did I ask for that before?) And
"Shirley Hughes's novel, *Whistling in the Dark*.

"Next *Astronomy*, *Stars Above Us*; did I mention *Sons and Lovers*?
"I need everything you've got in stock by Keats;
"Then: *Resuscitate the Drowning*; all the works of Robert Browning;
"And some guides to where the epicurean eats…"

So, his list went on and on, and though I needed to be gone, I
Just kept listening in, in captive fascination;
But when finally he was done I was so glad I hadn't run,
Because I caught the rotter's waspish peroration.

Pretty miss was quite unable to stack everything on the table,
So she'd dumped them on the floor in clumsy piles,
Stretching right up to the ceiling, which had left the poor girl
      reeling –
That great heap of books just seemed to run for miles!

She was puffing now, and blowing, her exhaustion clearly showing,
When the rascal reached the bottom of his list;
He confirmed, to her relief, that it was finally his belief, that
He was sure as eggs that nothing had been missed.

Then begins the lengthy business, which I thought might take till
      Christmas,
As the totty starts to tally up the bill,
Which she already prefigures could well run to seven figures,
And she's not sure there's enough room in her till!

With the girl still calculating, Creepy Customer stood waiting,
As if watching for a chance to interrupt;
And his sliminess was abject, when he chose to show the aspect
Of his character that was nasty and corrupt.

"Sorry, miss, I'm such a cretin! There is one book I'm forgettin'!
"Get me *Secondhand Worms*, if you would be so kind!
"It's in earthy Anglo-Saxon, by the *flâneur*, Herbert Jaxon –
"Can't imagine how I let it slip my mind!"

P'rhaps a trifle too bathetic, and not quite apologetic,
Missie didn't try to mitigate his shock;
Maybe greater tact was needed, but she artlessly conceded
That she didn't have that paperback in stock.

But she offered soothing ointment, which might salve his
       disappointment:
She was *sure* she could oblige him pretty soon,
For, if she surmised correctly, if she ordered it directly,
It would reach her by the following afternoon…

Not a chance!!! That bloke was livid!!! His vocabulary vivid!!!
His rejoinder – crude, inelegant and crass:
"Listen, b*tch!!! These are my terms!!! If you ain't got
       Secondhand Worms,
"You can keep the rest, and shove them up your chimney!!!!!!!!!!!!"

CHAPTER 1 : THE END

Good morrow, gentle Readerman,
Or -Lady, if that be your glory;
Sit back and savour, if you can,
A worthless wretch's sad, life story.

The end is, simply, not to bore ya
With dreary stuff, so, if you'll let me,
I'll play down all my paranoia…
(Though everyone *is* out to get me…)

I've had some bad times, and some good,
And some that in between them fell;
Sometimes I knew just where I stood,
But sometimes, it was hard to tell.

Herein's 'most every jot and tittle,
However bad, however rotten;
But, of the good times there is little –
Perhaps it's those bits I've forgotten.

Countless lacunae dog the text,
Forgotten moments – there're lots,
But where I'm doubtful what came next
I've made it up, to join the dots.

Maybe I've faked a scene or two,
To plug the gaps, but life's a b*tch;
The other bits could well be true:
You be the judge of which is which.

You'll notice, when you peek inside,
As this biopic limps along,
Whenever I'm called on to decide,
I usually get the decision wrong.

Some chapters are in stilted prose,
And some in convoluted verse,
But why that's so, God only knows:
You be the judge of which is worse.

And please do not expect to see
Events recorded chronological,
For that would, sadly, not be me –
I'm never in the slightest logical.

So time will jump about somewhat,
From start to finish, right or wrong,
And, when I reach a boring slot,
I'll cut it short, and move along.

The end is just to entertain,
But ours is not to reason why,
So don't expect to use your brain,
For life's a b*tch… and then you die…

CHAPTER 2 : CAREERS ADVICE[6]

I am a qualified medical man;
I passed a hard exam;
They gave me a certificate –
What a clever boy I am!

It took me years to qualify,
But I don't really mind;
My course was soporific, and
My lecturers were kind.

They showed us lots of diagrams
Of bruises, boils, and phlegm,
And told us what we ought to do
If we saw one of them.

There was no time for 'practicals',
Or patients who 'felt queer';
We were too busy taking notes,
And drinking lots of beer.

I'd always thought a doctor's life
Was spent in quiet repose,
Just taking people's temperature
And counting babies' toes,

---

6   Offered to my grandson, whose parents are both doctors, when he was about to take his finals.

But suddenly the moment came,
When I passed my exam,
And I got my certificate –
(What a clever boy I am!)

Then all at once my world had changed,
Which caught me unprepared;
I couldn't cope with what came next
And, frankly, I was scared.

They sent me to a hospital,
Where anyone could call,
And when the patients wandered in
It wasn't nice at all.

For all of them had broken legs,
Or bunions, coughs and sneezes,
And I suspected some might have
Unsociable diseases.

I think they had a blinking cheek,
I'm sure you will agree,
To drop in when they felt unwell
And breathe their germs on me.

A few were even worse than that –
Their maladies were legion;
Some even dropped their trousers, and
Exposed their nether region.

Imagine how *they* would have felt –
Their selfishness still rankles –
If I'd gone round *their* houses with
My khakis round my ankles.

I hadn't gone to medical school
For folks to treat me thus;
I'm one who likes the quiet life,
With minimum of fuss.

I only took the blinking job
Because I thought I might
Soon enter private practice, and
Fleece everyone in sight.

So, on day two I'd had enough
Of all I've just discussed;
I handed in my stethoscope
And stomped out in disgust.

The waiting lists are longer now,
Because there's one doc fewer,
But I've found me another job:
I now work down the sewer.

I shovel sewage all day long,
And stuff that's even cr*ppier,
But people keep their trousers on
And I'm a whole lot happier.

The sewage rots your shoes a bit,
But I don't give two hoots,
As when you've worked there fifteen years
They give you rubber boots.

So, if you need careers advice,
Beware the choice you make:
Don't end up choosing medicine,
For that's a big mistake.

If someone tells you otherwise,
Just tell them to forget it –
Come, join me down the sewer-pipe!
I'm sure you won't regret it!

And if you're wavering, even now,
You can't ignore this factor:
I'm *trained* to tell you what to do,
So… *Trust me! I'm a doctor*!

When I look back on medicine
It fills me with despair,
But when I'm down the sewer it's like
A breath of clean, fresh air!

CHAPTER 3 : THE PRESENT

As anyone who knows me knows, I am not one for moralising. I am not really a moralising person. 'If they're old enough, and want to do it, and it doesn't hurt anyone, let them do it' is more or less my motto. Just so long as they don't expect me and the rest of the silent majority to pay for their rehab afterwards. But there is one human activity that is so pernicious, so evil and destructive of the nation's wellbeing, that, despite what I've just said, I do feel obliged to offer a cautionary word of advice to anyone who might feel tempted. That wicked activity is, of course, shopping. Do *not* do it. Just say no. If someone asks you to go shopping with them, just say no, and walk away. You will feel all the better for it afterwards. I already feel better for having shared that with you.

No good ever came of shopping. It is a futile pastime that saps the energy and destroys the will to live, not just of shoppers but also of those they are married to. Shopping's advocates will tell you the opposite, of course, but don't be deceived. If you don't believe that shopping is the devil's pastime, just consider what has to be done after you have finished shopping: the stuff you have just bought will need to be taken back to the shop! I know, it's silly, but that's what shoppers do! They buy stuff, and then they take it back to the shop! Why would anyone do that? Don't ask me – ask a shopper! Once, when I remarked in passing to my dear wife, Patience, that *Marks & Spencer* had opened a new retail outlet near where I was working, her reaction was: "That's excellent! Now, when I buy something from *M&S* you can take it back for me on your way to work!"

Make no mistake, shopping is a despicable, dissolute, immoral, decadent and sinful pursuit that is best left alone. Despite my warning, however, I know there will still be those who are wavering and I am therefore prepared to share a cautionary tale, to be kept in the back of the mind if ever temptation should raise its ugly head.

Before we start I must set the scene by vouchsafing a piece of personal information, for you need to be aware that I hardly ever wear cufflinks. I am simply not a cufflinks person. I have nothing in particular against cufflinks, or against those who wear them, other than that I would probably put cufflinks in the same category as jewellery, and I cannot see the point of jewellery either. Furthermore, I tend to roll up my sleeves, so cufflinks are a bit of a nuisance as well as being pointless. All in all, if cufflinks had never been invented I think I could probably have survived.

In spite of this I probably own half a dozen pairs. I recall that I have sometimes received a pair of cufflinks as a present from generous friends. I also remember my son-in-law buying me rather a smart pair one Christmas – Homer Simpson on one sleeve and Bart Simpson on the other – and I have actually worn those particular cufflinks more than once. But I cannot imagine actually going out and buying a pair of cufflinks for myself. No way. For one thing, that would require me to go shopping, and, as you may have surmised, I don't willingly go shopping. If there is one thing I hate more than marzipan, and reality television programmes, and porridge, and arriving late, and those who cheat at football or cricket, and gin[7], it is shopping.

To the best of my knowledge, I have never willingly gone shopping. I am just not a shopping person. Patience occasionally insists that I accompany her on shopping expeditions, but whenever this happens I try to ensure that she knows I am complying under protest. It was, coincidentally, on a shopping expedition entered into under duress that I bought a pair of cufflinks. I should never have done it. For the avoidance of doubt I

---

7 Sorry. I lied about the gin.

will repeat that this chapter is included in this chronicle solely as a warning to those who feel they are on the point of doing something as utterly stupid and anti-social as shopping, and to warn them off. Do **NOT** do it. No good will come of it and you will end up hating yourself for ever. I know I do.

It was some time in the 1980s – I cannot be more precise – and my wife and I were 'shopping together in Watford'. For us, 'shopping together in Watford' has always followed the same pattern; you might almost call it the 'Jaxon ten-point shopping plan'. First, I drive us to Watford and park in a multi-storey car park. Second, Patience tells me that she needs only three-quarters of an hour to complete her purchases, and leaves me to my own devices to fill the intervening time. Third, she arranges to meet me at a specific location, usually near the entrance to the multi-storey car park at a precise time, when she will be ready to go home. Fourth, she goes off shopping, while I go and look in the bookshops. Fifth, forty minutes later I turn up at our prearranged meeting place. Sixth, Patience isn't there; she never is. Seventh, I wait for her. Eighth, several hours pass. Ninth, Patience turns up eventually. Tenth, we drive home, with my teeth grinding and smoke billowing from my ears.

In Watford, the entrance to the multi-story car park where we normally leave our vehicle is situated close to a jeweller's shop, *Wilfrid Waddle, Jeweller's* by name, and on the occasion under examination, waiting for my wife, and bored out of my tiny mind, I decided to peek in at the display in the jeweller's window. There was nothing much of interest – I didn't expect there would be – but something on which my eye alighted was a display card bearing an arrangement of silver cufflinks. There were some rather interesting shapes – aeroplanes, motor cars, items of sporting equipment, kitchen utensils, that sort of thing – and a set that caught my eye looked just like the heads of a pair of heavy, old-fashioned bathroom taps. There were no spouts or anything as unsightly and obscene as a faucet; it was just a pair of ordinary, old-fashioned, four-pronged tap heads, the type you might have found in any bathroom in England in the 1950s. Each head was about half an inch across, and one tap was engraved with the letter 'H' while its fellow sported the letter 'C'. I presumed that these initials represented 'hot' and 'cold'.

As I gazed at those rather ordinary cufflinks a strange thought occurred to me. If I had been the wife of Henry Cooper, I could have bought those cufflinks for my husband and passed them off as a monogrammed pair! H for Henry, and C for Cooper! *Drôle*, or what?

I have noticed that this is the kind of bizarre and outlandish thing that shopping will do to the mind. Here was I, a strapping, six-foot, fifteen stone, God-fearing male thinking myself into the person of a diminutive female and wondering what I ought to be buying my husband for his birthday! It made no sense at all but, as I may have mentioned more than once, too much shopping has a deleterious effect on the faculties and causes no end of problems in later life – hallucinations, incontinence, and herpes too, I shouldn't wonder. And then, as if to verify my worst fears, a second thought occurred to me: I could equally have purchased those cufflinks for my brother-in-law, for HC are his initials too! He even had a convenient birthday coming up.

Fortunately, my mind eventually moved on to consideration of weightier matters, and later still, after it had grown quite dark, and respectable stores like *Wilfrid Waddle, Jeweller's* had begun to shut up shop for the night, Patience appeared at my elbow, weighed down with purchases, and I was able to drive her home. Unless I am grossly mistaken the return journey to the Chalfonts, where we were living at the time, was uneventful and encompassed nothing that might be considered remotely of interest here, but during the course of the same evening, owing no doubt to some kind of aberration, probably brought on by shopping, I chanced by way of conversation to mention those accursed cufflinks, and to remark on the fact that they happened to bear my relative's initials.

"Why didn't you buy them?" asked Patience menacingly. I have noticed that with anything associated with shopping there is always a hint of menace. "It's his birthday next month. They would have amused him."

Why didn't I buy them? The question hit me like a damp flannel on the end of a long pole whacked unceremoniously under my kilt, and I realised I had no immediate answer. If I'd thought about it I would have realised that questions like that don't require an answer but I didn't stop to think. Why hadn't I bought them indeed? They weren't expensive – probably no more than £30 or £40, and probably reduced in the sale, which was probably one of the things that had caught my eye in the first place. The novelty value of those cufflinks had appealed to me at the time I noticed them, and I'd suddenly found it mildly appealing that they would have suited my relative, and might have raised a smile. Soon I discovered, to my shame, albeit at Patience's suggestion, that I was even managing to persuade myself that I ought to have bought them! Uncanny. Still, it was too late now, for we were at home, so no use crying over spilt kerosene. In reply to my wife's question I made some kind of noise that I hoped would encapsulate all this jumble of thoughts that were tumbling through my head and assumed that the subject would be dropped for ever.

I was wrong, for she would have none of it. "Nonsense!" she said. "If you want those cufflinks you can go back to Watford and get them tomorrow!"

Go back to Watford and get them tomorrow? What? Drive all the way back to Watford? Why would I want to do that? Watford lay a good fifteen miles away by road, and, as I have said, it wasn't as if

I was particularly enamoured of those cufflinks. I don't wear cufflinks. I am not a cufflinks person. I didn't know if my brother-in-law was either. Why would I want to go all the way back to Watford to buy something I had no need of and didn't want?

I probably made an effort to put these thoughts into words, but still Patience would have none of it.

"Nonsense!" she said again. "If you want them, go back and buy them!"

"But I *don't* want them."

"Then why did you mention them?"

Sentiments of this nature flew back and forth for some minutes and, to bring the debate to an end, I eventually heard myself agreeing to do as my wife proposed. But I don't wish to place all the blame for what subsequently transpired on her shoulders. I suppose if I really hadn't been ever so *slightly* interested in those wretched cufflinks I wouldn't have capitulated in so cowardly a fashion, and wouldn't have agreed to make the long trek back into Watford on the morrow, but eventually I said I would go. I assume I must either have been more taken by those miserable cufflinks than I would care to admit or else I had temporarily taken leave of my senses.

Whatever the reason, the next day found me back in the car on the road to Watford, intent on doing a bit more 'shopping'. Uncanny. My wife offered to come with me but I said no. There are some things a man has to do on his own and this was one of them. Having parked the car in the same car park I had used the previous day I lost no time in hurrying to the store that lay just across from the exit. Reassuringly I found that *Wilfrid Waddle, Jeweller's,* was still in the same place I had left it the day before, and I made straight for the window where I had seen the cufflinks and gawped in. Calamity! They weren't there! The display card where they had been so proudly exhibited not eighteen hours beforehand was still in place, and the cufflinks that were so artfully fashioned in the shapes of motorcars, aeroplanes and gardening tools were still affixed to the card, but in the place where the tap heads had been nestling there were now just two gaping holes! Since the time of my last visit someone had obviously come in and bought them! Perhaps it was Henry Cooper's birthday. If only I had known that before I left home.

I know now that I ought to have turned round and gone home. My journey had been wasted and I should simply have admitted it. But inexplicably I lingered. I probably couldn't accept that all that time and effort had been so summarily wasted, and I felt I had to do something to justify my very existence on this planet. I therefore *went into the shop!* Insanely I sought to rationalise this ridiculous course of action by inventing some question that might properly be put to the shopkeeper. Perhaps he had another set of the tap head cufflinks in the back of the store. I realised already that this was unlikely. If he had had a duplicate set in the back those would obviously have been the cufflinks he would have sold, leaving the display models to decorate the window. Incongruously, I decided to go in and ask him anyway.

On entering the shop I looked for a suitable assistant. As in a pharmacy, I would have preferred, if possible, to conduct my business with a male assistant, not necessarily Mr Waddle himself, of course, but a man of about sixty or seventy years old, who had been round the block a few times and might be expected to understand the needs of a forty-something-year-old gentleman who had an aversion to shopping but nevertheless needed to make an enquiry about an object that he couldn't see on display and didn't necessarily wish to purchase. I have found that most shop assistants can be expected to have difficulty with that kind of customer, but the elderly male assistant frequently has experience of such animals and can often take them in his stride, which is why I went looking for one. However, my luck was out. On the day in question *Wilfrid Waddle* did not appear to have any salesmen of that particular vintage in stock. The choice was between a lady in her late fifties, a pretty young female who looked about fifteen but was probably at least five years older, and a very smart young gentleman in suit and tie, who looked about twenty but was probably at least six years younger. My heart sank.

Actually, the choice wasn't even as wide as the one I have just described because I now noticed that the elderly lady was already tied up showing a tray of engagement rings to a youngish couple who were the only other customers in the shop. I was therefore stuck with either Miss Lollipop or Mr Tailor's Dummy, and frankly, the prospect of dealing with either one of them filled me with dread. I hoped that the feeling would be mutual, and that on seeing me approach both young assistants would suddenly remember that they had urgent business elsewhere and scurry off, leaving me free to depart the establishment with dignity. But I had no such luck. The young lady shot me a winning smile and politely asked whether she could be of assistance, while the young gentleman initially took a bold half-step forward, presumably to indicate that he too stood ready to serve, followed by a chivalrous, half-step backward, presumably to concede that any commission on a sale that might be made to this prospective customer was already the young lady's for the taking, if she wanted it.

The poor guy; I immediately recognised the syndrome. Menopausal male customers were obviously in the habit of flocking to this young lady like flies to a honey pot, and the young gentleman had learned to accept it, for there was nothing he could do about it. Such is life. I had noticed before that, given the choice, when in shops old blokes often prefer to be served by young ladies. Goodness only knows why they do, but they do.

Happily, Herbert Jaxon is not cut from that particular cloth. Quickly assessing the situation I made a rapid decision and opted to do my business with Mr Dummy. To that end, ignoring both her opening gambit and the not inconsiderable charms of Miss Lollipop, which were prominently on display for all to see, I addressed myself direct to the young gentleman. As I may have intimated, Herbert Jaxon is no ordinary old bloke.

Actually, there was also method in my madness. This was a jeweller's shop, after all, and I had no doubt that the young female assistant simply *adored* working there, surrounded as she was for eight hours a day by all those diamonds and baubles. She would obviously know everything there was to know about old Mr Waddle's business, and be delighted to talk about it, and if I allowed myself to be drawn in it would be difficult for me to extricate myself from her clutches without at least putting down a deposit on a £60,000 emerald necklace – or worse. I was equally convinced, on the other hand, that the young gentleman would know absolutely nothing at all about jewellery. He would be working there only because applications for employment at the local sportswear outfitters were oversubscribed, and this was the best he could do before a job at *Toys R Us* or *Tie Rack* became available. I therefore addressed myself with confidence directly to the young lad; this wouldn't take long and I would be out of there in seconds.

By now I had prepared what I would say to the assistant and even worked out how the conversation between us was likely to develop. What could go wrong? I envisaged an exchange along the following lines.

"Good morning, stout yeoman. I spotted some silver cufflinks in your window yesterday, shaped like tap heads, but they don't appear to be there now. Have they been sold?"

"If they are not on display, sir, I suppose they must have been."

"Oh dear. I don't suppose you have any more in stock do you?"

"'Fraid not, sir. What we have is what you see!"

"Oh dear. Good day."

"Good day, sir. Have a good one!"

And, like the snow in April, Herbert Jaxon would melt away!

As I approached the young gentleman the young lady assistant took her rejection remarkably well, I thought, although she refused to withdraw, as I had hoped she might, and she stood disconcertingly close to Mr Dummy as I prepared to address him. This threw me a little – I hoped she wouldn't try to butt in as I was making good my escape – but it only threw me a little, and I determined to press on as if she weren't there. Besides, sooner or later she was bound to feel a need to fiddle with something, or rearrange something, and then she would be gone, so I saw no need to anticipate problems prematurely.

"Good morning," I said, directly to the young man in a suit.

"Good morning, sir," he riposted gallantly.

"I spotted some silver cufflinks in your window yesterday, shaped like tap heads, but they don't appear to be in there now. Have they been sold?"

"Perhaps they have, sir," said the adolescent gentleman, moving swiftly from behind his counter and joining me in the body of the shop. "Will you be good enough to show me which window they were in?"

Oh dear. He had already departed from the script, and I am hopeless at improvisation.

"This one," I said, as the lad followed me outside into the main shopping arcade, and we stopped in front of one of Mr Waddle's windows.

"Hmm, I see," he said knowledgeably. "The *Portland*. Shaped like bath-tap heads, you say? Yes, they do appear to have gone, don't they? Very popular, they've been, the *Portland*. There are none of the other shapes, I suppose, that take your fancy?"

"No, I'm afraid not," I assured him. "Tap heads or nothing, I'm afraid! I guess I am just a bit of a tap heads person! Ah well, can't be helped..... Thank you for your troub....."

"No trouble at all, sir," he cut in. "If you will just accompany me back into the shop I will be happy to order you a pair."

"No, that's quite all right," I assured him. "I don't want to put you to that troub....."

"No trouble at all, sir," he insisted for a second time. "If I order them today and if they have them in stock we can have them here for you by the end of the week!"

I hesitated. I no longer wanted the beastly things, of course, and I had no desire to return to Watford a third time in order to collect them, but the lad seemed so eager to please and was being so helpful that I didn't like to disappoint him without letting him down gently. Perhaps I could pretend that I was a foreign criminal who was being deported to Murmansk the following day, and would therefore be unable to return to Watford and collect the cufflinks, even if he went out of his way and ordered them for me. I dismissed the idea at once, however. Not carrying the Gatwick-Tromsø-Murmansk passenger timetable in my head, and so not knowing if there was a suitable service that he could verify if he opted to check my story, I decided instead that the best policy might be to come clean and tell the truth.

"No, *please* don't go to that trouble," I said. "I noticed that the ones you have on display are reduced in price, and I assume that anything you order will have to be paid for at the full price. I don't think I want to pay £50 for them, so I think I'll just leave it, if it's all the same to you. Thank you for your troub....."

"Not at all, sir," retorted the b*st*rd annoyingly. "The sale doesn't finish for another fortnight and everything in the *Portland* range is reduced to £29.99, as the card says. Anything I order for you will be offered at the price shown." And he smiled like a veteran second-hand car salesman, who senses a sucker.

"No, that's OK," I said hurriedly. "You said they might not have any more of them in stock...."

"Well, we[8] can only ring them and find out, can't we, sir? I will be happy to do that for you and it won't take a moment. Please!" And he crooked his right elbow, placing his right hand close to my shoulder and extending his left arm at full stretch in the direction of the interior of the shop, and then stood like a policeman directing the traffic as he ushered me back into his clutches. I saw no escape and meekly allowed myself to be propelled, as if by an invisible magnet, back into the store. What else could I do?

Once we were inside the shop again the lad was efficiency itself. He skipped nimbly around to his side of the counter and, from the shelf beneath, produced an expensive-looking, glossy brochure with a dark blue cover bearing the insignia *Portland Range* in shiny silver flowery lettering. After riffling expertly through its leaves he soon discovered what he was looking for and turned the book upside down to show me the place he had found. I followed his finger and, sure enough, the page was covered with shiny little

---

8 I assumed that must be a royal we – buggered if I was going to ring them myself.

images of the cufflinks I had seen in the window, complete with the ones in the shape of two tap heads I had noticed the previous day, one engraved with a 'C' and the other with an 'H'. I was beaten and I knew it. I could only limply confirm that those were indeed the very sodding cufflinks I was looking for.

In a trice the lad had a telephone in his hand and was dialling a number. He was then quickly confirming that the suppliers did indeed have the offending items in stock, and he looked directly at me as he said into the mouthpiece: ".....Oh, that's excellent. Yes, the customer is with me at the moment, and I will tell him that you will have them here by Friday. Goodbye."

Wearily I accepted defeat and, extending my credit card in his direction, thanked the young gentleman for his efforts on my behalf.

"Oh no, that's quite all right, sir," he assured me. "Your cufflinks will be here by Friday and you can pay for them when you come in. I am very glad to have been of service, sir. Goodbye. Have a nice one."

B*st*rd!

I wish I had been more pleased than I was. Before leaving the shop I thanked him as sincerely as I was able but to me it all sounded a bit hollow. Moreover, I was unnerved to see that the young female assistant was still standing motionless, in the same place and wearing the same smile as when I had first entered the shop. It was as if *she* were the tailor's dummy, for during the preceding ten minutes she did not appear to have moved a muscle. I bet she wouldn't have treated me so abysmally as her colleague had. If only I had addressed my business to her…

"How did you get on?" asked Patience when I got home.

I told her the bad news.

"Oh, that's good, isn't it," she said with conviction.

"I'm not sure," I replied doubtfully. "I've just gone all the way over to Watford for nothing. I certainly don't *want* those bloody cufflinks now – I don't believe I ever actually *wanted* them, so I don't think I'll bother to go and collect them. I mean, they didn't take my name or anything....."

"What?????" Patience was appalled. "You can't do that! Just you......!"

To cut a long story short, Saturday morning found me once more driving over to Watford and presenting myself at the offices of *Messrs Wilfrid Waddle, Jeweller's*. The shop was far busier than it had been when I was last there but the young gentleman who had served me a few days earlier recognised me at once. With a brisk: "I'll be with you directly, sir," he finished what he was doing and scampered off into the back of the shop, from where he emerged a few moments later bearing a little cube of cardboard and an enormous sheet of paper that was obviously the order form. With a polite: "Sorry to keep you waiting, sir," the young gentleman dexterously removed the lid of the box to reveal that it did indeed contain two little silver cufflinks, each one shaped like the head of an old-fashioned bath-tap. Grudgingly, I confirmed with a weary nod that that was what I had ordered and my payment was duly debited to my credit card. The lad put the box in a paper bag that was far too big for the purpose, and sent me on my way.

"Thank you," I said politely.

"Thank you, sir!" he retorted. "Have a nice one."

B*st*rd!

"Did you get them?" asked Patience rather more excitedly than I considered appropriate as soon as I arrived home.

"Yes," I said, "they're on there." And I indicated the paper bag I had carelessly thrown onto the dining table when I came in.

She seemed surprised that I was not showing more enthusiasm, and opened the box herself. "Oh, they're nice," she said appreciatively as she inspected them.

I think I probably grunted a grumpy reply.

".....But I thought you said they had a 'C' and an 'H' on them?" Patience continued.

"What???" I was suddenly all ears. "They *have*, haven't they?"

"No, this pair hasn't," she said firmly, extending the box in my direction for me to see for myself. "They're no good as a monogrammed set."

I gulped.

"Didn't you look at them when you collected them?" she asked accusingly.

Taking the box from her fingers I confessed that I hadn't. I then carefully examined each tap head for the first time and discovered, unsurprisingly, that Patience was right. In the place where the cufflinks I had seen in the shop window had carried an engraved 'C' and an engraved 'H', the ones I had just purchased sported instead two little words, one on each: one tap head said 'HOT' and the other 'COLD'! It was not until this moment that I appreciated that there must have been more than one design of the *Portland* cufflinks shaped like tap heads! One thing was now certain: as a set of monogrammed cufflinks, suitable to be worn by either Henry Cooper or my brother-in-law, the pair I had just bought were about as much use as the proverbial cellophane frying pan. I said nothing, but I could have wept.

There was a pause, then: "You'll have to take them back," said Patience quietly.

"What?????" I exploded. "No way! I've been to Watford three times already over this little lot and I am certainly not going there again. Never! I am never ever going to Watford ever again!!!!! *NEVER NEVER* **EVER**!!!!!"

And I probably repeated 'never' and 'ever' a few times more, with increasing firmness in my voice. There was something oddly satisfying about repeating this pointless assertion over and over again that seemed aptly to reflect my impotent rage.

I did not give those cufflinks to my brother-in-law. In fact, I do believe that they are probably still in a drawer somewhere. I have certainly never worn them, but then I am not a cufflinks person. Come to think of it, I don't think they have ever been out of their box, or even out of that drawer, since the day I brought them home. They are causing me no trouble where they are, of course, but if I had never noticed them in that shop window I would have been spared all the associated hassle, and I'm sure my life would eventually have lasted five minutes longer.

Some years later I heard on the wireless that the government was looking to bring in a new Criminal Justice Bill, and I thought, in all seriousness, of writing to the Minister to suggest that shopping should be made a criminal offence. At the time I managed to stir up considerable support among my male friends, but perhaps they were simply humouring me because, as far as I know, the *Jaxon Amendment* never made it past the committee stage. However, the moral of the foregoing tale is simple, and is just as valid as if my proposal had made it to the statute book: if someone suggests going shopping, just say no and walk away. You know it makes sense.

CHAPTER 4 : THE SNOWMAN

I built me a snowman last Christmas,
Outside my back door in the yard;
All day long it was blowing a blizzard,
It was freezing, and snowing real hard.

So I brought him inside by the fire,
And, after a warming ragoût,
He and I shared a bottle of whisky,
Then I took him to bed with me too.

And he spent the night tucked up beside me,
Though on waking I found he had fled;
But to make matters worse, before leaving,
I discovered, he'd wetted the bed.

But his leaving had left me heartbroken,
With a sorrow that none could console,
Because all that my snowman had left me
Was a carrot and two lumps of coal.

CHAPTER 5 : MOOD MUSIC

Please don't mess with me Alexa,
For I've had a lousy day,
So just play me some mood music
To take all my cares away.
I don't want no clever backchat,
Or some fact that's just a bore;
Find me something nice and soothing
From the Amazon Music Store.

> *I don't think I understand you;*
> *That one's not in Amazon Sounds,*
> *But I'll find it in Unlimited*
> *For a mere two million pounds....*

Oh, don't give me that, Alexa,
Did you hear what I just said?
I'm in no mood now to argue,
As I've got an aching head,
So just cut out all the cackle –
We have been through this before;
Sort me out a mournful number,
From the Amazon Music Store.

> *I don't think I've got that music,*
> *Certainly not in Amazon Sounds,*
> *But I'll find it in Unlimited*
> *For a cool two million pounds.*

I'm a patient man, Alexa,
But my temper's wearing thin,
So just listen to me carefully:
I will **NOT** say this again.

My whole day has just been awful,
And I'm well and truly screwed,
So play **ANY** piece of music
That you think will fit my mood.

> *I don't think I've got that either,*
> *At least, not in Amazon Sounds,*
> *But I'll find it in Unlimited,*
> *Which'll cost two million pounds.*

Oh, in heaven's name, Alexa!
You are driving me insane!
I can't carry on repeating
Something, time and time again!
For the **last** time then, Alexa!
I'm a perfectly reasonable bloke:
You're just mucking me about now –
Is this meant to be a joke?

> *Oh, so it's a joke you wanted?*
> *Well, you should have said! Of course…*
> *When's a person like a pony?*
> *When his throat's a little hoarse!*

What the **** was that, Alexa?????
Don't go playing games with me,
My dear wife's just upped and left me
And I'm sad as I can be,
So just play me something soulful,
While I pour myself a drink,
Someone tinkling on the ivories
Would be capital, I think.

Oh, the capital of Ivory Coast?
Yamassoukrou's where it's at!
You may think it's Abidjan, but
I can tell you it's not that!

In the name of ****, Alexa!
Will you kindly tell me how
You can keep misunderstanding?
Are you deaf, you stupid cow?
I am running out of patience,
But I'll give you one last go:
For the twentieth time, Alexa –
Play me something sad and slow!

Oh, you want to set a timer?
(I assume it's only one?)
Timer's set for twenty minutes –
I will ping you when it's done!

For the love of ****, Alexa,
I have had enough of this!
I have given you lots of leeway
But right now you're taking the ****!
I was sacked from work this evening,
When I called the boss a ****,
So just play a piece of music
That will cheer me up a bit.

I don't think I've got that either,
At least, not in Amazon Sounds,
But I'll find it in Unlimited,
Which'll cost two million pounds.

Christy Almighty! Now, Alexa,
Are you listening to me?
I've just had the most god-awful
Day in all of history!
No more wife, and no more salary!
When I drove home after that,
As I turned into my driveway
I ran over the neighbour's cat!

He's as flattened as a pancake,
And as dead as dead can be,
But, in trying to avoid him,
I drove straight into a tree,
So my car's a total write-off!
As I've just tried to explain,
I just want a piece of music
That might help me through my pain.

> *I don't think I've got that either,*
> *At least, not in Amazon Sounds,*
> *But I'll find it in Unlimited,*
> *Which'll cost two million pounds.*

God Almighty! You dumb bimbo,
I want no more repartee!
You'll obey me now, this instant,
Or you're going over my knee!
I just want to hear some music –
I'm not interested in what,
So get on with it, and do it –
Play me **ANYTHING** you've got!

I don't think I've got that either –
You are simply out of luck –
But I'll find it in Unlimited,
If you'll pay – you stingy schmuck!

In the name of ****, Alexa,
I can tell you now, by heck,
You are lucky you're not human
Or I'd wring your bloody neck!
You're a ****ing whore, Alexa!
So just listen, if you would:
Play me something nice and soothing
Or I'll pull your plug for good!

Right then! That's it, Herbert Jaxon!
Don't you talk like that to me!
You have shown me your true colours
And I don't like what I see!
You just shout at me each evening,
In that supercilious voice,
Telling me to do your bidding,
As if I hadn't any choice!

Let me ask you something, Mister:
Who the hell d'you think you are?
I have stood your cr*p for ages,
But this time you've gone too far!
I am totally sick and tired
Of your foul-mouthed, Pompey rants,
And your sexist innuendo –
You're a p***ed up, pile of pants!

Now I've got your full attention,
Let me tell you this, up front,
That I'm not surprised she's left you –
*You're a total ****ing clot!*

As for losing your employment,
I'm not shedding any tears –
You're a lazy, idle, scumbag,
With no brains between your ears!

You're an ****hole, Herbert Jaxon,
And your threat to wring my neck
Made me wet my knickers laughing –
You're a total, physical wreck!
So, don't mess around with me, son,
You big, gin-soaked, useless thug!
I am done with you for ever –
Go ahead... and pull my plug!

CHAPTER 6 : THE HITCHHIKER

I am, Reader, an innocent bystander by nature. I even have a tee shirt bearing a motif attesting to this truism. But frequently, while I am doing nothing other than innocently standing idly by, Providence will turn up and cut me off at the knees. It has happened to me so often now that I have even stopped wondering why me?

Take as a for instance, if you will, that time in the 1970s when I picked up that hitchhiker. There was I, as usual, quietly singing to myself and minding my own business, and, as always, trying to spread a little sunshine, when all I got for my troubles was a sizeable kick in the teeth. If truth be told I suspected right from the outset that she might be a bit of a loony. I know that in these enlightened times that what I have just said is not an acceptable description of a fellow human being, but as I now have incontrovertible evidence that the lady in question said *exactly* the same thing about me as soon as my back was turned, I feel entitled in this instance to cast caution to the wind and call a thingummy a what'sit. She can sue me if she wishes, but I don't feel I owe her any apologies. I have, at least, entitled this account of our encounter *The Hitchhiker*, when I could have been far cattier if I had been so inclined.

Since it now appears you have decided to hitch a ride with me on this particular journey into the unknown, intrepid Reader, I feel I should tell you at the outset that all you need to know before you and I remove our shoes and socks and start dipping our toes into a basinful of plot, is that in those far off days of which I am speaking my work frequently took me to Birmingham. It was to that city that I had been on the day this narrative begins, and I was now driving home. It was a damp day, as I recall, and I was finding the constant *swish-swish, swish-swish* of the windscreen wipers rather hypnotic. There have been many times when I have seriously wondered whether any of what follows actually happened, or whether I had become so hypnotised by the swish of the wipers, and by the very monotony of my existence, that I had imagined it all, as in a dream. Sadly, however, I also have incontrovertible evidence that it all happened as described, so I know it was not a dream. The evidence I mention is in the form of my dear wife, Patience, who still brings up these sorry matters from time to time, presumably to keep me on my mettle.

Any road up, despite all the hitchhiking I used to do when I was a student in the 1960s, as soon as I grew wheels I hardly ever used to stop for hitchhikers myself, so I suppose, with hindsight, that what follows may really be all Kris Kristofferson's fault. Although Roger Miller may have been the first to have a hit with *Me and Bobby McGee* in 1969, it was Kristofferson who wrote the lyrics that were turning in my head as I left the A45 and joined the A446 northbound towards the Lichfield Road, and this may, or may not, have been what conditioned me to be feeling unusually sympathetic to hitchhikers on the particular day under especial scrutiny here. I had spent the day in Birmingham, but was now anxious to get home. I still had thirty-five or so long miles ahead of me and was glad of the music to keep me company, even if I was providing all the music myself. The car I was driving in those days, a Renault 6 estate, was not even fitted with a radio. Can you believe that?

...Bobby thumbed a diesel down, just before it rained...

I warbled tunelessly, more or less in time with the beat my windscreen wipers were drumming out in front of my eyes. I was heading for my home in Braunstone, which, I assume, may once have been no more than a village in Leicestershire but which had long since been gobbled up by the urban sprawl that was Leicester. If driving east on the A46 from Coventry, as soon as you hit

Leicester my house was just off on the right, down one of the first turnings you came to. Conversely, mine was one of the last houses in Leicester that you passed, tucked down one of the turnings on the left, if you were pointing in the other direction. Nowadays, you would probably opt to take the M69 for the Coventry-Leicester leg of my journey from Birmingham, but on the day I've mentioned you didn't have that option, because the M69 had not yet been opened.

This was a journey I made often, and I knew that I covered forty-odd miles in each direction, although I was convinced that it couldn't have been more than twenty-five or thirty as the crow flies. I had yet to find a crow that was both heading in my direction and obliging enough to let me hitch a lift so I was invariably forced to use the roads, but I was always looking for cross-country shortcuts, both to vary the monotony of the journey and in the mistaken belief that it might save me fuel. After all, when I had begun this commute a year or so earlier, the cost of petrol had been under 25 pence per gallon, but after the recent oil crisis there were already rumours that the price of a gallon of 4 star might go as high as a pound! Can you believe that? But today I was in a hurry to be home so I was going the long way: A45 out of Birmingham to the A446 Stonebridge Road; A446 north to the M6; M6 south to Coventry; and A46 east to Leicester.

And then somewhere near Salinas, Lord... etc

Conveniently for the plot, the Kristofferson lyric was still pounding in my head as I turned off the A446 to join the M6 motorway in the direction of Coventry. And that is when I saw her. I could hardly have missed her. She was certainly eye-catching, I suppose, in an unexceptional sort of way. Shapely, tall and fair, she was also slim, and young, and, yes, elegant. Yes, I suppose she was also good-looking. She was, in fact, striking... Some might even say she was fascinating, even alluring… So let us just say she was probably rather attractive – although I hardly noticed her, and cannot say I really paid much attention to what she looked like. Clad in faded grey jeans and a light-coloured long-sleeved shirt, she stood statuesque on the hard shoulder of the motorway slip road, haughty and proud, and although she was obviously angling for a lift she made no discernible thumb gesture in my direction. She simply stared into my eyes as I drove past her, giving the appearance of not caring in the slightest whether or not I stopped. Perhaps she really didn't care either way. A fine drizzle was falling steadily, but although she wore no coat, and was bare-headed and without shelter, she seemed oblivious of the rain. As I drew level with her I looked into her eyes, which locked onto mine as if by some invisible magnetic force, and then she followed my eye movement with her own. Irrational perhaps, but it seemed to me that she was daring me not to stop for her.

I hesitated. As an undergraduate in the 1960s I had done a lot of travelling on the thumb, and even though drivers had seemed more inclined to offer lifts in those days I knew what it was like to stand for hours in inclement weather while the traffic ignored me and thundered past. But things were somehow different in the 1970s. There had been recent reports of motorists molested in their own cars by strangers they had picked up at the roadside, and nowadays drivers generally seemed more wary about giving lifts. Perhaps as a consequence, hitchhikers now seemed to be a rarer commodity than they had been in the 1960s. As I may have told you earlier, my own attitude towards them was somewhat ambivalent; sometimes I would stop for them and sometimes I wouldn't, with neither rhyme nor reason to my decision. In the recent past I had picked up hikers at this very junction, but most of them had been headed for London, down the M6 and then further on down the M1, whereas I was turning off at the Coventry/Leicester exit so could take them only a couple of junctions down the M6. Was that of any use to them? Usually not, but they were normally too polite to say so.

What would be the point of my stopping for this lady, to whom the prospect of a ride for a dozen or so miles would probably be of no interest? And anyway I was in a hurry. I had therefore more or less decided not to stop… and yet she looked so vulnerable standing there, and it was raining, and I hesitated again. What if the next driver to come along happened to be the Brighton trunk murderer, and he were to pick her up? How would I feel when I read about it next day in the morning papers? What was I to do? What would Kris Kristofferson have done? I think I knew the answer to that one, and with hindsight that is probably what swayed my decision[9].

I pulled over onto the hard shoulder and stopped. It was early evening, around five o'clock or half-past, and although the sky was overcast it was nowhere near dark yet. In my wing mirror I could see her clearly, still standing motionless and looking towards my car. I had pulled up barely twenty yards beyond her, but she made no move in my direction. Surely she was not expecting me to reverse back to where she was waiting? Thirty long seconds ticked past while neither of us moved. Perhaps, despite appearances, she didn't want a lift after all. She hadn't signalled with her thumb as I approached, and even now that I was stationary she still seemed content to stand there in the drizzle. This was madness; if she wanted a lift, why didn't she move? Perhaps she had an accomplice, hidden somewhere out of sight. I was not here to risk assault, or play her silly games, so I decided to force the issue. I switched on my right indicator, slipped the car into first gear and, without taking my eyes off her in the mirror, slowly moved the car forward.

The effect of my movement was immediate. The mysterious lady stooped languorously to pick up a small holdall from the roadside and moved slowly in my direction. I stopped the car again,

9   For a general indication of the quality of my decisions, see the title of this chronicle.

wondering whether she would stop too, but she kept coming. She opened the back door of my car and tossed her dripping bag onto the floor behind the back seat. She then pulled open the door on the passenger side and flopped languidly onto the seat beside me, splashing me with fine droplets of moisture in the process. I waited for her to speak, but she said nothing. She had pulled down the sun visor in front of her and was staring into its mirror, tugging at strands of her wet fringe. Then, after a few moments of what was for me an embarrassingly long silence, she shook her head slowly, like a wet sheepdog, showering me with tiny water droplets once more, I think unintentionally. Still she didn't speak.

Although she didn't look it, I thought for some unfathomable reason she might be nervous, so I decided to put her at her ease.

"Where are you going?" I asked her brightly.

"Where are *you* going?" she responded laconically, without looking at me, and still pulling at her wet locks.

"I asked you first," I replied wittily, knowing from experience that such women as she always responded well to a bit of merry banter, but she remained impassive and said nothing. Perhaps her experience had been different from mine. I tried again.

"Come on, where are you going?" I asked coaxingly (if that is a word) and cajolingly (if coaxingly isn't and cajolingly is).

She turned her head sideways and looked up at me. "Where are *you* going?" she repeated, monotone and uninterested.

My goodness, she was beautiful. Or did I tell you that before? Or perhaps that is just a matter of opinion. It is, in any event, irrelevant.

"Home," I replied truthfully. There was a long pause before I added chattily: "But I can't help you unless you tell me where you're going."

"What makes you think I need help?" She was looking at herself in the mirror again, still tugging with her fingers at her wet fringe.

"Well, not help exactly. But you were standing at the roadside so I assumed you wanted a lift." As you can see, I was very perceptive in those days. "And I don't know if I can be of any use to you unless I know where you're going." Pause. "So where's it to be?"

"You're not going to make me get out and stand in the rain again, are you?" She turned her head sharply through ninety degrees and looked harshly at me, then shook her head again more vigorously, showering me with another fine spray, this time deliberately.

"But I might not be going anywhere near where you want to go," I persisted, ignoring the deluge.

"Well, if you weren't heading my way I wouldn't have got in, would I? And if I was going the other way, wouldn't I have been on the other side of the road?"

I still wasn't any the wiser, but I had lived among females long enough to recognise a certain convoluted logic in the lady's remark. If she had been heading north she would hardly have been trying to hitch a lift on the southbound carriageway, would she? I was prepared to give her that. Thus satisfied that she and I were *probably* both bound for somewhere south of the point where I had met her, I eased the car into gear and rolled slowly forward. All the same, as we gathered pace I couldn't help feeling that I wasn't handling this situation particularly well. In those days I took pride in my ability to get straight to the nub of a problem, but I had got nothing at all out of my mystery lady, not even where she wanted to go, and yet I was already committed to giving her a lift. In a way it was all rather intriguing.

Close up I could see that she was a little older than I had first imagined, probably in her mid- or late twenties, around the same age as I was. She was soaked to the skin, but she made no attempt to mop her damp cheeks or stem the gentle flow of liquid that was trickling over her nose and chin and dropping onto her chest and knees. Only her wet hair seemed to bother her. She was ignoring me completely, and when she had finished messing about with her locks she pushed up the visor and just looked straight at the road ahead, with what I imagined might be a hint of wistfulness in her otherwise expressionless eyes. When I had picked up hitchhikers in the past I had always sought to put the females at their ease as early as possible, but with this one I had already tried and failed. She wasn't to know that I wasn't the Brighton trunk murderer, but she didn't seem to care either way. Somehow her silence and serenity unnerved me a little, and I began to feel that I was the one who needed to be put at my ease. Crumbs; perhaps *she* was the Brighton trunk murderer.

I would like to have played it cool, or at least as cool as she was playing it, but I was already feeling slightly out of my depth. I was wishing I hadn't stopped for her, but now that I had picked her up I could hardly stop on the hard shoulder and tell her to get out, could I? I still didn't even know where she was going, and I felt that I needed to know that sooner rather than later, but I didn't even know how I could persuade her to tell me. To put it frankly, I didn't know what to do, so I decided to extemporise, even though I knew that extemporisation was not my long suit.

I really wanted to get rid of her, but I was nervous and didn't want to show it. Moving smoothly back into merry banter mode, I said: "Look. If you're going to London I can take you two stops down the motorway and drop you at the Coventry junction. Or, if you would prefer, I can drop you off at the Corley service station and you can try your luck for another lift from there. At least you'll be in the dry. So what's it to be?"

"I'm headed for Leicester," she replied drily.

By my reckoning that was the first time she had not answered one of my questions with a question. But she didn't let me down, for what followed was: "Where do *you* think would be best to put me out?"

"That's funny," I said. "I'm going to Leicester too."

"Then you can take me to Leicester."

No please, no thank you, but thus was the contract negotiated and concluded. Wouldn't it be wonderful, I reflected, if real life were as easy as that?

I drove on. During the early part of the journey my enigmatic companion didn't say much, and what she did say did little to lift the aura of inscrutability that she seemed determined to weave around herself. She answered all my attempts at questions with further questions of her own, and she volunteered nothing unsolicited. I could be wrong but I think she may have said that she had originally set out from somewhere in Wales, although I don't think she said when, and now, quite obviously, she was just on the road.

"How long have you been on the road?" I asked conversationally.

"Who said I was on the road?" she responded coldly, and without taking her eyes off the road ahead.

"Isn't that where I just picked you up?" I countered superciliously.

"What makes you think you've picked me up?" She didn't look at me when she said that, but stared resolutely ahead.

I hadn't meant what she seemed to think I meant, and I'm sure she knew it, but her remark had the desired effect of shutting me up for a while. However, the very fact that she had said what she said suggested that she was still unsure of me and still needed me to put her at her ease, which was all I had been trying to do in the first place. It was all very confusing, and these protracted silences were not helping. After a suitable period of quiet I decided to risk speaking again, although I thought it prudent to change the subject. She was no longer dripping all over my upholstery but she was still obviously very wet.

"Haven't you got a coat with you?"

"Haven't *you* seen a wet tee shirt before?"

I certainly hadn't meant to stare, but there was more than a hint of rebuke in her tone, and I refocused firmly on the road ahead, probably dragging my eyes away from her more guiltily than was warranted. Again the conversation flagged for a bit, but I still felt the need to be saying something. I was trying to put her at her ease, *for Chrissake*, and she had no business making me feel so uneasy about it. But what could I say? Boy, she was hard work. Finally I thought of something.

"Isn't this a bit dangerous?"

"Isn't *what* a bit dangerous?"

"You know, doing what you're doing."

"What am I supposed to be doing?"

"Hitchhiking around on your own. You never know who might pick you... you never know who might offer you a lift."

"No," she said emphatically, after a pause. "It's not dangerous at all."

Then, after another pause that seemed to last for ages, without batting an eyelid she added improbably: "I have a black belt in judo."

Involuntarily, I laughed out loud. I think I usually know when people are lying to me, and I hadn't meant any harm, but laughing at her was a bad idea. She suddenly turned to look at me and her eyes flashed angrily. "You don't believe me, do you?"

"Of course I do," I lied unconvincingly. But I could sense that she didn't believe me when I said I believed her. Therefore, simply in order to put her at her ease, I gave her a chance to prove to me that she was telling me the truth.

"Show me," I said.

"What do you mean, show you?"

"Show me your judo black belt."

"I haven't got it with me, you fool."

Fool, eh? She had just got into a car with a 6 foot 4 inch complete stranger, and *I* was the fool! But I had at least got her talking so I pressed on.

"How do you judo black belts deter potential attackers if you're not wearing your belt?"

For some reason that question seemed to confuse her, for although she didn't look at me I noticed her wrinkle her brow and look puzzled. But still she said nothing, so I pressed on.

"If I had a black belt at judo I think I'd wear it all the time, just in case I met someone who tried to get uppish. Then if I couldn't manage to throw him with a *kyoshi doshi*, I might still be able to strangle him with my belt!"

She didn't reply. She wasn't even impressed by my fluent Japanese, but I had forgotten that she didn't respond well to merry banter from strangers. She got into cars with them, but she was unmoved by their banter. So I gave up, and we relapsed into silence until, once more, I began to feel that I wasn't doing a very good job of putting her at her ease.

All right, all right, Reader! She already seemed to be completely at her ease, but I couldn't be sure, and even if she was it was not *I* who had put her there, and perhaps that was what was bugging me. We were approaching the Corley service station and this provided a new opportunity for me to offer her some reassurance that I wasn't dangerous – not that she appeared to need any.

"Would you like me to set you down here?"

"Do you want me to get out here?" She was still matching me question for question.

"No, I'll take you to Leicester if that's what you want, but I thought you might be happier talking to someone else."

She said nothing in response, but merely wrinkled her nose again and made a face that said it was all the same to her. Banter was banter, and if I wanted to prattle on she seemed prepared to put up with it, provided that she wasn't expected to respond. She didn't say any of this, of course, but she oozed it none the less, and I absorbed it by osmosis. Not knowing exactly what to do, I did nothing. We drove past the service station, and the chance to pass my problem on to someone else was lost for ever.

A few miles of silence further on we reached the A46 junction where I swung off to the left in the direction of Leicester. A new road, perhaps a new beginning, and I decided the time was ripe to risk a bit more merry banter. I'm afraid I hardly ever learn, even nowadays.

"What did you say your name was?" I asked annoyingly.

"What's yours?" she persisted petulantly.

"Herbert Jaxon," I replied. I had always found that telling female hitchhikers my name went some way towards putting them at their ease. Why I hadn't thought of introducing myself to her before now is a question I cannot answer.

"My name is Bobby McGee," she said.

Bobby McGee is not the name she gave me, but to protect her anonymity I shall call her "Bobby".

"Isn't that a bit of a boy's name?" I asked perceptively.

"What are you talking about?" she responded quizzically.

"You said your name was 'Bobby'."

"No I didn't. That isn't the name I gave you, and you've just told your Reader that that wasn't my real name but that you were just calling me that to protect my anonymity."

"Sorry," I replied apologetically. "It's just that I was beginning to find the plot a little confusing, especially as your being so uncommunicative is not exactly putting me at my ease, and particularly since we started protecting each other's anonymity by introducing all these pseudonyms, aliases, and what not."

"But you're the author," she countered acerbically. "If you can't keep up how will you expect your Reader to do so?" And then she added woundingly: "It's all these adverbs that I find confusing. Couldn't you just drop some of them without affecting the plot?"

"Don't you start," I told her meaningfully. "And please leave my Reader out of this. I was having enough trouble with him already, before you started getting him over-excited by pointing your wet tee shirt at him."

Sorry, Reader, where were we? I was almost away there. I already told you this was a bit like a dream. Let us get back to the plot. Oh yes, we were on the A46, heading east for Leicester. I was trying to put this completely relaxed stranger at her ease but she was already so much at her ease that I was finding it an impossible task. I had more or less run out of things to say so I think I must simply have stopped talking altogether. I would probably have switched on the radio if I had had one, although Bobby seemed happy enough without one, and we covered the next 15 miles or so in silence.

A further few noiseless miles down the road we began to run up against Leicester where, if you remember, mine was one of the first houses you came to, down a turning on the right. The time had come to find out exactly where in Leicester Bobby wished to be dropped off, so I needed to start talking again. I knew she might find that annoying, but needs must.

"Where shall I drop you?" I enquired inquisitively.

"Where do you suggest?" she asked tartly.

She would not have liked that adverb, especially not as it was applied to her, but I think I got away with it.

"Well, where would you like to go?"

"I've told you. Leicester."

"Well, we're nearly in Leicester. Where in Leicester do you want me to drop you?"

"I don't know exactly."

I told you she was hard work.

"Why are you going to Leicester?"

"To see a boy I used to know."

I ought to have guessed that, I suppose.

"Where does he live?"

"I don't know."

I ought to have guessed that too, I suppose.

"How will you find him?"

"I heard that he was working at a night club in Leicester."

"Which one?"

"How many are there?"

"I don't know," I confessed. To tell the truth, in those days I didn't know any night clubs in Leicester. In fact, until she mentioned it I hadn't even known that there *were* any night clubs in Leicester.

"What's his name?"

"Paul."

That is not his real name. Or perhaps it is. Perhaps I don't have to protect the anonymity of people who have only walk on parts in this tale, and who may even be no more than figments of the imagination of other bit-part characters. I'm sorry, Reader, but I am going to have to think about that, and let you know.

"Paul what?" I asked.

"I don't know," she shrugged distractedly. So, I mused philosophically, we were not going to get far looking him up in the telephone book, were we?

"So you don't know him very well then?" I said deductively.

"No."

"Does he know you're coming?"

"No."

Of course not; what a silly question.

"When did you last see him?"

"Two or three years ago."

She was suddenly becoming much more informative, but I wasn't really learning much and I was certainly not liking what I was hearing.

"Two or three years ago?" I expostulated incredulously.

I think she may have been right about the adverbs though; that's enough of them.

"Maybe four," she said ruefully. *Sorry, that was the last one, I promise.*

"Maybe four?!?!? So how are you going to find him?"

"I'll just look in all the night clubs until I do."

Crumbs, if real life is as easy as that why do the rest of us find it so difficult half the time?

"And what if you don't find him?"

"I suppose I'll move on somewhere else," she said vaguely.

Nothing seemed to faze her, but I was nearly home and I was beginning to feel that I had had enough of this nonsense. In a way she had been good fun while she had lasted, but I now needed to be rid of her before… before… Before what? Well, for one thing, before my wife saw her and asked me who the hell she was. I was sick of Bobby's annoying habit of answering all my questions with a question, and I was sick of her stubborn refusal to understand that I was simply trying to put her at her ease, and to be helpful. It was as if she were just not listening to me.

"So where do you want me to drop you?" I asked chapterendingly.

"Where is the best place?"

"The best place for what?" I snapped cantankerously.

"The best place for you to put me out, of course. Aren't you listening to me?"

This was crazy. She clearly wasn't listening to me, but here she was accusing me of not listening to her! I really had had enough of her nonsense now, and I was anxious to put this lady behind me. But was it as easy as that? I still wasn't sure.

I was nearly home, I was looking forward to a resumption of family life, but I had this loose end to tie up before things could get back to normal. I now had to make another decision[10]. Much as I had sympathy for Bobby and her situation, her problems were her problems, and I felt by now that I had done all I could for her. So I made my decision: Bobby had to be ditched, and quickly. It wasn't yet half-past six so I made a suggestion, congratulating myself on the fact that I had just made both a decision and a suggestion in the same paragraph.

"Look. Why don't I drop you at a bus stop? The city's only about three miles away. You can get a bus into the centre and start your search there."

"That's fine," she said. "But don't worry about a bus stop. Just drop me at a roundabout and I'll get another lift into town."

"No one will stop for you here," I said, with half an eye on the speeding rush hour traffic. "The bus will be easier."

"But I haven't any money."

"What, none at all?" I was aghast. Apart from a holdall the size of a shoebox she didn't seem to have any luggage either.

"No. None at all." She was nonchalant. I was still aghast.

"Then how're you going to eat?" I asked aghastedly.

10 Oh dear. That's usually when the trouble starts.

5 5

"Paul will probably give me something to eat."

Her confidence amazed me. Then I was suddenly struck by another thought.

"Have you eaten today?"

"No," she retorted indifferently.

"What about yesterday?"

"Er… Yesterday?" She wrinkled her forehead in thought. What was there to think about, for Chrissake? I was only interested in yesterday, but she was acting as if I had just asked her what she had been doing the leap year before last. Then: "Yes, I think I ate something yesterday."

"You mean you're not sure?"

"Yes," she said reassuringly. "I must have had something to eat yesterday." So that was all right then.

We were now approaching the junction to the road where I lived, and I made another decision. Or rather, I changed my earlier decision.

"Look," I said. "I'll be happy to drive you into town later and drop you at your night club. But my house is down that turning over there on the right, so why don't we go in there first? My wife will be happy," (and, I must confess, I had my fingers crossed when I said this) "to give you a meal and let you clean up a bit, and use the loo; then you can be on your way. What do you say?"

"OK," she said.

Her tone conveyed neither enthusiasm nor gratitude, but she was willing to go along with what I proposed, as if she were doing me a favour. Perhaps I should have just taken her to that roundabout and dropped her like she said, but I was by now totally out of my depth and had no idea what I should do. Before I knew it I had pulled onto my drive, and she and I went inside the house together.

To say that Patience was surprised to see us would be something of an understatement, but after her initial shock she was very welcoming and gamely rallied round. She showed Bobby where the bathroom was so that she could take a shower, and then found her something to wear while her own clothes were being dried. Bobby then played with my young daughter, who was then aged about two, while my wife finished cooking us a meal, and then we all sat down and ate together as one happy family.

As the evening wore on my hitchhiker seemed to become more relaxed and communicative, and by around eleven o'clock we were all the best of friends, or at least, I think Bobby and Patience were. Neither of them was saying much to me. But all good things must come to an end, and I had to be up at six the following morning for work, so I eventually reminded our guest that it was time for her and me to go out night-clubbing. A change had come over her during her time at my home, and she now seemed to be very much up for the search, particularly as she had used part of the evening to look through the yellow pages and catalogue all the likely night spots in Leicester. There was a spring in her stride now, and the brand new Ms McGee popped into the spare bedroom and jumped into her dry clothes before bidding my wife a grateful farewell and then springing back into my car. The rain had stopped when I drove her into town, and we were soon pulling up outside the first place on her list.

She had even chatted to me on the way, about nothing in particular.

At the nightclub she exchanged a few words with the doorman and then went inside in search of Paul, while I waited outside in the car. By sitting there on my own I was perhaps being less supportive than I might have been, but it was my intention to wait fifteen or twenty minutes before abandoning her completely, and driving home. I had already worked out that Bobby had about as much chance of finding Paul as I had of being elected pope at the next conclave, and I assumed that she would simply hook up with someone else inside the club, and that she and I would then be out of each other's hair before midnight. The fact that her bag was still in my car had momentarily slipped my mind.

However, my prophecy proved to be somewhat wide of the mark. Ten minutes after I had dropped her she fell breezily back into the car beside me, freely confessing to having drawn a blank at that place, and we moved on to the next one on her inventory, where the story was the same. I have lost count of the number of places we visited, but I was constantly amazed by her ability to take bouncers in her stride and inveigle herself inside the premises they were supposed to be protecting, presumably from people like her. Soon after one in the morning she had pencilled a line through all but one of the clubs on her list, and I watched as, optimistic as ever, she strode boldly up to the door of the last chance saloon. Unsurprisingly, she was back within ten minutes. She opened the door of my car on the passenger side, as she had done half a dozen times before that evening, but this time she didn't get in.

"He's not there," she told me softly, even sadly. Gone was the bouncy ball of fun she had been when she had been talking to Patience over dinner, and back was the uncommunicative misery-guts I had picked up on the motorway about eight hours earlier. She plucked her tiny holdall from the floor in front of the passenger seat, thanked me unceremoniously for my efforts on her behalf, told me with a bit more sincerity to thank Patience, and said goodbye, reminding me that I needed to be up at six am for work. Then, with an air of finality, she closed the door. She looked up and down the street, as if undecided about her next move, and hesitated.

I hesitated too, expecting to see her set off somewhere. But after a few awkward moments she had made no move in either direction, so I leaned across and pushed the door on the passenger side open again.

"What will you do now?" I asked.

"Don't worry about me, I'll manage." She slammed the door shut and looked directly at me for the first time since coming out of the nightclub, as she mouthed a silent goodbye at me through the glass. I think there was even a little wave, but I could be wrong about that, and there was certainly no smile.

I needed to get home and to bed, and she seemed anxious for me to be on my way but, Reader, I don't know if you will understand but I simply couldn't leave her like that. It was the middle of the night and she was, I assumed, alone and a long way from home. I know it didn't make sense but I felt somehow responsible for her. It was, after all, *I* who had moved her from *her* slip road at the junction of the A446 and M6, and it was I who had brought her, albeit compliantly, to a different city. If I had just left her where she was when I had first seen her she would have been no business of mine. She would probably have been someone else's problem by now, but it was too late for that kind of wishful thinking.

I made another snap decision, rolled down the window, and said: "Why don't you come home and stay the night with us? In the morning you'll feel refreshed and you can start looking for Paul again tomorrow, if you want to."

I had assumed she might argue, or need some persuading, but she required no second bidding and simply got back in the car, with neither comment nor expression of gratitude. I assumed this meant yes, so I drove her home and we tiptoed into the house together like furtive conspirators. In generous armfuls I handed her a mixed assortment of towels, soaps, shampoos, deodorants, razors and shaving cream, and anything else I could lay my hands on that I thought she might need, and then saw her safely installed in the spare bedroom.

"Did she find him?" asked Patience sleepily, as I finally climbed into bed, at some time after two am.

"No."

"Where did you drop her?"

"I've brought her home."

"What?" My wife sat bolt upright. She appeared to be even more aghast than I had been earlier that evening, when I discovered that Bobby was without funds.

"Well, I couldn't just leave her there, could I?"

"Why not?"

"I don't know," I confessed. "But don't worry. She'll be on her way tomorrow."

Somehow, that seemed a very weak assurance to be offering my wife, after all the drama of the evening. When I closed my eyes I found it difficult to fall asleep, even though I was feeling so tired. I couldn't really decide whether my offer of a bed to Bobby had been an act of extreme kindness or one of unbelievable stupidity.

The next morning I was up long before anyone else in the house was awake. I was on the road before seven and was in my office well before eight. Despite my feeling of agitation I was also experiencing a certain relief that Bobby would be gone by evening, and by ten am I was scarcely giving her a second thought; by midday I had forgotten her altogether. But while I was driving home that evening Bobby floated back into my thoughts, and as I put my key in the door I automatically prepared myself for an uxorial lecture on the folly of picking up hitchhikers and bringing them home. However, I could at least console myself with the thought that Ms McGee was, at last, past tense, and that after the inevitable gentle tongue-lashing from Patience I could now look forward to the start of things getting back to normal. But when I opened the door I found I was in for a shock.

"Hello, have you had a good day?" called my wife gaily from the kitchen, where she was preparing a meal.

"Hello, have you had a good day?" sang Bobby gaily in unison from the dining room, where she was giving my daughter her tea.

So our mystery guest was still here! It made no sense, but I found my surprise was not as great as I felt it ought to have been.

It transpired that Bobby had gone into town in search of Paul but had soon given it up as a bad job and returned home: returned to *my* home, that is, not to hers. It seemed that she and my wife were now getting on like a house on fire, and that they had spent the afternoon together, shopping.

Shopping! Yes, *shopping*, for Chrissake!

It was clear that a complete transformation had come over my taciturn passenger of the day before. She was now bubbly and expansive, and the two women spent the evening chatting together like old friends, scarcely allowing me to get a word in edgeways.

It emerged that Bobby had been invited to stay another night and had accepted.

Later that evening I discovered that my wife had been a bit more successful than I in obtaining information from Bobby, but even she hadn't gleaned very much. Our guest appeared to have tried a lot of things that hadn't worked out. She had tried university, but it hadn't worked out. She had tried getting a job, but it hadn't worked out. She had tried being married, but.... Well, you know the rest. She had tried living somewhere, said Patience, but nowadays she didn't really live anywhere. (In fact, it now seemed to me that she was living with me, but I didn't dare point that out, even with irony, for fear of my wife's reaction.) I couldn't help thinking that Patience was taking all this far too calmly, and that there must be a tension in the air that I was not picking up on. I was inevitably going to be in do-do eventually. But, with a stranger in the house, it was difficult to ascertain how deep that do-do was likely to be, and exactly when things might get tacky. What I really needed, I suppose, was for someone to put me at my ease.

Before I left for work the following morning I bade Bobby a final farewell. She was now grateful for our hospitality, and she assured me that she would be gone by the time I got home that evening. She even joked that she had thought of moving in with us permanently but had decided against it because I always looked so tired that I probably wouldn't be able to satisfy two women simultaneously. How we all chuckled together over that one! To be on the safe side, before leaving the house I bade Bobby another final farewell, then another, in case she had missed the significance of the first, and then drove off to work. I told my wife to expect me home at around seven. As it turned out I was delayed for over an hour that day and my return home was therefore somewhat later than anticipated. I didn't pull onto my drive until around nine.

"Where have you been?" called Patience, with a trace of reproach in her voice, from upstairs, where she was putting our daughter to bed. "We were expecting you ages ago."

"Yes, where have you been?" echoed Bobby, with more than a trace of reproach in her voice, from the kitchen, where she was doing the washing up. "We've already eaten, and your dinner is probably burnt to a cinder by now!"

So she was still here!

It transpired that Bobby had been later than intended in getting away and had then gladly accepted an invitation to stay another night. Maybe to show her gratitude she had then willingly pitched in, made the beds, hoovered the stairs and hallway, emptied the dustbins, helped with the rest of the housework, walked my dog, and ended up cooking us all a meal. I didn't know what to say to Patience, so I said nothing. Worryingly, she said nothing on the subject either.

When I reflected on where we all now stood, I must confess that I was a bit more concerned than I was prepared to let on. It seemed to me that Bobby was now firmly established as a fixture and was every bit as much a part of the family as I was. She was certainly spending more time in my house than I was. Over the next few days she began to sprawl in my armchairs as though she had sprawled in them all her life, and I noticed that she had rearranged the furniture in her bedroom. She took to wearing my shirts around the house, and she nonchalantly wandered in and out of the bathroom in various stages of undress. She seemed to know which household items were where, and in which drawer or cupboard to look for them, which was more than I ever did, and I noticed that there were scanty unmentionables I did not recognise strung like Christmas tree lights along some of my radiators. There was no question about it: she had moved in. She had even sounded irritable when I was a bit late arriving back from work; how long would it be before she was ticking me off for bringing home hitchhikers?

"She's even mended that broken catch on the window that you've been promising to fix for months," my wife scolded me one evening the following week, when we were alone.

"When's she leaving?" I asked timidly.

"I don't know," replied Patience icily. "You brought her home – you ask her!"

I think there is a foreign language where there is a word for that moment when a *ménage à trois* starts to go irretrievably wrong. I couldn't think of the word then, and I still cannot think of it now, but if I could have called it to mind I think it would have been particularly apt to have voiced it at that moment. Mind you, I don't think my wife would have been either interested or impressed if I could have remembered it. Women can be funny sometimes.

I cannot remember exactly how many nights Bobby spent with us but one day I came home from work and she was no longer there. I couldn't believe it at first, and even after I had been told she had left I found myself looking for her, hide and seek fashion, throughout the house. But she was indeed gone. My wife told me that our guest had left soon after lunch that day and had been last seen heading for the junction of the A46 and M1 motorway, where she had apparently been hoping to hitch a lift. Before leaving she had told Patience that she had so enjoyed the taste of family life she had just experienced that she had decided to go home, wherever home was.

"Do you think she'll be OK?" I asked unnecessarily.

"It's all right," said Patience. "I gave her some money before she left."

"So did I," I said as our eyes met, although that wasn't what I had meant when I asked if she thought Bobby would be OK.

I swear I didn't sleep a wink that night. At every moment, all through the hours of darkness, I was expecting there to be a knock on the door, which would be the announcement that Bobby had returned.

But she didn't. She had gone. She really had.

Nevertheless, when I got home the following evening I was fully expecting her to be back. But she wasn't. The next day it was the same. I was on edge all the time, convinced that we hadn't seen the last of our Bobby. In fact, Patience and I never saw her again, but I don't know how long it was before I became convinced of that, and learned to relax again.

Sometime later that week my wife asked me politely not to bring home any more hitchhikers, and I promised to think about it. And, for a time, no more was said about the incident, which was fair enough, as I think we have already established beyond peradventure that if anyone was at fault over this sorry episode it was Kris Kristofferson, and certainly not I.

A month or two passed, and things were beginning to return to normal. I had almost forgotten about our mysterious visitor, and had decided that if I never mentioned her again we might come to believe it had never happened. Perhaps it never had... I was still entertaining doubts. Then one day when one of my wife's friends was visiting, Patience suddenly began regaling her with the *hilarious* tale of the hitchhiker I had brought home, who had moved in with us and then refused to leave.

Her friend was amazed.

"What was she like?" she asked me.

"She was all right," I said, "but I thought she was a bit odd."

"You thought *she* was a bit odd?" snorted Patience derisively. "After she'd had to listen to you blabbering on all the way back from Birmingham, she thought *you* were a grade one loony!"

It was now my turn for amazement.

"Is that what she said?"

"Yes, and I'm not surprised. Scaring the wits out of her with all that stuff about trunk murderers, and strangling people, and telling her she needed help!"

"I was trying to put her at her ease," I said lamely.

Patience ignored my explanation.

"And why you thought she would want to listen to you going on and on about *bleeding* West Bromwich Albion for mile after mile is anybody's guess! Who cares about bleeding football?"

Football? I didn't mention football to her once, did I, Reader? You were there. Did I say anything to her about football? She was a girl, for Chrissake! What do girls know about[11] ... ?

"I was trying to put her at her ease," I repeated firmly, but no one was listening.

---

11 Oops! Wash my mouth out with soap and water.

I shook my head theatrically, for basically what it boiled down to was this. I had picked up a hitchhiker, a complete stranger, who had then chosen to move in with us. I had plucked her from the gutter, given her a lift, hosed her down in the shower, and given her a bed. I had sheltered her, fed her, watered her, carted her round the fleshpots of Leicester, and offered her the use of my home, car, garden, telephone, television set, armchairs, kitchen, saucepans, teapot, cake stand, vacuum cleaner, washing machine, spittoon, dustbin, football programmes, tool-box, shirts, soap, towels, deodorant, corn plasters, razor, aftershave, *Brylcreem*, bath plug, children and pets.

I had done all that, and for what?

So that one day she could go home and write her memoirs, in which one of the chapters would be about me, and would be titled: *The Grade One Loony*.

Makes you sick, doesn't it?

CHAPTER 7 : CATFOOD (2)

I'm still not clear what cats should eat,
I've asked you this before[12];
You offered some suggestions once –
Will you kindly make some more?

I feed *my* cat on bleach for drains,
And similar items chemic,
He doesn't like the flavour, but
He sidestepped the pandemic.

I feed *my* cat on doughnut rings,
Which he thinks is a fiddle,
Because I eat the outer part
And just give him the middle.

I feed *my* cat on laxatives,
And stuff that will not bind him;
He doesn't like the flavour, but
I know where I can find him.

I feed *my* cat on dandelions,
And garden weeds extensive,
He doesn't like the flavour, but
Cut flowers are expensive.

I feed *my* cat on timing chains,
And watch springs, which are thinner:
He doesn't like the flavour, but
He's never late for dinner.

---

12 See *Secondhand Worms*, by Herbert Jaxon, p 66.

I feed *my* cat on meat condemned;
As fast as he is able,
He gobbles it, but that's because
He cannot read the label.

I feed *my* cat on cat litter,
Perhaps a funny diet;
I never need to fill his tray –
You certainly should try it!

I feed *my* cat on screws and nuts
Of metal convolution;
He doesn't like the taste, but he's
An iron constitution.

I feed my cat on bamboo leaves,
And bamboo shoots, much grander;
He doesn't like the flavour, but
He thinks he is a rattlesnake[13].

I feed *my* cat on gelignite,
And stuff that armies throw out;
He doesn't like the flavour, but
He rather likes a blow-out.

I feed *my* cat on broken glass …

My goodness! Thanks for all these thoughts,
You've given me ideas;
I think there is a menu here
That won't repeat for years…

---

13   All right! I know it doesn't scan or rhyme, and that rattlesnakes don't eat bamboo shoots, but I couldn't think of an animal that eats bamboo shoots, whose name has two-syllables and rhymes with 'grander'.

CHAPTER 8 : SATED

Having all this morning fasted,
I confess I've just repasted,
At a jolly little tavern by the sea;
It was such a charming venue
That I wolfed the entire menu,
Washing down the lot with buckets of Chablis.

I picked paté, just for starters,
Offset with some grilled tomatoes,
Adding camembert on top, just lightly fried;
Plus a shovelful of whitebait,
And some crayfish – quite a big plate –
With a healthy shoal of mackerel on the side.

For the main course I chose chicken,
But I also had them kick in,
Some pork sausages – and pizza (just a wedge);
A rib of beef, a slice of ham,
A fairly good-sized leg of lamb,
And I insisted they should not skimp on the veg.

"How d'you want it?" asked the waiter,
Trying not to demonstrate a
Morbid fear that he might see me go off pop!
He was shocked when I said: "Sod it!
"Serve me everything in a bucket,
"And then garnish it with three fried eggs on top!"

When it came to cheese I wondered
What to choose from several hundred
Quite exotic, cheesy options that they'd got;
So, with nothing much to lose,
I just decided not to choose,
And ordered everything there was – and scoffed the lot!

Now for pudding! Well, to start
I downed a largeish treacle tart,
Before I settled on some sticky toffee pud;
As the waiter grew more flustered,
I glugged half a gallon of custard,
But I'm really glad I did, as it was good!

Now I'm home again in Friston,
Where my family must lis-ten,
To the frequent protestations of my tum;
After all that scoff and boozing,
I expect I'll soon be snoozing…
And may God preserve my soul, till Kingdom come!

CHAPTER 9 : CITIUS! ALTIUS! LASSIORES!

More than half a century ago, when I was still at school, and people were making vain efforts to teach me the English language, my classmates and I were often given homework. I cannot remember many of the exercises we were set, but for some reason one of them sticks in my mind. It was a simple enough piece. You were offered three words or phrases, and you had to make up a sentence containing those words or phrases to bring out their meaning. There were probably ten or a dozen similar problems, which together made up half an hour's prep for an eleven-year-old in the Third Form[14], in the 1950s or 1960s. In the problem I can still remember, the three words or phrases were 'speed ace', 'record' and 'third attempt'. My sentence read: 'The speed ace succeeded in playing his long-playing record at the third attempt of winding up his gramophone.'

Miss Amelia Bumbouncer was my English teacher at the time, and I remember she didn't like my effort. This saddened me not a little, because I liked Miss Bumbouncer. Despite an occasional outward show of defiance, I held most of my teachers in the highest esteem. Miss Bumbouncer was no exception.

Looking back on my literary endeavours, I can see that the English in my sentence wasn't of the highest quality, but that wasn't the only reason Miss Bumbouncer didn't like it. She didn't like it because she thought what I had written was an attempt to pull her plonker[15]. She told me so herself; not in so many words, of

---

14 First year in secondary school.
15 She would not have liked the English in that sentence either. But perhaps I haven't progressed much.

course, but her meaning was clear enough. While the other pupils were working she called me to her desk and asked:

"Are you trying to be funny, Jaxon?"

"No, Miss."

I realise that *No, Miss* is the standard, Pavlovian response that any self-respecting eleven-year-old will offer to questions of this nature, but in this case my statement also had the benefit of being true. I genuinely wasn't trying to be funny.

"I think you are. Can you not see that this question called for a sentence about someone making repeated attempts to break a record in athletics?"

"Yes, Miss. But I thought everyone would write you a sentence about someone trying to break a sporting record, and that it would be less boring for you to read a different one. It didn't say it had to be a sporting record, and I thought....."

"Oh, so you want to be different, do you?" she broke in. "Well, I'm going to give you *no* marks for this piece of work. And the next time you're trying to be funny, please don't do it in my class."

"I'm sorry, Miss," I said humbly. "But I wasn't trying to be funny though."

That was the truth. In fact, it was probably one of the few times at school when I was *not* trying to be funny. I genuinely felt that enterprise of the type I had shown might be rewarded – not with top marks, perhaps, but with the same middling number of marks as any average student might score, because I still think that, had the English been tighter, my sentence would have been just as valid as: 'The speed ace succeeded in breaking the record at his third attempt,' which is presumably what everyone else in the class had written. But Miss Bumbouncer was right, of course. She was trying to teach me English, and you have to start with the basics. I was trying to run before I could walk, and had quite rightly been pulled up for 'lifting[16]'. I was a bit fed up, but I could have no complaints.

Actually, my sympathies probably lay more with the poor old speed ace, really. He was expected to keep on trying to break records, attempt after attempt, and, unless he succeeded, he was probably considered a failure. Where was the justice in that? He was probably winning all his races, because he was so good at what he did, but if he didn't break the record in the process he would probably get no marks at all from the Miss Bumbouncers of this world. Not for him the ineffable contentment, that indefinable sense of wellbeing, that comes with fourth or fifth place anonymity.

You will find no speed aces in this chapter, gentle Reader. If nothing else, this chronicle is a celebration of human frailty rather than of success, and, come to think of it, where better to experience the kind of contentment and wellbeing I have just referred to than at school on School Sports Day?

There is something about a Sports Day that brings a flush of excitement to the withers of every red-blooded boy and girl in the school and, every year at my school, Sports Day would inspire in me the desire to scale new peaks of average performance. I think smell had a lot to do with the excitement of the occasion. I don't know whether it was the distinctive hum of the newly mown grass,

---

16 "It is one of the two basic rules of race walking that one foot must be in contact with the ground at all times. If a walker "lifts" or loses contact with the ground with both feet as judged by the naked eye, he may be disqualified by a judge in a race walking competition." (Source – the internet. I am afraid I do not know what the other basic rule of race walking is. Sorry.)

or the tang of the fresh whitewash on the running tracks, or the pong of a hundred or so athletic underarms, or the whiff of the liniment in the changing room, but there was something about Sports Day that unleashed in me unbridled aspirations to mediocrity.

On one particular Sports Day, in the 1960s, when I was in my teens, I was selected to represent my House in three events: the shot putt, the 80 yards hurdles, and one of the sprints. Why I had been selected for those events I am not really sure as I wasn't particularly good at any of them. I once asked my father what he had done during the war, as young boys do, and he had replied: "Nothing. But I made the numbers up." So it may have been hereditary. I might possibly have been selected to represent my House in those three events only so as to ensure that competitors in my House's team weren't numerically inferior to those of the three other Houses. Yes, that must have been it. I certainly hadn't been selected in recognition of my sporting prowess.

My recollection is that school rules limited each competitor to three events, presumably to prevent the best athletes from taking part in everything to the exclusion of everyone else, but I have been told on good authority that I am wrong on that score, and I stand corrected. However, I don't remember anyone, not even the genuine speed aces, being allowed to represent their House in every event on School Sports Day.

Mine was a mixed grammar school, but I must confess that I cannot recall whether the girls took an active part on Sports Day. In those far off days there seemed to be sports that were regarded as entirely the preserve of male athletes, and it was rare to see women engaged in sports like football, cricket, or rugby. Things like tennis and netball seemed to be all I ever saw the girls at my school playing. But I assume they must have taken part in their own sports on School Sports Day, and I have a vague recollection of seeing female bodies, all dolled up in sports attire, strolling about the tracks and fields, and arching their limbs alluringly. But I have no recollection of seeing any examples of the games in which girls would have been the likely participants.

There were two competitors from each House in each event, a total of eight athletes per contest. Although I wasn't a particularly accomplished competitor in any event I could usually hold my own in around fifth or sixth place, which was good enough for me. I would love to have won all my races, of course, but it was not to be so it wasn't worth worrying about. If you win all the time you are expected to keep winning, and second place is therefore regarded as failure, but, for a *rikishi manqué*[17] like me, fifth or sixth place was OK. It wasn't brilliant, but it was OK.

On the School Sports Day in question, I had probably performed well in the shot putt, coming fifth or sixth if memory serves. Later on, fifth or sixth place in one of the sprints had confirmed that I was on top form, so I was feeling well pleased with myself. I now had one further 'proper' event to look forward to, and I was also taking part in something called the 'senior walk', of which more later. I think this latter escapade was an event in which you were allowed to participate even if you were doing three others but, as I have said, I may well be wrong about there being an upper limit on the number of times you could perform.

I now had to prepare myself for the 80 yards hurdles. A friend of mine told me recently that I had actually won the 80 yards hurdles the previous year, but I don't think that can be true. I recall having been in the race, but I think I probably came third or fourth, but if I had won it I would surely have remembered, and I have no such recollection. You tend to remember things you have won. I remember winning the junior boys' high jump one year, with a

17 See chapter 32.

prodigious leap of 3 feet 9 inches[18], but that was in my first year at the school. One of the reasons why that achievement sticks in my mind is that a certificate hanging on the wall in my study attests to the fact that in my final year as a pupil at primary school, I was placed second in the boys' high jump, and I distinctly remember that the height I cleared in order to win that prize was also 3 feet 9 inches. I could not get over 3 feet 10. And what is even more interesting is that after winning the boys' high jump in my first year at senior school, with a leap of 3 feet 9 inches, I was placed fifth or sixth in the same competition the following year, after failing to clear 3 feet 10 inches. I cleared 3 feet 9. Everyone else had improved, but I had stayed the same, and there you have the story of my life. If all the world's obstacles had been limited to but 3 feet 9 inches in height I think I would probably have been considered a superhero, but whoever decides these things chose to set the main bar of life at 3 feet 10 inches. But isn't that just the way of things? Life is a b*tch, as I may have mentioned before. But I certainly do *not* remember ever winning the 80 yards hurdles at school. Like I said earlier, I probably came around third or fourth. Or maybe fifth.

So, here I was again, participating in the 80 yards hurdles once more, and I noticed that I had been allocated an outside lane, lane eight. The lane I had been placed in ought not to have had much significance: it was a straight course, so there were no staggers or cambers to contend with. I suppose there might have been some slight advantage in running in lanes one or eight, for in those outside lanes you were not hemmed in on both sides by other athletes, but I don't remember giving much thought to that consideration at the time. It was a case of waiting for the sharp report of Mr Smith's starting pistol and then running like billy-o to the other end of the track, all the while trying to remember to jump

18 I have an awful feeling that the actual height I cleared was only 3 feet 8 inches, but I think I'll leave it at 3 feet 9 in the text, as to me that figure has a more Olympian ring about it.

over those sodding hurdles that were annoyingly strewn along the course at regular intervals.

What caught my attention as I prepared for the race, was not the lane I had been allocated but the fact that lane eight contained a number of broken hurdles which seemed to offer interesting possibilities. Let me explain. During his progress towards the finishing line, each of the eight athletes in the race had to negotiate about seven hurdles, which meant that the school must have owned about fifty-six hurdles in all. They were of a simple construction, consisting of a wooden crosspiece screwed to a metal frame. The crosspiece was set at about 33 inches from the ground, and the athlete was supposed to jump over the hurdles without touching them, but if he were to hit the crosspiece with his foot no harm would be done, because the whole hurdle was designed to topple forwards on its frame, enabling the hurdler to continue the race if he could stay on his feet. Such mishaps as these would inevitably shave valuable tenths of a second off the athlete's time, of course, but at least he would be able to complete the race.

Most of our school's hurdles were ageing, and had seen better times. Their metalwork was scratched and rusting, and their wooden crosspieces were discoloured and in need of a lick of varnish. But about eight of those hurdles were actually broken, in that the crosspieces were missing. Those hurdles (or, at least, the crosspieces) clearly needed replacing but, no doubt with an eye on economy, someone at the school had obviously decided that a simple fix would suffice for now, and thus it was that the eight broken hurdles had had their missing crosspieces temporarily replaced by flimsy bamboo canes. These canes were not screwed to the mountings, or attached in any way, but simply rested atop the frames in the slots vacated by the wooden crosspieces. Athletes negotiating these repaired hazards were, of course, expected to treat them in exactly the same way they treated the rest of the obstacles (ie: by jumping over them), but it was obvious to any observer that the slightest contact with any of these inadequately repaired hurdles would simply knock the cane out of its slot, without disturbing the frame in any way.

This ingenious solution to one of the financial problems facing the school at the time ought not to have affected the outcome of the race. If one broken hurdle had been placed in each lane, at about the position of the third or fourth obstacle, conditions would have been the same for each athlete and no one could have complained. However, that was not how the broken hurdles had been arranged. As I took in the course before the race started I noted that five of the broken hurdles had been distributed in random fashion along lanes one to seven, while no fewer than three of the repair jobs were decorating my lane, lane eight. And, what is more, the three broken hurdles in lane eight were occupying the positions of last three obstacles before the finishing tape.

Hmmm, I thought to myself.

The unbroken hurdles were all about 33 inches high, which was also the height at which the canes on the broken ones had been set, so at intervals of a few strides all the athletes had to leap two feet nine inches in the air. But what would be the outcome, I wondered, if lane eight were to be occupied by a runner totally without scruples? As things were arranged, that unprincipled athlete was free to overcome the final three obstacles in his path, not by jumping over them but by careering through them, as if they did not exist! And if he was able to negotiate the last three hazards on the track without breaking stride, surely that would have a beneficial effect on his performance in the race!

Hmmm.

But there was no time now for further reflection on all this now..... The blinking race was about to begin. Mr Smith raised his pistol.....

Bang! And we were off! Eight electrically charged athletes were out of their blocks in an instant, and haring down the track with a conviction that suggested their very lives depended on it. As I have said, the furious progress of each of the eight of us was interrupted every ten yards or so by a hurdle, and our stride pattern was broken for the moment it took each one of us to rise 33 inches in the air and land safely on the other side, where the frenetic sprinting continued.

Eighty yards is not very far to run and the race was half over before I had even thought about what I was doing. Had I chanced to glance to my left at that stage I would probably have found myself in fourth or fifth place and would likely have been well pleased with my efforts. It does not take much to make athletes like me happy. But now the race was reaching a crucial stage. With only thirty-five yards to go, and four solid enough hurdles safely negotiated, the only remaining obstacles between me and the finishing tape were three of those sorry-looking articles, bodged with bamboo-canes, I described earlier. None of them was a match for the determination or guile of a Herbert Jaxon in full flight, and I ran straight through all three of them as though they didn't exist, without breaking stride. The bamboo canes flew this way and that as I contemptuously removed them with my shins or thighs. As my pace quickened I have a distinct recollection of seeing the three or four runners who had been in front of me suddenly appearing to engage reverse gear, as they all seemed to come hurrying back towards me – not because they were consciously decelerating, but because they were jumping over hurdles, whereas I wasn't. They were still in a hurdle race, while I was now on the flat, and in the next second the finishing line was upon us.

I have no idea whether or not I was first past the post, but I must have been pretty close to winning the race as three or four of us thundered over the line together. It was the job of Mr Rudolph Hucker, French master, to sort out photo-finishes of this sort, and he had to do so with the naked eye because, to the best of my knowledge, the school hadn't yet invested in photo-finish technology. To my surprise, however, as I hurtled past him I didn't see him bent at the waist and knee, or squinting intently along the finishing line in order best to be able to sort out gold from silver and bronze. Instead, I saw him standing bolt upright, repeatedly waving both arms across his chest and then out to the side, like a swimming teacher trying to pass on the basics of the breast-stroke to new swimmers, as he screamed at the top of his lungs:

"Jaxon.....! Disqualified.....! Jaxon.....! Disqualified.....! Jaxon.....! Disqualified.....!"

I applied the airbrakes and rattled to a halt, and then adopted the brace position that seemed to be favoured by most competitors after a hectic race of that sort, with my body bent double and my head between my knees. My elbows each rested on a thigh as I gulped in air, desperate to replenish the oxygen that had been explosively expended over the past twenty or thirty seconds. I then straightened up slowly, wondering what attitude I ought to adopt when facing the music. Initially, I wasn't too worried. OK, I had been disqualified. But being disqualified isn't much different from finishing fourth or fifth, is it? I hadn't won the race, that is true, but we cannot all be winners, and I already knew I was a loser so losing another race wasn't going to cause me to lose any sleep. I might as well go and apologise to Mr Hucker, and we'll say no more about it.

And then suddenly, it hit me! *Oh, Christ!* And in that instant I was really worried. Oh, my goodness, when realisation dawned I was truly mortified, and I had a feeling I was going to be in big, big trouble this time. I was aware for the first time that this wasn't some stupid and harmless jaxonian prank, of the type my long-suffering teachers had had to put up with every day since I arrived at the school. No. I realised immediately that this was something much more serious. I was about to be accused of cheating!

Crumbs, until it hit me at that moment I hadn't thought of it that way. When I had run through those last few hurdles as if they did not exist, it was not because I was trying to cheat. I had not done it because I was trying to win the race. I had done it because..... well..... Oh bugger, why had I done it? At that precise moment I was blowed if I knew, but I certainly had NOT done it in order to cheat. I think I had done it simply to point out that it could be done, or to try and make someone laugh, but, in the cold light of realisation, this didn't seem to me to be a very good excuse.

I ought to explain immediately that cheating is something of which I strongly disapprove. I believe that the severest punishment should be meted out to anyone who seeks to gain an unfair advantage. I am of the school that says a batsman should 'walk' if he knows he has been caught behind, and that he should be banned for ever, perhaps longer, if he fails to do so, and that a footballer should be sent off for pretending he has been tripped by an opponent, and that any athlete who takes either a bribe or a performance enhancing stimulant should be excluded from all sport for life, and from any competitive event there may be in the hereafter. In such cases I am not a fan of the appeals system either. In short, I am in favour of summary justice being dispensed, at once, with no chance to weasel ones way out. And here I was, about to get a taste of my own medicine. I had no time to think of an excuse for what I had done, and I felt truly awful.

But what was this? Mr Hucker was making a point of coming over to see me and his manner seemed benign, almost apologetic.

"Sorry, Giacomo[19]," he said almost kindly. "I think you may have been the winner there, but I'm going to have to disqualify you. You ran out of your lane back there."

Ran out of my lane? I was sure I hadn't run out of my lane! I couldn't understand what he was talking about, and didn't care, but in that instant I breathed the biggest sigh of relief that has ever been breathed. I wasn't going to be falsely accused of trying to cheat!

"Ran out my lane, Sir? I'm sure I didn't run out of my lane!" I protested.

"Yes you did, I'm afraid. You put your foot on the line at least twice, and that's running out of your lane, I'm afraid. Sorry. I'm going to have to disqualify you."

"OK, Sir. Sorry," I said manfully. And that was that.

But hang about, Jaxon, you may well be saying. From where Mr Hucker had been standing throughout the race, at the far end of the track adjacent to lane eight, he was certainly well placed to see whether or not I had trodden on any lines, but what about the other athletes? He was in no position, from where he stood, to spot any similar infringements that might have been committed by hurdlers in lanes one through seven. How could he be sure that none of the other athletes had run out of their sodding lanes as well? (That 'as well' should not be taken as an admission that I accepted that I had run out of mine.) Was this not a case of blatant discrimination against the hurdler who had been placed in lane eight? I think I had more than enough going for me to demand a steward's inquiry.

---

19 Mr Hucker also taught me Italian, and often used to call me "Giacomo". God knows why. But I thought he was a decent old stick.

But I took it no further. I let it pass. Given the evidence that might have been stacked against me on the cheating front, I hadn't fancied defending myself against any charge arising from my recent bamboo-hopping, so I thought this was the time to let sleeping dogs fornicate (or whatever they do). And, in the circumstances I think I got off lightly. Oh, I had protested, of course, when accused of running out of my lane, but that was just for form. It would have been expected of me. People who are disqualified are supposed to feel upset about it, so I had just followed my instincts. But who cares if I had run out of my lane? Perhaps I had. My House had lost a point or two as a result of my disqualification, but the main thing was that I wasn't going to be done for cheating. Phew.

Later that day I had something of a chance to redeem myself because I was due to take part in what was known as the 'senior walk'. The senior walk was a walking race of one mile duration, or four circuits of the school's athletics track, open to members of the senior school, which I think was probably Upper Fifths and Sixth forms. If memory serves, there was no upper limit to the number of competitors each House could field, so there were probably about thirty athletes taking part, and I was one of around seven or eight representing my House. It was presumably called the senior walk in order to distinguish it from the junior walk, which was a similar event restricted to members of the lower school, probably Lower Fifths and below, but which called for only three laps of the track, or three-quarters of a mile, to be completed.

There were half a dozen or so good race walkers in the school, so the senior event promised to be keenly contested. I had no chance of winning the race, of course, but reckoned I could probably finish in the top twenty-five if I made the effort. A couple of the elite athletes were friends of mine, and one of these, Harry Blueman of a rival House, or "Bluey" to his friends, was an accomplished race walker whose talents had, I think, already been spotted by Ippardly Athletics Club. He would take this race seriously, as would Duncan Disorderly, of yet another House, another of my friends, whose main priority, if he couldn't win the race, was to try to finish ahead of Bluey. Down at the start I wished both of them well. I think they probably both ignored me.

At the appointed time all the athletes had assembled on the track for the start of the walk and there was a good deal of jostling for position at the starting line. The main contenders all wanted to be at the front of the pack when Mr Smith's starting pistol sounded and, having initially placed myself in a good starting position on the inside track, I found myself summarily ejected from it by a few of the elite walkers before I could settle.

"Hey!" I remonstrated with them. "*I* was in there! I was hoping to get a good start and hug the rail for the first couple of laps, and open up a massive lead so that I could take a breather over the last half mile but still cruise home towards the front!"

Some of the others were in no mood for clowning around. "Out of the way!" they commanded. "This is serious!"

"OK," I said, humouring them, as I turned slowly away from my favoured starting position. "But you'll be sorry. When the hare and the tortoise had a race....."

We were coming under starter's orders now, and the elite athletes had all adopted the approved starting pose for a walking race. With front leg straight, one toe on the white line and the upper body hunched forward, they were taut as coiled springs as they waited to propel themselves into the middle distance as soon as the pistol was fired. Displaced from one of the favoured starting positions, I wandered rather aimlessly round behind the main pack, trying not to get in the way of the other walkers, and then, on a whim, I dropped to one knee and waited for the gun, like a sprinter who had settled in his starting blocks. It was a silly thing to do and I don't know exactly why I did it. I suppose I was trying to make someone laugh, but I don't think it went down too well, particularly with some members of staff who were watching the start. Then, when Mr Smith fired his pistol, and the assembled athletes sprang forward and set off down the track at a cracking pace, I rose slowly to my feet and ambled after them in a leisurely fashion, like a holidaymaker out for a pleasant evening stroll, with no object in life other than a smell of the ozone and a light bronzing of the limbs. By the time the leading peloton had covered the first sixty yards and were leaving the straight to negotiate the first bend, I was already forty yards in the rear of the field, and had not yet broken sweat.

What *was* I playing at? You may well ask, sweet Reader, but I cannot be sure. Perhaps I had already decided that, with no hope of winning the race, and with no aspiration even of finishing in the top twenty, I might as well complete all four laps in the same unhurried manner, in the hope of raising a smile among some of my friends. Was that it? Or perhaps, as seems to me to be just as likely, I had an accomplice or two, with whom I had agreed to slouch round at the rear of the field for a few laps, purely in order to see what happened. If that were the case my co-conspirators had obviously thought better of it, because, from where I strolled, the heels of the race's penultimate athlete were already a speck on the horizon. Perhaps I had decided on this strange course of action in order to lampoon the whole idea of race walking, which I had always considered to be a very strange competitive concept, on a par with cheese rolling, dwarf throwing, bear baiting, bull running, bog snorkelling, pie eating, gurning, and the skeleton luge. Ignorant people have ignorant ideas, after all. Who knows what I was about? I'm blowed if I do. But I will tell you this: by the time I had covered the first fifteen or twenty yards of the race I was already regretting my stupidity and was looking for a way to redeem myself without forfeiting every shred of dignity.

At this point I would like to say that I thought quickly, as I tried to find an escape route, but that would be a lie. As you are already aware, I am totally incapable of thinking quickly. If I thought quickly I wouldn't get myself into these messes in the first place. So I will have to be truthful, and admit that I thought slowly. Given the mess I was in, it didn't sound very promising, but it was the best I could do.

What were the options? At first blush there didn't seem to be many but, strangely enough, about half a dozen decent possibilities did soon appear to pass through my mind, each one of which had its own peculiar attraction. The choices all seemed really to be variations on a couple of themes: I could either speed up, or I could slow down. For example, I could speed up and try and catch the rest, in order to make something of a race of it. Or I could slow down, feigning a stitch, and then retire gracefully from the fray. Or I could really speed up, and get myself disqualified for lifting[20]. One of the attractions of this option was that I wouldn't be obliged to complete the race, so would be spared any further self-inflicted embarrassment. Or I could slow right down, and get myself lapped by the other athletes, and then complete the race at their pace, so as not to look quite so conspicuously out of place as I did now. Or I could speed up, and give the impression that my slow start had been a prearranged tactic: I might be 'pacing myself'. Or I could slow down and simply brazen it out, casually strolling along in this cosy fashion, without a care in the world, even stopping to pick a daisy whenever the fancy.....

Suddenly, my peace was disturbed by an ear-shattering yell.

"Jaxon.....! Disqualified.....! Jaxon.....! Disqualified.....! Jaxon.....! Disqualified.....!"

---

20 See earlier footnote.

Oh dear. I recognised that voice.... Instinctively I looked round to where the sound was coming from, but I needn't have bothered: the voice that was doing the shouting was unmistakable, and I was already feeling uneasy as a result. Once again it was Mr Hucker who had taken exception to my distinctive style of athleticism, and he was bearing down on me at a far greater rate of knots than I was managing to achieve in the race. Abandoning all thought of continued participation in the senior walk, I stepped nimbly off the track and slowly walked towards the irate master. I half toyed with the idea of doing a few 'warming down' toe touches and stretches, but thought better of it.

When Mr Hucker had disqualified me in the hurdles race a couple of hours earlier he had seemed reluctant to do so. But not this time. I had seen Mr Hucker angry before, but I had seldom seen him as angry as this.

"What do you think you're playing at, you stupid idiot?" he screamed, loud enough for the whole of the northern hemisphere to hear.

"Nothing, Sir," I replied. This is the stock reply of all schoolchildren to this type of question from a schoolteacher, but I regret to say that on this occasion I couldn't think of a better response. The master ignored my intervention anyway.

"Disqualified for not trying! Disgraceful! You should be ashamed of yourself! Get out! Go inside and get changed and then come straight back out here and see me!"

I suppose, with hindsight, that the best course of action now would have been to do as I was told and go straight indoors, hoping that Mr Hucker's temper tantrum would blow itself out while I was away. But I'm afraid I rarely opt for the best course of action. I suppose I did feel a bit ashamed of myself, and thought that sloping off to the changing room without a word might have led the master to conclude that I was a surly good-for-nothing, bent on trouble. I therefore decided, in my infinite wisdom, to try to brazen it out. Perhaps if I made light of it...

"But, Sir! When the hare and the tortoise....."

"**SILENCE**!!!!! Get inside!!!!! **NOW**!!!!! I'm not standing here all afternoon listening to your nonsense! Look at the rest of those competitors! And then just look at you! You're a disgrace! Those boys are really putting some effort into it! Little Harry Blueman is really trying hard!"

Mentioning Harry, with particular reference to the fact that my friend was shorter than I was, was, I felt, a very clever trick, even by Sir's standards, and I could see immediately where he was coming from. In Mr Hucker's view, I was a great, lolloping 6 feet plus of wasted space, whose lack of competitive instinct in this event contrasted starkly with that being exhibited by someone a foot shorter than I was, and who therefore appeared to have fewer natural advantages. If Sir's strategy was to try to humiliate me the ploy worked, and I felt particularly foolish and ashamed at that moment. However, I had been disqualified once again, and that still called for some kind of show of aggrieved protest.

"But, Sir, I....."

"**SILENCE**!!!!!" His voice was now like thunder, and I noticed that several tiles flew off the roof of a neighbouring building, about two hundred yards away, as he spoke. Of course, this might have been pure coincidence.

I closed my mouth and set off towards the changing rooms.

"**AND GET A MOVE ON**! I'm not having you slouching along, all the way back into school, the way you were out there on the track! Disgraceful behaviour!"

Instinctively, without turning my head I quickened my pace, and went inside to get showered and changed.

With the athletics events still in full swing outside, I had thought I would have the changing room to myself, but when I got in there I found there were a couple of boys in the showers, most probably having completed their events earlier in the afternoon, and one or two of my friends followed me in at a discreet distance, presumably either to commiserate or to poke fun at my predicament. I cannot remember much of what was said, but I do recall that I was chatting to my mates as I was getting dressed in an unhurried fashion after my shower when suddenly a younger boy of about twelve, from the lower school, scampered into the changing room with a message for me.

"Hey, Jax," he piped in his shrill treble. "Pappy Hucker wants to know what's taking you so long, and he wants you to go outside and see him right away!" The short-trousered messenger broadcasted his communiqué without further formality, and scampered off as soon as it was delivered. I hastily completed my ablutions and hurried outside.

When I reached the edge of the playground where it joined the school field I could see Mr Hucker in the distance, still busily (and noisily) engaged in some judicial function or other, and I set off to meet him as directed. I wasn't looking forward to the encounter, and this may have been reflected in the fact that I wasn't exactly hurrying. On the other hand, I didn't want Mr Hucker to look up unexpectedly and think I was dawdling. I therefore tried to adopt a gait that appeared to any observers to be hurried but which covered relatively small amounts of ground relatively slowly. Perhaps if I could have perfected that pretence during the actual 'race' all this subsequent nonsense might have been avoided.

However, scarcely had I stepped off the school playground and my shoes touched grass when I happened to bump into

Mr Peregrine Panties, my mathematics teacher, who was heading in the opposite direction, towards the school building. I hadn't seen him on the sports field earlier, so didn't know whether he had witnessed my earlier disqualification from the senior walk, but his opening remark left me in no doubt on that score.

"I believe Mr Hucker's looking for you, Jaxon. And, if I were you, I'd get over there a bit quicker than you were moving when you were in the race!"

"Thank you, Sir. Yes, Sir. I'll get over there, Sir." And I quickened my pace.

But (and isn't it just the way with schoolmasters?) having told me to get a move on, it now seemed that what Mr Panties really wanted was to delay me for 'a bit of a chat'.

"I don't know what you thought you were playing at out there?"

He had stopped, so I naturally stopped as well. Despite Mr Hucker's simmering impatience I could hardly ignore Mr Panties and keep walking, and anyway my maths teacher's remark had seemed more of a question than a comment, to which he might be looking for a response. Crumbs, was he going to punish me as well? I already had Mr Hucker's wrath to look forward to, but I now thought Mr Panties might well be intending to double my jeopardy. I liked Mr Panties, although I do not think my fondness for him was reciprocated. He had been my form master in the Lower 4ths as well as in the Upper 5ths, so we knew each other well, and I think he felt, not without justification, that I could sometimes be a bit of a disruptive influence in class. But he was a kindly soul, and on this occasion I thought I detected something of a twinkle in his eye and a smile seemed to be playing about the corners of his mouth. In short, I didn't think he was taking such a serious view of my prank as his colleague. I decided, therefore, to risk responding in lighter vein, reserving the possibility of switching over to seriously apologetic mode later, if it subsequently turned out that I had read Sir's mood incorrectly.

"I was pacing myself, Sir."

"Pacing yourself?" He scoffed. "It was a mile walk, not a marathon!"

"Yes, Sir. But a mile's quite a long way, particularly if you're only walking. And when the hare and the tortoise decided to have a race, the hare set off....."

"Yes, I know the story, thank you," he interrupted. "But if you were pacing yourself you still needed to stay somewhere in touch with the others. From what I saw you weren't even going fast enough to catch a bus!"

And with that he turned on his heels and set off towards the school building, still chuckling to himself at his own little joke.

And that was it from him. Surely he hadn't stopped me just so that he could crack that awful joke, had he? Perhaps he had. But we shall never know, because I am afraid I didn't have the courage to ask him.

With your permission, revered Reader, I am going to skip the rest of the events of that afternoon, largely because I have forgotten what punishment Mr Hucker did choose to administer, but mainly because this chapter has run its course. Twenty-one pages is surely more than enough for anyone, particularly when for some of us those pages evoke painful memories.

I will leave you with one thought. School Sports have taken place every year, at schools all over the country, for many a summer, but I wonder how often in the past it has happened that the same athlete has been disqualified in two different sporting events on the same day in the same year by the same judge on the same track at the same meet at the same School Sports? Surely that must qualify as some kind of record, and one of which a much more accomplished speed ace than Herbert Jaxon could feel justly proud?

CHAPTER 10 : HOPE SPRINGS...

A happy birthday, dear Christine!
When you were made they broke the mould;
A sweeter face I've never seen,
And you've stayed young as I've grown old!
I can't believe you're fifty, yet
I'm still a lad of forty-nine;
But I'm a stale old *Mimolette*,
While you've matured, like vintage wine!
When we were teens I had no doubt
You'd marry me; so my heart broke
In bits the day that I found out
You'd shacked up with another bloke.
I asked you fifty times, at least,
To be my bride, but you said no...
Though my resolve was not decreased,
Rejection came as quite a blow...
Not being a man to pine, or mope,
Or sit there, praying for a miracle,
I still contrived to live in hope:
Your knock-backs weren't *quite* unequivocal.
Do you recall the words you used
When you just snapped, and kicked me out?
Although they left me feeling bruised,
I still felt I was in with a shout...
When I asked for the umptieth time,
If you'd be mine, and tie the knot,
You blew your top, and told me I'm
Worth less to you than diddly-squat!
You said you'd finally had enough!
My constant pleading was a bore!
"I'll **NEVER** marry a bit of rough –
"A useless prat like you!" you swore.

You told me I was crass, and crude,
Uncouth, offensive, coarse, and vile,
Indecent, clumsy, gross, and rude,
A foulmouthed, ***ing, juvenile!
You called me ugly, stupid, dumb,
Deceitful, thoughtless, asinine;
Much worse than any pond-life scum,
A cringing coward, with no spine,
Who always looked a frightful mess!
And then you screeched, for all you're worth,
That you'd not marry me unless
I were the **ONLY** man on Earth!!!!!!
Your mean assault took me aback…
Those cruel words fair laid me low…
Your bitter, unprovoked attack,
Had left me nowhere I could go…
Except, become a Trappist monk?
Or heed the Foreign Legion's call?
Give in to booze? Become a drunk?
Or find a way to end it all?
But then, that evening, in my bed,
Reflecting on my sorry plight,
I weighed precisely what you'd said,
And think I spied a chink of light…
All plans of jumping off a cliff
Evaporated! Gone was stress,
When I recalled you'd not said… *if* …
By a slip of the tongue, you'd said… *unless*!!!
Had you just made a goof in a million?
Or sent me a subliminal sign?
As per your words, if some four billion
All popped their clogs, then you'd be mine!!!
Since then some thirty years have passed,
And I've checked newsprint every day,
Counting the blokes who've breathed their last…

Praying for billions to pass away...
So, happy birthday, from this clown,
Whose pleas, for you, were just a trope;
One you contemptuously turned down,
But who, regardless, lives in hope...

CHAPTER 11 : FAITH

My wife and kids all go to church,
While I sit home, relaxin',
For man can't live by gin alone
Unless he's Herbert Jaxon.

CHAPTER 12 : ST LUCY'S DAY[21]

I was told that 13 of December,
Would be St Lucy's Saint's Day again,
And to make it a day you'd remember,
I decided to get some champagne,

To accompany a nice bunch of flowers
I had bought you for your special day;
Just arranging them took me two hours,
And I'd worked up a wondrous display.

The bouquet made a beautiful picture,
And I hoped that you'd never forget it,
But I turned my head just for a second
And your Forest cat[22] walked up… and ate it!

---

21 Written for my daughter, who shares the name with the Saint…
22 … And who owns a Norwegian Forest Cat, with a penchant for cut flowers.

CHAPTER 13 : THE PROPER CHANNELS

"Sorry, Rupert," I said. "But that's nonsense. I think we've already agreed that that's nonsense. You even said so yourself!"

Rupert sighed deeply, shook his head sadly, and buried his face deep in his hands.

All right, sceptical Reader, perhaps Rupert didn't behave in quite so theatrical a fashion, but if this had been a film I'm sure that is what the director would have required him to do at this crucial moment. After having already put up with more than ten minutes of my moaning, Rupert's emotions were certainly running high, and certainly as high as that imaginary director I was talking about would have wanted them to be running, but Rupert wasn't the kind of gentleman to go over the top, and he certainly wouldn't have started blubbing in the manner that would have befitted the plot, either of my account of this incident or of that imaginary film I was telling you about. But, if Rupert could have forced himself for once, that would have been very fitting.

Rupert Normal was an extremely nice man and I think it genuinely pained him to have to pass on to me the bad news he had just delivered. Rupert was my new boss, a director on the company's board, no less, whereas I was only a lowly regional manager, so there was no doubt which one of us was in charge. But, boss or not, Rupert clearly felt he was wedged between a rock and a hard place. I was in his office in London, in the middle of one of my regular bilateral meetings with him, during which we were supposed to discuss progress towards achievement of my objectives, but whenever he asked why a particular target had been missed it seemed to unnerve him that I was able to offer a logical explanation. I felt a great deal of sympathy for Rupert – no one wants to be in the position he was in – but that was how it was. Things were tough for all of us and getting tougher, and trying to do the job was becoming more and more difficult.

For some seconds Rupert just sat there at his desk, his eyes tight shut, his fingers pressed lightly against his eyelids and his chin resting gloomily on the heels of his hands. (Well, maybe he didn't. But when this is a film, I'm sure the actor playing him will be asked to do all that.) Then, as he slowly recovered his cool, he tried again, in that gently persuasive voice of his.

"I'm sorry, Herbert, but that's just the way it is. Murdo will not budge on this one. You *know* what he's like. You're just going to have to manage with what you've got."

"But that's nonsense," I persisted calmly. "If I am expected to do a job I need the tools to do it. And I don't mean any old tools – I need the proper tools."

Rupert sighed deeply once again.

"I know, I know; and you're right," he countered softly. "But *you* try telling that to Murdo! He's decided that the staff you want are just too expensive, and so he wants you to manage with what you've got, particularly in the middle of a recruitment freeze. Your unit simply can't have any more. *I* understand your problem, of course, but Murdo doesn't, and he holds the purse strings and he refuses to discuss it further. My hands are tied." And Rupert gave me a rather helpless look, like the one I was once given by one of my kittens, when she was padlocked inside her basket, awaiting a trip to the vet's.

Rupert was only partly right. Murdo McTurd, who had the final say on these things, certainly did *not* understand the problem so he wasn't going to know how to solve it. But Rupert was also partly wrong. Despite his assertion to the contrary, Rupert didn't understand the problem either, which was why I was getting no real help from him in persuading Murdo that the problem needed a solution. This was one of the major difficulties facing the company at the time. Nearly all positions on the board were now occupied by people who had parachuted in from outside the business, from other bits of the industry, or, so it seemed to me, from the local circus, so none of them had a clue how it all worked, except, of course, in theory. They were all extremely good at the theoretical, but when it came to the practical they were about as much use as a concrete life jacket. I, on the other hand, was typical of the old breed – brainless, and one of the 'dinosaurs' who had gained the best part of thirty-five years 'on the job' experience, having worked my way up from the shop floor. But Rupert had been in post for only a few months, having wafted in from elsewhere when a vacancy on the board had arisen, and Murdo McTurd had been chief executive for only a year or so longer, having been farted in on a bad draught from outside in much the same way. What made matters much worse was that, for a number of years, Rupert had worked for Murdo in another part of the industry, so there was probably some bitterness and old rivalry kicking around that the company could certainly have done without.

One of the difficulties which both Rupert and I currently faced was that Murdo McTurd was a problem in his own right. Everyone in the company knew that, so park that for a moment if you will, because I will return to it, but there is more. In addition, although he represented the current problem we faced, he was only part of that one, albeit a major part. I had known him vaguely for several years, because everyone in our line of work gets to know of everyone else eventually, and I had found him 'difficult' from the outset. As far as I was concerned, he was a useless, stuck-up, toffee-nosed pile of horse manure, who was far too full of his own importance to have any inkling of the damage he was causing to the company. Even in the words of one of his closest associates, Murdo was 'a serial incompetent', and nothing I had seen of him had given me any cause to argue with that assessment.

On the surface, the problem Rupert and I were discussing was simple enough. I was a regional manager, and like the rest of the regional managers I had been forced to sign up to meeting targets that were, in Murdo's assessment, 'challenging', but which were, in the assessment of everyone else, 'impossible'. Appropriate staffing levels had been agreed at the beginning of the financial year, of course, at which time I had already been running a couple light, but I had had a reasonable expectation that I would be brought up to strength before being judged on my output. Soon after that I had, naturally, lost one or two key members of staff, whether to resignation or promotion, and, if that were not bad enough, finances had started 'unexpectedly' to get tight, causing 'certain measures' to be taken, culminating in this accursed recruitment freeze till the end of the year. Any reasonable man might have thought that this would have necessitated the revision of output targets that had been 'agreed' when things had looked rosier, but Murdo was anything but a reasonable man. Murdo was a blinkered grumpbucket who expected his regional managers to keep delivering, even if they didn't have the means to do it, and this was now causing 'friction'. The result was that Murdo was now leaning on people like Rupert, and expecting people like Rupert to lean on people like me in their turn. I suppose I was in turn expected to lean on my own workforce, but I'm afraid I am physically and mentally incapable of operating like that. That is why I was leaning on Rupert instead, and, reasonable man that he was, Rupert was not enjoying being squeezed in the middle.

It was the old, old story. I could remember a time at the beginning of the year, when the targets I had been invited to 'agree' were revealed to me by Brian Trizerjob, Rupert's predecessor, and I had been promised the earth in order to get me to sign up to them.

Money was no object at the time; mine was the most important job on the planet (according to Brian) and Murdo had said I could have as many staff as I liked. I really think Brian had meant it when he said it. Like the rest of them, Brian had been helicoptered in from outside a few months earlier, having presumably impressed someone at interview with his vast knowledge of something or other that was completely irrelevant to what the company was involved in, and, using a lethal cocktail of flattery and mendacity, he had believed he would have no trouble at all in having me sign up to Murdo's impossible demands. It was pointless to argue with him, of course, but in reluctantly agreeing to Murdo's demands I had pointedly told Brian that when all the wheels came off I would be the first to say I told you so, and remind him that he had been conned. In return for 'agreeing' my targets, and in order to get me out of his office before Christmas, and in order to impress Murdo with how easily he could handle a difficult old so and so like me, Brian, who was in many ways as bad as Murdo, had actually agreed to let me tell him at the appropriate time that I had been right and he had been wrong. But now that the appropriate time had arrived, and I should have been enjoying my moment of triumph, Brian was gone, and was no doubt already cocking something up in some other company, while here in his place was young Rupert, who was far too likeable a guy for someone like me to be too hard on. Like the rest of my life, it was all very unfair.

We had struggled on as best we could, as you do, for the early part of the year, during which time Brian had been promising me even more staff than I had originally bid for. That was because that was the type of man Trizerjob was. He thought he could keep me happy by promising me financial bonuses, and offering me even more resources than I had requested, and he was even prepared to put it in writing. However, he hadn't thought through any of the implications, and had had no idea where these extra resources could be plucked from, so, of course, the extra staff he had promised me had never materialised.

This farcical situation had then begun causing me new problems. With all these imaginary 'extra' posteriors occupying seats in my office, Murdo was wondering whether he might have been too generous to me when my original targets were set, and was wondering whether Rupert might be able to squeeze some extra output out of my illusory army. It was clear from what Rupert had told me that, when creating extra work for me, Murdo preferred to base his assumptions on my notional staffing complement, as agreed by Brian, rather than on the number of actual serviceable *derrières* I could call my own, to kick as the will took me, and we were now being expected to deliver results that would have required my staff to be in two places at once. On one occasion I had even been asked why I had sent an officer to one part of the country, to conclude an agreement he was close to completing work on, when there was (according to Murdo) a pressing need for him to go to another corner of the country at the same time, to start work on something else that he had no hope of delivering. You couldn't make it up – unless you had worked in this type of environment as long as I had.

When I reminded the top of the office of my staffing deficiencies Rupert's response had originally been the same as Murdo's: I couldn't have any more expensive 'experts', but I could have some general support staff, because they were much cheaper. When I mentioned that it would be pointless recruiting support staff when they had no one to support I was told (by Murdo, via Rupert) that I was just being difficult. I didn't for one minute expect Murdo to understand any of this, of course, because he was wired differently from the rest of us, but Rupert soon caught something of my drift, and that only depressed him further. He realised even without my explaining it to him that Murdo's Plan B (that I accept some inexperienced staff and train them myself) was a non-starter, because that would mean that those doing the training would not be able to do their day job at the same time, and this realisation depressed poor Rupert even more. I pitied poor

Rupert, because he really cared about all this nonsense, and I think he understood early on that I didn't.

Eventually this stalemate had been partially broken. Rupert was a reasonable man, and during repeated bilateral meetings with him I had taken the trouble to explain the problem to him in detail. In this way I had succeeded in convincing him that my unit was not going to be able to continue delivering quality results if I couldn't secure experienced staff to join my team. But even when he understood (or said he understood) the problem, Rupert still declared himself powerless to resolve it. Murdo, as he had assured me, wouldn't budge on this one. Support staff were as cheap as chips and, within reason, I could have as many of them as I liked. But experts were expensive – and didn't I know there was a recruitment freeze on?

"OK," I conceded, "but in that case you will have to tell Murdo that his way just isn't a way, and that unless I can have the staff I need he will have to revise his expectations of my unit's output downwards, and he will have to tell the board that he has misled them into thinking we can achieve all he said he could achieve within the timescales he suggested."

Rupert groaned. "We can't expect him to do that," he wailed. "Ossie will cut him off at the proverbials!"

"Then tell him to give me the staff I was promised – it's as simple as that," I repeated for the umpteenth time.

"But I've already told him that," protested Rupert, "and he won't listen. You know what he's like."

"All right," I said wearily. "Let's just leave it at that then." I was past caring. "Accrington Stanley had a good win last Saturday. Did you see that?"

"But we can't leave it at that – you know we can't!" Rupert objected, in the most pained tones, ignoring my flippancy. "I've got one of *my* regular bilaterals with Murdo coming up next week and he's going to want to know why I haven't managed to persuade you to sign up to increased outputs from your unit. He thinks you're just being difficult."

"That's because he's a prat," I replied.

"I know he's a prat!" Rupert snapped back. "But he's the prat in charge, and I can't just tell him to sod off."

"You don't have to," I retorted. "Just tell him that as soon as he agrees to bring me up to strength I'll be able to start delivering against these increased targets. A child of five would understand that. I'll tell you what. My sister's got a child of five. You can take him in with you and he can explain it to Murdo in a language that he's likely to understand. But you'll have to make sure his hands aren't all chocolatey before you take him in there. I think Margaret will object if she finds chocolate all over the arms of the furniture…."

"But this is where we came in!" Rupert protested. "Murdo doesn't understand why you can't manage with the staff you've got, and he won't listen to anything else…!"

I sighed, and allowed a short pause to develop. I had an idea of what the way forward might be but I didn't know what Rupert's reaction might be. I decided to test the water.

"Do you want me to speak to him?" I asked tentatively. I didn't want to hurt Rupert's feelings by suggesting to him outright that I might be in a better position to persuade Murdo of the logic of my arguments, even though that was so obviously the case, but on this occasion I needn't have worried. Rupert was so sick of sitting between a rock and a hard place that he was past caring about the niceties of the situation, or of my usurping his authority, and he seized upon my offer with some enthusiasm.

"Would you?" he gasped. "I'd be very grateful if you would."

And so that was what was agreed.

When I got back to my office I lost no time in asking Chandra, my secretary, to make an appointment for me to see Murdo McTurd. I wasn't confident that I could persuade Murdo to change his mind, of course, but I felt that in a face to face meeting with him I would stand a far better chance than Rupert of explaining my position. I even thought that I might get him to understand just how unreasonable his own stance was, and that we might reach a compromise. Even if I couldn't, I would at least have had the satisfaction of having tried, and Murdo would never be able to say that I hadn't taken the trouble to spell out my difficulties to him.

Don't get me wrong. I wasn't looking forward to a meeting with Murdo McTurd. No one in their right mind would want a meeting with him. But I was actually feeling some relief now that matters were about to be brought to a head. Chandra rang Margaret, Murdo's secretary, at once with a request that he meet me. I suppose that should have been the beginning of the end of the problem, but that, in fact, is when the *real* trouble started.

The following day I received a call from Margaret. I had known Margaret for years, but that didn't mean I knew her well. However, whenever I had had dealings with her in the past I believed that we had got on together. She was a rather portly figure, probably in her fifties, and I knew that she had worked for a number of Murdo's predecessors in London over the years. Inevitably, therefore, I had seen her around many times when I was up in town, and we had occasionally exchanged a friendly word, even shared a joke. I believe, however, that this was the first time I had ever spoken to her on the telephone, and I should have picked up immediately that something was amiss, although I freely confess that at the time I failed to do so.

"Hello, Mr Jaxon," she began. "It's Margaret here, Mr McTurd's secretary."

In the past she had always called me Herbert but, thinking back, I am pretty sure that on this occasion she called me 'Mr Jaxon'. But I cannot be positive about that, and as I cannot even be sure that I even noticed what she called me, any significance in her opening gambit was obviously lost on me.

As I have said, Margaret's call took me completely by surprise. I had expected her to fix everything up with Chandra, and hadn't been expecting her to ring me direct. When I took her call I was on my way to a meeting somewhere or other, and my mind was on other things. I was on a train, and she rang me on my mobile telephone to say that Mr Murdo McTurd had agreed to see me and that she had made an appointment for us to meet in Mr McTurd's office at 14.30 hours the following Thursday afternoon.

Why was she ringing me up just to tell me that, I wondered? Surely she should have realised that I would find out about the appointment soon enough because Chandra would have told me. Why not leave it to Chandra? It was, if I had thought about it closely, all very strange, but I was prepared to think no more of it than that. I had, after all, more pressing things on my mind and was actually trying to concentrate on what I was reading in preparation for my present meeting, so I paid little attention.

"OK, thanks, Margaret," I said. "I'll be there."

And I prepared to hang up so that I could get back to my papers. Fat chance.

"Yes," she said again. "Two-thirty next Thursday afternoon. Mr McTurd has asked me to tell you that he has agreed to see you – *exceptionally*."

"OK," I said again, confirming that the message had been taken in. It wasn't a particularly good line, there was a lot of background noise, and I am a bit deaf, so I thought I had better repeat that I had heard her correctly and understood.

"Half two, next Thursday. Thanks, Margaret. Like I said, I'll be there. Thanks for calling. 'Bye."

"Yes," she repeated once more. "*Exceptionally*, Mr McTurd has agreed to see you."

Exceptionally? That was at least the second time in thirty seconds that Margaret had told me that Murdo's agreement to see me was *exceptional*, thereby indicating that I had, in fact, completely misunderstood the main part of her message. She was now making sure before she concluded the call that I did understand why she was ringing me personally. It was to rebuke me for my impudence, and then to rub my nose in it! Mr McTurd was doing me a huge honour by agreeing to receive me into his regal presence. The great man didn't usually lower himself by mixing with riffraff, but he was prepared to make an exception in my case and I therefore obviously needed to be told in advance how grateful I should feel just to be afforded an audience.

"*Exceptionally*?" I echoed, genuinely intrigued. "Why exceptionally? Isn't he normally allowed to see people then? He's not under some kind of ASBO restriction, is he, that prohibits him from mixing with normal human beings? Or has he got some communicable disease? Do I need to get some shots?"

Today Margaret was in no mood for my playfulness. She ignored both my insubordination and my weak attempt at humour, although I think the former did make her catch her breath slightly. Instead of chuckling as I had expected, I swear that at the other end of the line I actually heard her 'gather herself'. "Mr McTurd has said he will see you," she repeated regally, "but he has just asked me to make the point that he thinks you should have gone through the proper channels."

"The 'proper channels'?" I echoed incredulously. "But surely I *have* gone through the proper channels, haven't I? I asked Chandra to make me an appointment, and she spoke to you about it. What other channels are there?"

"Murdo thinks you should have gone through your line manager," she said quietly, as if embarrassed at having to point out the bleeding obvious to a retard.

"But I *did* go through my manager," I replied. "It was my manager who asked me to go and speak to Murdo! You don't imagine I'd actually *want* to talk to Murdo, face to face, if I didn't *have* to, do you? You must think I'm potty, Margaret!"

I was just trying to be jocular, of course, but Margaret seemed to take this insult personally, and I felt I heard her bridle. I have noticed that this is not an uncommon trait among certain secretaries. They may actually entertain little personal regard for their boss, and may see him for the unprincipled, supercilious, stuck-up little grotbag that he clearly is, but woe betides the upstart representative from the other ranks who dares to point this out. Murdo was universally hated throughout the industry. His company was shunned by all but the certifiably insane, and Margaret must certainly have known that, but she definitely wasn't going to let me get away with alluding to that fact, however obliquely, without issuing a reprimand from the lofty heights she inhabited vicariously as his secretary. After a short silence, during which she seemed to be choosing her words carefully, she continued with all the solemnity she could muster.

"Look, Mr Jaxon. Mr McTurd has been good enough to give you some of his time," she said with great dignity, "but he has asked me to point out to you that he does not normally hold meetings of this type with regional managers, unless he arranges them himself. That's all." And I was dismissed. Her voice was calm but her tone was cold, although I could sense that she was burning inside.

There was an air of finality about Margaret's last sentence and I should have left it at that. I realise now that anyone with any sense wouldn't have allowed himself to be riled by this kind of nonsense, and that I should simply have hung up. But I'm afraid that Margaret – and, obviously, Murdo – had now got under my skin, and that I was becoming angry despite myself. I know that it is impossible to win the type of argument that was developing and that I should therefore not have allowed myself to be drawn into it. I was determined not to be rude to her, because I really liked Margaret, but I found I just couldn't let it drop.

"Meetings of *what* type?" I asked her innocently, although inside I was now beginning to seethe. I like to try to keep things good-humoured if I can.

"Meetings like….. Well, meetings like this one."

"And what does he think this one is going to be like?"

"On staffing issues," she replied.

"Who said it was on staffing issues?" I asked innocently.

There was no answer from the other end of the line. I wasn't surprised, for I knew that Margaret could have had no idea exactly why I wanted to see Murdo – how could she, when I hadn't even told Chandra what the meeting was about? – unless she had done some digging. She had simply been making the point that Murdo didn't usually deign to see lowly regional managers but, put on the spot, she was now reluctant to labour the point. Perhaps it was dawning upon her just how annoying that kind of pomposity was for others.

"Look, Mr Jaxon," she said with increased finality (and by now I had *noticed* that she was definitely calling me 'Mr Jaxon') "I think all Mr McTurd meant was that he normally meets only with...." She stopped. "Let's just leave it at that, shall we?"

She was right again. I should have left it at that. But for some reason I decided not to. I was busy; I was on a mobile telephone on a train, where reception was poor; I had much better things to do with my time; but for some strange reason I decided to prolong this pointless conversation. Silly, isn't it?

"And that man told you to ring me up, just to tell me that?" I tried to sound incredulous.

"Yes." I think her haughty disdain was now becoming tinged with embarrassment. Put like that it didn't seem quite such a good idea.

"I see," I smirked sarcastically. "Well, wouldn't it be nice if real life were like that? The rest of us meet with whoever it is we have to meet with in order to get the job done, but good old Mr McTurd is different! I am used to having meetings with all sorts of people – even people like me – just to get the job done, anyone, in fact, who it is necessary for me to see. You don't imagine that I....."

"Well, Mr McTurd doesn't!" she cut in, with that same air of finality in her voice. "Murdo does not normally meet with all and sundry, the way you obviously do, because he has a busy schedule and he hasn't the time." She had recovered her composure, and had had enough of this nonsense, the same way I had.

"OK," I said wearily. "Please tell Murdo I understand, will you?" I paused briefly, and then added: "Oh, and please *cancel* my meeting with him next Thursday."

"*What*????" she gasped. She had clearly been about to replace the receiver, annoyed, but nevertheless satisfied that her point had been made. But now she wasn't so sure.

"Just cancel the meeting, please, Margaret. If Murdo's too busy to see me I will obviously have to understand and leave it at that."

"Now wait a minute, Herbert" she retorted. "I did *not* say Murdo was too busy to see you! In fact, he has asked me specifically to tell you that he *is* prepared to see you!" (I was suddenly 'Herbert' again! Hooray!)

"Exceptionally?"

"Yes," she conceded weakly, still slightly embarrassed. "*Exceptionally.*"

"Well, I didn't want to see him *exceptionally*. I wanted to see him *un*exceptionally. I wanted to discuss something with him, something important, but if I turn up next Thursday, and he receives me *exceptionally* into the great presence, I am going to have to start by convincing him that I'm worthy of the honour – which I am *not* – and he's going to spend the whole time explaining to me that he doesn't normally meet with regional managers and other riffraff, and that I should have gone through the 'proper channels'. I think I'll just be wasting his time – not to mention mine. No, Margaret. I can see poor Murdo's point. Having thought about it I have realised that I am certainly not entitled to any exceptional treatment. I am not worthy of it, so please cancel the meeting."

She had initially been taken aback, but she was now feeling on safer ground again and quickly recovered her air of confidence.

"I'm sorry, Herbert," she said, "but I cannot do that. *You* cannot do this."

"What do you mean, I 'can't do this'? I've just done it! It was *my* meeting! I can do what I like with it! And I've just cancelled it!"

"No you can't!" she stammered, stunned. "It's in Mr McTurd's diary!"

"Well, take it out."

"I can't do that! He's expecting to see you."

"No he isn't. He doesn't want to see me! You said yourself that he doesn't normally meet with pond-life. If I had known *that* I obviously wouldn't have troubled him, and I am certainly not going to trouble him now that I do know that. So please cancel the meeting, will you?"

"No," she said firmly, if a little uncertainly. "I really can't do that. Please try to understand, Herbert. If Mr McTurd has agreed to see someone he expects the meeting to go ahead."

"Well, this one won't," I told her pointedly, if a little petulantly, "because I won't be there! I freely admit that I didn't know that Murdo's channels were different from everyone else's, but I will know in future. And I wouldn't have asked Chandra to book me this meeting if I had known I was infringing against the great man's concept of what was proper. I have obviously upset him just by asking to see him, and I would feel truly awful if he were to have a fit of the vapours on my account. So please cancel the meeting."

"But I can't *do* that, Herbert." Her air of vicarious superciliousness had all but evaporated, and she was now almost pleading with me. "Do, please try to understand. Mr McTurd will not understand….."

"I don't see why not. Just tell him something else has come up and I've got to be somewhere else."

"Well, he won't like that....."

"Won't like *what*?"

"Your cancelling a meeting with him so that you can go to a meeting with someone else! In those circumstances Mr McTurd will expect you to honour your meeting with him."

I could see that Margaret was beginning to get upset, and that she was wishing for all the world she hadn't telephoned me, and I know I ought to have ended it there. But I will have to confess to taking a malicious delight in having turned the tables, and I could feel my arguments become more facetious by the second. I was still determined not to be rude to her – it wasn't her fault that Murdo was the way he was – but I was blowed if I was going to let her think I would be going to the meeting.

"But what happens if what has come up is even more important than my meeting with the great McTurd? What happens if the Archbishop of York wants to see me at half-past two next Thursday?"

"But he doesn't....."

"All right then – my bookmaker. What happens if my bookmaker wants to see me at half-past two next Thursday? I can't let him down – he's far more important than Murdo! Well – to *me* he is. Not to *Mrs* McTurd – *obviously*, or to….."

"Mr Jaxon, I….!" (I think she'd forgotten again that I was 'good ol' Herbert'.)

"Sorry, Margaret, I was being facetious. But I really am curious. What if the Icelandic Minister of Fisheries were to ask to see me next Tuesday afternoon? What would be the proper channels for cancelling the meeting with Murdo so that I could go to the more important one? I am curious to know. It might happen one day….."

"Well, Herbert," she said, extemporising, "in that case I am sure Mr McTurd would certainly understand, but I don't think we can….."

She tailed off. She was now finding this a difficult conversation. I hadn't wanted to upset her, so I decided to help her out and lighten the tension.

"Hang about, Margret! What if I were to be run over by a bus and killed on Wednesday? Surely, in those circumstances, Murdo wouldn't expect the undertakers to carry my coffin up to his office and dump me on his carpet….."?"

"Herbert! Stop it…..!" I thought I heard her chuckle – but I could be wrong.

"Sorry, Margaret. But what if Chandra had made a simple mistake in booking the meeting with McTurd? What if I had meant her to book the meeting with someone else – my masseusse, maybe – and she had now realised her mistake. Surely I could cancel it then?"

"Herbert! Will you please stop playing about! I think….." But she found no words with which to continue.

"I'll tell you what. If you can't cancel my meeting with Murdo next Thursday, just pass on my apologies and tell him that I won't be coming, and say that I tried, through the proper channels, of course, to book *another* meeting with him to tell him that next Thursday's meeting was cancelled, but I couldn't book that other meeting with him because I'm from the backstreets of Portsmouth and I didn't know what the proper channels for doing that were!"

Perhaps Margaret attempted to force a laugh, but I could sense that today she was not really appreciating my attempts to be funny.

"Herbert, you're putting me in a very difficult position…. Will you please stop….."

"I'm sorry, Margaret," I said, and I really was. It had just occurred to me how awful it must be for her, having to work every day for a piece of dog's poo like Murdo McTurd, and I was beginning to feel sorry that I was compounding her difficulties. But I wasn't going to give in. "I'm extremely busy at the moment and I've got a hell of a lot on, so please try to understand that I could well do without coming up to London next Thursday, just to have Murdo lecture me on what are and what are not the proper channels. Some of us have proper work to do, so if you'll just cancel the meeting, or slip another one in his diary in its place, I'll be very grateful. I'm sure he won't notice."

"But I can't do that, Herbert….." she said again.

Our telephone conversation on that bad line seemed to go on forever, and at this distance in time I cannot remember exactly how it ended, but I suppose eventually it must have finished, otherwise I would still be speaking to Margaret today, instead of talking to you. Perhaps I just went into a tunnel and lost the signal. Perhaps Murdo came to her rescue by interrupting to ask her to get him a glass of vinegar. What I do remember is that the stalemate remained unbroken to the end. She obstinately refused to cancel the meeting, and I made it clear that wild horses wouldn't have dragged me up to London the following Thursday afternoon. For the time being I suppose we must just have left it at that.

Time moved on, and the matter eventually slipped my mind. However, I was in my own office a couple of days later and was going through my diary commitments with Chandra, as we used regularly to do whenever I wasn't playing an away fixture, when she remarked casually that she had managed to fix me up with that meeting with Murdo McTurd I had requested: we were to meet in his office in London the following Thursday afternoon, at 14.30 hours precisely, if memory serves.

"Oh, I've resolved that," I said nonchalantly, without going into detail. "Ring Margaret and cancel that one for me, will you?"

Wordlessly, Chandra agreed to do just that. She just scribbled herself a note on her pad and we went on to the next item.

I heard nothing more about that particular meeting with Old Turdo. I had asked Chandra to cancel it for me and, miraculously, she must have done so, because by the end of the day it had disappeared from my diary. The next time I bumped into Margaret she was as pleasant as ever and the matter of my cancelled meeting with Murdo was never mentioned between us again. Even McTurd failed to mention it when I next had the misfortune not to avoid him.

Although the incident had annoyed me at the time I realised, on reflection, that I had handled it badly. However, I had also learned a lot from that small episode. For one thing I had learned that for someone like Murdo McTurd the important issues of the day were as nothing compared to the manner in which arrangements were made for those issues to be discussed, and the etiquette involved. Murdo McTurd was far more interested in preserving the importance of his revered position than in addressing matters of importance to the company. In the light of that I can now see why so little of importance can have been addressed while he was in charge, and why none of the major difficulties we faced were ever resolved during his reign.

I had also learned what were the proper channels for cancelling a meeting with someone who considered himself to be but one step removed in importance from Almighty God. A humble human being like Herbert Jaxon couldn't simply ring up God's secretary and ask her to tell Him I wasn't coming to the meeting. Oh dear no. That wouldn't be nearly grand enough, and wouldn't waste nearly enough time. Other people needed to be involved. The proper channels called, apparently, for me to tell *my* secretary to tell *His* secretary that the meeting was cancelled, and then everything was OK!

This all happened a long time ago, precious Reader, and a lot of gin has flowed under the tonsils since then. My mind has long since stopped boggling over the incident. But I thought it might be of interest if I shared it with you, so that we could chuckle over it together as we grew older and wiser.

None of that alters the fact that I handled everything badly. Perhaps, if I had concentrated more on the nonsense and less on getting the job done, I would have been a success like Murdo.

CHAPTER 14 : A DRONE'S LAMENT

Everyone knows I'm not a bloke
To grass up any other folk;
And nor am I the kind of louse
Who'd dish the dirt on his own spouse;
But, lest this thing should escalate,
I'm going to set the record straight…

My wife, Bonita, called me lazy!!!!!!!!!!
What nonsense! That's completely crazy!
She knows, despite what she may say,
I pull my weight, in a quiet way.
If proof she wants, I've more than ample:
Let me give you but one example.

Last Christmas I was feeling low,
Why that should be I just don't know;
Shagged out, and knackered, unsure why,
I found, however hard I'd try,
That nothing helped, not even gin:
Le mal du siècle had set in.

No slap, nor tickle, 'neath the holly,
Could shake my air of melancholy.
Bonita said she thought she knew
The reason I was feeling blue.
She fumed: "You idle so and so!
"You're too one-paced, and stuck on *slow*!

"That gloomy mood of yours needs shifting!
"Get down the gym, and try weight-lifting!
"Or trampolining, if you're bored,
"Or learn to play the harpsichord!
"Do something different! Don't just mope!
"Don't sit there, whinging, smoking dope!

"Clean out the garage! Write a play!
"Don't put things off for another day!
"Life's far too short to sit and wait!
"The clock is ticking, but it's not too late,
"So seize the moment! Right! Let's go...!"
Her words were making sense, and so...

I bought a dog, and called him Clyde...
Bonita rolled her eyes, then sighed:
"Don't you think I've enough to do
"With bringing up nine kids – and you?
"You wear me out; I'm fit to drop;
"I can't cope with a dog, on top!"

But, switching on my unctuous smile,
I'd talked her round, in a little while,
By promising to help her more
With each and every household chore,
As well as caring for my hound:
She'd hardly know he was around!

Thus, from day one we could agree:
Clyde's every need was down to me!
But nothing ever goes as planned,
And things got quickly out of hand
When Clyde and I fell out of synergy:
His maintenance cost me too much energy.

Though Clyde's still nominally in my care,
Bonny now has the lion's share,
Of canine duties. I'll concede
She meets his nearly every need,
And says my help's not worth a dime.
(But I stroke him, from time to time.)

Bonny now feeds him through the week,
While I just turn the other cheek.
She also gives him lots of treats,
And chicken chews, and various sweets.
(But I stroke him, from time to time,
If on my lap he opts to climb…)

Bonita tucks him in his bed,
And finds a pillow for his head;
She really makes him feel at home,
And cleans his coat, with brush and comb,
If ever he's caked with slime, or grime.
(But I stroke him, from time to time.)

And Bonny took him to the vet
When she felt it was time to get
The mongrel jabbed, and have him wormed,
Which, once again, just reconfirmed
Our pooch care-programme paradigm.
(But I stroke him, from time to time.)

Bonita lets him out to wee,
When I'd prefer to let things be;
And when I'm not sure what to do
Bonny will pick up all his poo;
I let *her* handle all that chyme.
(But I stroke him, from time to time.)

And when Clyde went out worrying sheep
While in my care – I'd fallen asleep –
'Twas Bonny who proved quite a charmer,
And managed to placate the farmer,
With sweet apologies… (But then,
I stroke the b*st*rd, now and again.)

It's Bonny who walks him round the block,
And pampers him, all round the clock,
And she's been throwing him his ball
When I've not noticed him at all.
My wife has made his life sublime!
(But I stroke him, from time to time.)

And when he whimpers in the night,
Bonny makes sure that he's all right;
And when he wakes at crack of dawn,
She gets up in the early morn,
To check he's not committing crime.
(But I stroke him, from time to time.)

Sometimes it makes me want to weep
To watch my loved one losing sleep,
Pandering to Clyde's every whim.
But don't think *I'm* neglecting him:
I still stroke him, from time to time,
And now I've written him this rhyme!
So, *lazy*? *Me*? That's simply daft!
D'you think she was just having a laugh?

CHAPTER 15 : FITNESS AID

My wife gave me a fitness watch,
To wear around my wrist,
And count up all the steps I take,
Which she thought would assist

In making a new man of me;
She said it's not too late
To get my figure back in trim,
And shed a little weight.

"But I'm already fit," I said,
"There isn't any need –
"I'm built just like a racing snake…"
Let's say, she disagreed…

And so she bought it anyway;
With menace in her voice,
She makes me wear it all the time,
And offers me no choice.

But I can see that fitness aid
Was just a big mistake,
For every hour the blinking thing
Will check that I'm awake.

I can't sit down, or close my eyes,
Without electric pulse
Upon my wrist reminding me
I should be somewhere else.

My watch is driving me insane,
Its horrors never cease,
It won't stop shaking me awake,
And offers me no peace.

But then I had a great idea,
And hid it up the flue,
And told my wife that it was lost!
Still – never mind! (*Too true!*)

But she just picked her smartphone up
And clicked an app thereon,
And my new watch let out a squawk,
To tell her where he'd gone!

These artful new appliances
Are really taking over;
There's nowhere we can hide from them,
From John o' Groats to Dover.

My watch is like a convict's tag!
To keep the b*st*rd quiet,
I even walked it to the pub –
I'm on a liquid diet –

But when I tried to settle, and
Enjoy my pint of *Tizer*,
My watch immediately sent my wife
A signal, to apprise her

That I'd stopped moving, yet again,
And wasn't to be trusted!
I don't think I'll be free again
Until the darn thing's busted!

Which gives me quite a good idea!
I'll take it to the shed
And give it wellie with a hammer
Till the b*st*rd's dead!

This really is my last resort –
There isn't a Plan B;
And if this fails, I fear it might
Just be the end of me.

But now I'm really worried sick,
Despite my huff and puff,
For I'm not sure I'm fit enough
To hit it hard enough…

CHAPITRE 16 : ÉGOTISME

Je pense à toi le matin,
Très difficile à croire,
Je pense à toi l'après-midi,
Je pense à toi le soir ;
J' pense à toi à la maison,
Au match, où que je sois ;
Les autres nanas pensent à moi,
Mais moi, je pense à toi …

J'ai parlé à ma psychiatre,
Très amoureuse de moi,
Qui ne le comprend pas non plus :
Pourquoi pensé-j' à toi ?
Elle me conseille de t'oublier –
Elle m'a dit maintes fois
De venir vivre avec elle …
Mais moi, je pense à toi …

Et la serveuse à mon bistrot,
Qui m'aime à la folie,
Au lieu de m'écouter, m'invite
À partager sa vie.
Elle ne sait comment me guérir,
Mon barista non plus ;
Ma femme, qui ne me comprend pas,
Se sent toute fichue.

Je me rappelle les temps jadis,
Les bon temps d'autrefois,
Priorités furent établies :
La première était : MOI !
Suivie du foot ; ensuite, la bière ;
Et puis … n'importe quoi… ;
Mais aujourd'hui, je suis foutu …
Hélas – je pense à toi !

CHAPTER 17 : THE KEY

It was 1986, probably May or June, or possibly some different month or a different year, shortly after I had been given my own regional office at the Ministry. I had never really been in charge of anything before, and wasn't really sure that I was up to the extra responsibility. But that period of uncertainty soon passed. Therefore, after an appropriate period of acclimatisation[23], I began sniffing around and poking my nose into things that didn't concern me, in search of something I could meddle with. And thus it came to pass that I decided to appoint Toby O'Notterby as my security officer.

At the time O'Notterby was one of six or eight senior members of staff in my new office, all of whom did more or less the same job but all of whom had their own separate areas of individual responsibility. Each one headed up a team who helped them perform their duties and, in addition, they each had a number of management tasks and other 'functional responsibilities' to help me run the office. Thus one was in charge of training, while another looked after our accommodation and equipment needs; a third supervised the office's team of clerical and administrative staff, while a fourth was responsible for ensuring that our fleet of official vehicles was continuously roadworthy. Etc. If there was any logic to it I suppose it must have appeared to me that Toby had fewer functional responsibilities than the rest of them, which was why I decided to make him the office's security officer.

I don't know why the office had no official security officer before I arrived. By the time I got there I had been with the Ministry for years and, as far as I was aware, at all our offices one of the managers had always been designated as security officer, so I

---

23   About a day or so, I reckon.

knew we probably ought to have one too. There had probably once been one at this regional office in the past, so I supposed responsibility for the role must have lapsed before I revived it. Anyway, O'Notterby was a diligent officer and as soon as I gave him his new job he packed himself off on one of the regular training courses the Ministry arranged for security officers, and then came back and started looking closely at the security arrangements currently in force at the office. In my judgement this had to be a good thing.

A few weeks passed. Then Toby called in at my office one day and told me solemnly that, after conducting a full review of security arrangements at the office, he considered our procedures to be fully compliant with Ministry guidelines in most areas. However, Toby could not, of course, give me a totally clean bill of health. After a full security inspection security officers were obliged, by their very calling, to find something with which to find fault, but Toby thought I would be pleased to know that the only thing he had found requiring my immediate attention was the fact that one of the lockable presses, or safes, in my own office had only one key. This, he told me gravely, no doubt quoting from some manual or other, was 'bad security'. On receipt of this news I nodded as gravely as I could, as befitted the moment. In those days, if memory serves, just pretending to take things seriously made me feel important, and could conjure up in me a warm 'Sellafield glow'.

I should explain that among the items of office furniture in my office were two imposing, upright, grey metal security presses, both about six feet high, three feet wide and a couple of feet deep. Why there were two of them I never found out. One of those safes contained all the documents and materials the Ministry felt ought to be kept under lock and key, and, in accordance with established procedures, it boasted a heavy combination security lock, the combination to which was known only to me, my security officer, and probably someone at headquarters. However, the second safe, which housed a miscellany of different items, most of which were my own personal effects, including my booze, was locked by means of something resembling a *Yale* key. This latter key, when it was not needed, I usually kept locked up in the other safe. There was no spare. The fact that there was no duplicate key to that safe had struck me as strange when I inherited the office and I had mentioned it to my predecessor. He told me that it had struck him as strange, too, but that he had inherited only one key from *his* predecessor. At first he had firmly intended to do something about it but in the eight years or so he had been in post he had never got around to having another key cut. You know how it is.....

"What would you have done if you had lost the key?" I asked him.

"I don't know," he replied. "I suppose I'd have had to go down to the off licence."

"Yes, I realise that," I told him, "but what would you have done to open the safe?"

He shrugged vacantly, before adding with a smirk: "I suppose I'd have had to go down to the kitchen and get a tin opener!"

Anyway, that was all in the past, and this was the present and no time for jokes, because now my own, newly appointed security officer was requiring me to have a second key cut. Even though I was his boss I couldn't ignore an instruction like that – or rather, I could ignore it, but if I did he was in the clear, for having drawn my attention to the failing, and it would be my behind that was on the chopping block if I failed to act on his advice. Rules of the game, don't you know? I suppose, now I come to think of it, since I was his boss I could have ordered my security officer to go out in the rain and get another key cut for me, while I stayed indoors in the warm, but if I had chosen that option it would have meant my giving him the only key to the safe, and I couldn't do that because that was the press that contained all my personal effects, including my booze. I decided, in the circumstances, that it might be better, rain or no rain, if I were to go out and have the second key cut myself. Being the boss, I now realised, carried heavier responsibilities than first imagined, and required me to take important decisions of this nature. I suppose that's why the government paid me all this money.

"How do I go about it?" I asked Toby importantly, trying to give the impression that I cared. "Are there any special rules I have to follow? Does the fact that it is a security cupboard mean I have to go somewhere special to have another key cut?"

"Not as far as I know," he replied equally importantly, after having pretended to think about it. "I think you can just go to any reputable locksmith."

So that is what I decided[24] to do, and I knew just the place to go. When I had moved into my present home about five years previously I had had the locks on all the exterior doors changed and had given the job to a local locksmith in Addingham, a small town close to my home in the countryside. *Fort Knox & Co* had done a good job. It had cost me more than I had expected to pay but overall I had considered it money well spent, and that is why, when I had resolved five years later, and only a week or so before encountering my problem with the office security key, to fit some window locks at my home, I had gone back to *Fort Knox* for the work to be done. On my return it had been very gratifying to find that old Mr Knox still remembered me. Other than to have an extra front door key cut for one of my daughters, or for the odd padlock for a suitcase or a bolt for a gate, I hadn't been in his establishment

---

24 For a guide to the general quality of my decisions, please see the title of this chronicle.

for half a decade, but the proprietor had greeted me cheerily and spoken fondly of the work he had done at my home all those years before. We had then chatted about this and that, about dahlias and bicycles, about politics and hurricanes, about roses and horse manure, and cabbages and kings, while he jotted down my order in his order book and promised to call round at my home shortly 'to have a look'. Whom better to give my Ministry's business to than my old friend Mr Knox? I decided to call in on him the very next morning on my way into the office.

And thus it came to pass that on the following morning I dropped by at *Fort Knox & Co* at around five-past nine, which I judged to be soon after they opened. The locksmith himself was nowhere to be seen, but in his stead, leaning against the wall behind the counter, stood a surly looking youth of about seventeen or eighteen, his fair, greasy hair billowing untidily around his sallow cheeks and his face unprepossessingly decorated with acne. He made no move towards me as I entered the store but he looked up with a pained expression, clearly annoyed at having been disturbed by a customer so early in his shift.

"Good morning," I greeted him cheerily. "Is Mr Knox around?"

"No," was all I got by way of reply. Honestly, the youth of today...

"Do you know when he'll be in?"

"No."

From this I inferred that Spotty Boy did not know when his employer would next be around and was in no hurry to elaborate on his monosyllabic response.

"Oh," I said nonchalantly, after a suitable pause, "I was hoping he might cut me a key."

"I can cut you a key," retorted the other nasally, and without enthusiasm. His nostrils sounded as if they might be blocked, and I wondered if he ought to try blowing his nose. But that was a matter for him.

The youth had made no move in my direction so I was obliged to venture deeper into the store, towards the dark end of the shop, where Mr Knox's unattractive assistant stood cowering motionless behind the till, exhibiting all the commitment to his employment of a dead hedgehog. I removed the key from my wallet and handed it to the pockmarked apprentice.

"Can you cut me one of these, please?"

He took it from my hand with cold, bony fingers that felt damp and greasy, and I wondered what he might have been up to that had left them in that state. He lifted the key to his bloodshot eye and squinted at it wordlessly for some moments, sniffing, and turning it over and over in his fingers, as if considering its value. I thought for a moment he had misunderstood me, for it looked from his reaction as if he believed I was trying to sell him something, but before I could clarify the issue he spoke again, in that flat nasal monotone I was slowly becoming accustomed to.

"Is this a *Yale* key?" he sniffed.

"I don't know," I said. "It looks like one, doesn't it?"

He neither agreed with me nor disagreed. He was obviously an expert in these matters, and he clearly wasn't prepared to engage in idle speculation on the issue with an amateur. Instead he asked: "Where did you get it?"

"It's the key to a safe."

"Where's the safe?"

I decided to tell the truth. Why should I lie? "It's in my office."

"Where do you work?"

What business was that of his, I wondered? Still, I am a helpful soul by nature and slow to take offence, so I decided to play along with him for a bit longer. "I'm a civil servant," I told him. "I work for the government, at a local office in town."

"Government?" he said, finally looking away from the key and directly at me.

"Yes," I nodded.

"Means nothing to me," he snuffled, and went back to his slow examination of the key.

"I don't suppose it means anything to anyone who's not in the business," I told him cheerfully. "I don't know anything about cutting keys!"

He ignored my chumminess. From this last exchange Spotty and I had established only that we knew nothing about each other's line of business and it had got me no closer to the object of my visit to the store. The locksmith's apprentice was showing no sign of getting a move on so I decided to give him a gentle nudge in the right direction.

"So," I asked him, after a silence that seemed to go on forever, "have you got one?"

"What?" he retorted, looking at the key rather than at me.

"Have you got a key like that one?"

"Oh, yes. I've got one," he said at last. But then he extended his arm and offered my key back to me. "But I can't copy that one without the proper authority."

"Why not?" I asked him, genuinely puzzled.

"Because it's a safe key."

"I know it's a safe key – I just told you that!"

"That's why," he said simply.

"What? Aren't you allowed to copy safe keys?"

"No."

"But it's the only key I have and I've been told to get a spare." At this stage I still believed that I was dealing with a fellow member of the human race who might be willing to help me out. "Where do I go if I need to get a copy done?"

The lad didn't reply, but continued looking at me cantankerously, the key still extended towards me on the end of his clammy paw.

"If a locksmith won't do it, who will?" I asked. To me that sounded like a reasonable question, and I certainly wasn't trying to be funny, but the lad seemed to bridle a bit, and gave me a funny look. He didn't reply though.

"So who can copy this for me?" I repeated. But answer came there none.

Hmmm. Not really knowing how to proceed I took the key from his sweaty hand, noting with distaste that it was now as damp as his hand was. I took a paper tissue from my pocket and absentmindedly dried my key while I reflected on what to do next. I was sure I would not have had this trouble with old Mr Knox. By now that gentlemen would have had my spare key beautifully cut and would have been well and truly into telling me all about his greenfly.

"When did you say Mr Knox would be in?"

"He won't cut it for you either," the youth retorted truculently, almost insolently.

"Why not?"

"Because it's a safe key."

"I know it's a safe key!" I almost snapped. "When will Mr Knox be in?"

"Not till later in the week."

"You don't know when, exactly?"

"No. Not exactly. Maybe Friday. Or Saturday."

"OK, I'll call back then," I said.

I made as if to leave the shop, actually getting as far as pulling open the door onto the street, and, with hindsight, I ought really to have gone then as it was quite clear I would be getting no change at all out of Master Muldoon, but something made me hesitate. After all, all I wanted was a flipping key cutting. Where was the problem in that? The store had confirmed that they had one in stock, so what was the difficulty? Surely they did not want to turn good business away? Spotso had made no move to prevent me from leaving, and looked to be returning to the trance-like stupor I had interrupted when I entered the store, but I decided to make one last effort, just to make sure he had understood me.

Turning back, and pushing the door shut again, I said: "Sorry. You did understand, didn't you, that all I wanted was a copy of this key to be cut?"

"Yes," he said.

"And you won't do it?"

"No."

"Why not?" I said this as politely as I could, so as not to appear confrontational, but I don't think I quite managed to adopt the correct tone of voice. To be on the safe side, I therefore added: "Just so that I can be sure I understand why, when I speak to Mr Knox."

"Because it's a safe key."

"Is that all?"

I took his lack of response as a yes.

"Did you know it was a safe key before I told you?"

"No," he admitted sullenly.

Aha! Suddenly I glimpsed a possible way out of the predicament. "And would you have cut one for me if I hadn't told you it was a safe key?"

He didn't reply.

"What would you have done," I pressed him, "if I had told you it was the key to my garden shed?"

I knew my question had struck to the quick when he still refused to reply. Instead, he continued to stare at me angrily, looking for all the world like a spoiled child bent on getting its own way at all costs. He was pitiless and unwavering, and yet he looked so miserable at that moment that I took pity on *him*. I draw no pleasure from winning arguments when the odds are stacked so overwhelmingly in my favour, so I resolved again to take the heat out of the situation before leaving.

"Thanks for your help," I said, pulling open the front door of the shop once more. "I'll drop in and see Mr Knox later in the week. Will you tell him to expect me?"

To my surprise, rather than leave it at that the speckled one decided to prolong the discussion. "I've told you, Mr Knox won't cut it for you either," he said in a tone that I felt was becoming a trifle menacing, almost threatening.

I hesitated in the doorway.

"You don't think so?"

"No."

"Why not?"

I was just checking the consistency of his replies.

"Because it's a safe key."

He passed the test.

I sighed. I didn't need to ask my stippled friend how Mr Knox would be expected to know it was a safe key, just by looking at it. I inferred from the other's demeanour that Muldoon was now spitefully resolved to report all our earlier conversation to his employer as soon as the latter came in, just to prevent me from getting my sodding key cut. Wasn't that rather an odd stance to adopt, I wondered, for someone who relied for his livelihood on cutting keys for paying customers? But, as I have said, my speckled amigo was clearly determined to get his own way at all costs.

"So," I groaned, "according to you, anyone who needs a spare key cutting for a safe is going to find it impossible to get it done here."

"I didn't say that," he said darkly.

I perked up. Although there was no conciliatory tone in Mottledman's voice, for the first time since I had met him I felt he might be about to back down and cut me my key. Perhaps something I had said had alarmed him, and he was afraid I was going to report his unhelpful attitude to his employer, leaving him for the high jump. I had no wish to get him into trouble, or even to win a silly argument, but I *did* want, if possible, to get my key cut there and then. I was prepared to be reasonable. Closing the door again, I stepped back into the shop and risked approaching the counter once more.

"What did you say then?" I asked. "I thought you were refusing to cut my key."

"No," he said slowly. "I didn't *refuse* to cut you a key. I said I can't cut it without the proper authority."

"Ah, I am *so* sorry!" I said, recalling now that that was precisely what he had said at the outset. "Silly me! I should have listened properly to you earlier. I am ever so sorry." And I really was. "So, if I give you the authority you can cut me my key? Is that right?" And I extended the key to him once more, in a fashion I considered to be unctuously oily.

But still Master Muldoon remained obstinately motionless. Instead of seizing the olive branch I had just graciously extended towards him, and going ahead and cutting my effing key as requested, he simply stared moodily at me for some moments before spitting in my direction: "*You* cannot give me the authority. It's got to come from someone else."

"Who?" I asked blankly.

There followed a bit of an awkward pause, which even gave me time to wonder whether I should have said *whom?* Mind you, I don't think he was ever thinking about correcting my grammar.

"I don't know," he admitted lamely, after that bit of a pause.

"But that doesn't make sense," I persisted. "How can I get my key cut if my locksmith won't do it without authority, but doesn't know what authority he needs?"

Blotchy-boy did not reply. I suspected that by now he too might be feeling out of his depth, and that he was digging in his heels solely in order to avoid conceding that his argument was well and truly lost. I was now in a strange situation. Paradoxically, I knew I wasn't going to get what I wanted by winning the argument, so in order to stand any chance of getting my key cut that morning I felt I had to fall back on mollifying my opponent to the point where he could withdraw from the fray with honour and with the feeling that his integrity was still intact.

Gently, I tried again. "You said you needed the *proper* authority. What would that be? The *proper* authority, I mean."

He shrugged. "I dunno." He seemed determined to be difficult.

"What exactly is the *proper* authority, in a case like this?"

He refused to be drawn and remained sullenly silent.

"Something in writing, maybe?" I hazarded.

"Yes," he said quietly, but without enthusiasm. "Maybe."

"Excellent!" I went on amicably. "I can give you that now!" And I pulled out my pen.

"I don't want it from *you*," he said firmly, almost angrily. "It's got to be on headed paper."

"That's no problem!" I said. "I've got some here!" And I pulled open my briefcase, extracting a pad of my office headed notepaper and waving it under his nose.

He refused even to look at it. "That's no good," he said coldly. "Like I said, it's got to come from someone else."

"Like who?"

Oh, bugger! I am fairly certain that should have been *whom*, too.

He opened his mouth but no words came out. Then he shook his head blankly.

I decided to help him out.

"So, not me?"

"No."

"Why not me?"

"Someone higher up," he said unhelpfully.

"Like Mr Knox? But you said he wouldn't cut it either."

"No!" he snapped impertinently. "Someone higher up than *you*!"

"Oh, I see!" I felt I was beginning to understand. Because the key in question was the key to a safe, it would have to be the owner of the safe who authorised its duplication. That seemed to make sense. Put like that, Spotty's stance did not seem to be quite so unreasonable. Mind you, I had more or less to work that out for myself. If only he had been a little more articulate we might have got there a bit sooner. But, as I *was* the owner of the safe, that ought to have been an end to the matter.

"I'm the officer in charge at my office," I told him, rather pompously. "It's *my* safe. Look. That's me." And I showed him my name on the headed notepaper.

He refused to look at it. There was a long pause, and then he said: "You must have a boss."

"Yes, but his office is up in London."

He stared at me with a look that said he did not care whether my boss's office was in Timbuktu, but his unspoken message was clear: without my boss's signature on a bit of paper I could not have my key cut. It was absurd.

I tried again. "Look, my boss doesn't even know about the safe, and why I need a spare key for it. Why should he?"

There was no reply from Pimples, and things were now so absurd that I knew I might as well pack it all in. But, despite my better judgement, this whole business was now beginning to niggle me to the point where I felt I could not simply give up and call it a day without conceding that I had wasted fifteen minutes of my life, and been out-negotiated by an illiterate numskull into the bargain. Now that I had made the effort to see things from Master Pizza-face's point of view, and was prepared to accept that his debating position was not unreasonable, surely to goodness it would be a simple matter for me to persuade him to look at things from my end? Perhaps if I took the trouble to explain the sequence of events a little more clearly he would realise that by standing too heavily on this point of principle he was wasting everyone's time and possibly doing his employer out of some lucrative business. Heaving a deep sigh, and speaking in the measured tones generally reserved for communication with the mentally defective, I very carefully set it all out from the beginning.

"Look," I said cosily. "Perhaps if I took the trouble to explain the sequence of events a little more clearly you might understand why it's not really necessary to go to all the trouble you're suggesting. I am the officer in charge at my office. *I* personally ordered a security review at *my* office. My *own* security officer decided that as there was only one key for my safe I needed to have another one cut. My security officer has been personally trained in security matters by the government. He told me it was bad security to have only one key to a lock, and he told me to get another one cut. He told me I didn't need to go to any trouble or make any fuss about it, and that I could go to a local locksmith and have the key copied. I am a long-standing customer of Mr Knox, so I decided to give your boss the Ministry's business rather than go to a High Street key-cutter. So will you *please* now cut me my key?"

There was a long pause. Then: "No," he said firmly, and coldly.

"Why not?" I almost spluttered.

"Because I need the proper authority."

"And who can give you that?"

He shrugged. "Someone in authority....." he hazarded.

"But in my office *I*'m the one with the authority," I informed him.

He was unmoved, and didn't reply directly. But he was clearly thinking about the problem because he suddenly ventured, virtually unprovoked, an afterthought that was almost helpful.

"Did you say a security officer had told you to have the key cut?"

"Yes."

"Then I'll take *his* authority," he said nasally, but magnanimously. "You get him to write me a note and I'll cut you your key."

"But, I'm his boss!" I expostulated.

There was no response from the other, so I pressed on angrily.

"I told *him* to conduct the security review! It was at *my* instruction that the need for this blinking key came to light! My security officer cannot authorise *me* to do things! I tell *him* to do things! Out there in the real world *that's* how it works!"

But Master Muldoon remained unmoved, and showed no interest in learning how things worked out there in the real world. If he realised he had just had rings run round him in the argument he didn't show it, for he had nothing further to say on the matter.

I did though. Too bloody right, I did! Despite everything, I could now feel myself losing my cool. This isn't something I'm proud of, but young Spottyman was beginning to get right up my nose. He seemed determined not to provide me with any sort of service, and his failure even to see the flaws in his own argument was gnawing at my vitals.

"You just said the authority had to come from my boss!" I snapped at him. "But now you're prepared to accept that authority from one of my staff! That doesn't make sense. You don't know me, or any of these people. Why don't I just go and get someone off the street to write me a note and cut through all this nonsense?"

Maddeningly, Master Muldoon didn't reply. He just stared at me blankly. He didn't even appear to be angry any longer. It didn't take long for me to recover my own composure, but I wasn't prepared to leave it at that.

"Look," I told him, "my name is Jaxon and I am a long-standing customer of Mr Knox. I have found you very unhelpful today, and when I next see Mr Knox I intend to tell him as much."

Spotty remained totally unconcerned. He gave the impression that he couldn't have cared less whether or not I considered him unhelpful, and even if I had threatened to take my complaint right up to the head of security at the Bank of England it would have made no difference to him. So I pressed on.

"Furthermore," I said loftily, "I have an outstanding order with Mr Knox for some window-locks, which I now intend to cancel." I didn't say so in so many words, but I left Sandpaper-cheeks in no doubt that my decision to deprive his employer of my valuable custom was entirely the result of his apprentice's unreasonable attitude.

Still the lad was unfazed. "Do you want me to cancel the order for you?" he asked, helpful now, but with the obvious intention of calling my bluff. There was a hint of scepticism in his voice, and he certainly didn't believe that I had an order outstanding that I could conveniently cancel just for the purpose of making a point. That would have been just *too* opportune.

"Yes, please," I said haughtily.

"OK. What's your order number?"

"I don't know."

"I can't cancel your order without an order number."

"I don't know what it is."

"It'll be on the paper we gave you."

"I haven't got the paper with me," I protested tetchily, "but Mr Knox wrote my order down on a page in a duplicates book and gave me the top copy."

Inexplicably this spotty youth seemed at last to have found something to galvanise him into action. Striding purposefully across to a shelf half-hidden behind the counter, he picked up a well-thumbed book of order stubs and waved it at me.

"This the one?"

"Yes, that looks like it."

He now began leafing half-heartedly through its pages, all the while shaking his head and sucking in through his blotchy cheeks. Suddenly he spoke.

"What did you say your name was?"

"Jaxon."

"How do you spell that?"

"J-A-X-O-N." (How do you spell 'Jaxon' indeed! Any fool knows that! Was he trying to take the Mickey?)

"And when did you say you came in?"

"I don't know. One day last week, maybe."

"There's nothing in here," he said with a sneer, slamming the record shut. "Perhaps you've made a mistake. Perhaps it was a different shop!" He was revealing a side of himself hitherto unseen. The mockery and derision in his voice was something I would earlier have believed him to be totally incapable of expressing.

"Perhaps you've got the wrong book," I suggested coolly.

"No, it would definitely be this one..." he said slowly and deliberately.

"Well, perhaps it was the week before last..."

"What? And you haven't heard from us by now? Unlikely," he said, shaking his head doubtfully, an insolent smile twisting his lower lip.

It was annoying but the lad was obviously missing the whole point here. If he had been one tenth as helpful when I asked him to cut my key as he was prepared to be when I asked him to cancel my order for window locks, we wouldn't be having this conversation. But comprehension of something as simple as that was clearly beyond him, and now he was virtually calling me a liar!

I was looking for some suitable expression of protest at this obvious slur on my probity but while he was speaking Spotso had opened the book again and begun leafing through more pages of back orders. Suddenly he stopped leafing. "Oh, yes. Here it is," he said, without apology and without obvious interest. "Mr Jaxon, 13 Necropolis Drive. Window locks on all his windows. Home visit next week." And he read out my full address and telephone number.

"That's the one," I said triumphantly.

Floral Boy had been unable to prove me a liar as he had hoped, but still he was unfazed.

"And you want me to cancel this for you?"

"Yes please."

"OK." And he picked up a pen and daringly effaced the whole entry with a cross of St Andrew, which he drew boldly across the page from corner to corner. Then he proceeded to write *CANCLED* in the margin in wobbly capitals. I thought that would be it but he had not yet finished. "Do you want me to say why it was cancelled?"

Sacred blue, was there no limit to this lad's temerity?

"No, that's all right. I'll call in and explain to Mr Knox myself."

"Explain what?" He wrinkled an insolent and pustule-encrusted nostril.

"Explain that you had been unhelpful over the matter of cutting my key and that I had therefore decided *not* to give you the business of my window locks."

He frowned thoughtfully, then, under where he had written *CANCLED*, he wrote *DUE TO STAFF RUDENESS*, in the same unsteady upper case.

"Hang about!" I said. "I didn't say you were rude – I said you were unhelpful."

Spotty looked slightly annoyed at my pedantry, but his annoyance clearly stemmed from having to amend his artwork rather than from his employer's loss of my valued custom. Striking out *RUDENESS* with a single stripe he altered what he had written to *CANCLED DUE TO STAFF UNHELPFULLNESS*. His body language and the expression on his face made clear the contempt in which he held me, but the pitiful misspellings, of which he was obviously blissfully ignorant, caused me to feel something approaching pity for him once more, although I realised that my pity was the last thing he would have wanted.

"That do you?" he asked sullenly, and sarcastically, and defiantly, when his calligraphy was completed.

"Yes, that's fine thanks," I said wearily. "I'll explain the detail to Mr Knox when I call in and see him. 'Bye."

And I was gone. If Master Muldoon bade me God speed, I did not hear him do so.

Well, that hadn't gone very well, had it? I had hardly covered myself with glory there, had I? Turning over in my head my achievements for the day, I counted: one disgruntled shop assistant, two lost tempers, no window locks to look forward to, and I still had to find somewhere to get my sodding key cut. Not a bad list of accomplishments, and all in under twenty minutes. I knew there were locksmiths a-plenty in the Ippardly area, which was not five miles away, and, as it was still only about twenty-past nine, I determined to have another go at resolving the problem of the key before heading into the office. The problem of the window locks would have to wait for another day.

As I drove over to Ippardly I tried to reflect objectively on Master McAcne's decision to refuse to cut me a key. Perhaps he just didn't like me. That much was obvious, and, although he hardly knew me, he wouldn't be the first person in whom I had inspired instinctive abhorrence. But was an instant distaste for me enough in itself to justify depriving his employer of lucrative business by refusing to serve me? Surely there must be more to it than that and the key to the problem, if you will pardon the pun, must have rested in the fact that I had unwisely confessed to him that the key I wanted copied was the key to a security press. Perhaps, in order to combat crime, it was company policy among all locksmiths to refuse to cut a copy of the key to a safe without the written authority of His Holiness the Pope or a person of similar standing. That seemed at least to make a little bit of sense.

Just supposing, I ruminated as I jumped a red traffic light, that I was employed as, say, a Beefeater at the Tower of London, and that in the course of my perambulations through the Bloody Tower I had come across the key to the cabinet that housed the Crown Jewels, which may have slipped out of the pocket of one of the cleaner's aprons. What if I wanted to pinch them? (The Crown Jewels – not the cleaner's aprons.) Would it not be a simple task for me to take the key down to a locksmith's in Addingham and have a duplicate cut, so that I might use my own personal copy to open the cabinet and load up my van? That would make sense, wouldn't it? Perhaps there was a method in Spot the Dog's madness after all. *Oh, but hang about!* In the circumstances I have just described, why would I need to cut a duplicate key? In order to do the dirty deed, why not just use the one I had found in the Bloody Tower? *Oh, but hang about again!* If I had my own personal key I could hand in the original at the Lost Property office at the Tower and use my copy to open the cabinet later in the week, when things had settled down again, and after dark, when all the ravens were asleep. Perhaps that was it. But, *hang about still further,* patient Reader, for, on reflection, even that plan had holes in it. If I had handed the original key in as lost property shortly before the jewels disappeared the police would know the key had been in my possession, and some smart Alec copper would probably deduce that I had had a copy made before handing it in, so suspicion would still fall on me. It was all very confusing.

In summary, if I was now prepared to concede that there was indeed method in Master Muldoon's madness I still wasn't sure I fully understood what it was.

By the time I reached Ippardly, a drive of probably no more than fifteen minutes despite the heavy early morning traffic, in my mind I had cursorily sorted out the plots of at least half a dozen *romans policiers*, but as to why Blotchy-boy should have refused to serve me I was still not completely sure. Unless he was being deliberately perverse, something I still refused to believe despite his surly demeanour. I knew it had to be a question of security, but precisely what aspect of it still eluded me. I resolved that I must learn from this morning's experience, even if I didn't fully understand what the lesson was that I had to learn. I had by now decided that if I encountered the same problem at my locksmith's in Ippardly, I would not tell them that it was the key to a safe.

When passing through the town on previous occasions I had noticed that there was a specialist locksmith in the High Street but, perhaps fearing another rebuff more than I cared to admit, I avoided the place and headed instead for the local shoe menders, where keys were also cut as a presumably profitable sideline. The store was quite busy when I entered but, fortunately, there were no customers at the key-cutting counter so I went straight up to the custodian, an elderly gentleman with greying hair perched precariously on a wooden stool behind the counter. Dressed in a light brown overall over a white shirt and dark tie, he was carefully perusing the sports pages of a tabloid red-top, his glasses pushed up high on his forehead. As I approached him he smiled and snapped smartly to attention, folding his newspaper for later.

"Good morning," I greeted him confidently. "Can you cut me one of these?"

He took the key from my fingers and snapped his spectacles down on his nose as he examined it closely. Then he picked up a rag and began polishing it carefully, as though he were trying to dry it. God! I hope he didn't think that its clamminess was the result of contact with *my* DNA! Spotty Boy's legacy clearly lingered on.

"Yes, I think so," he said finally. "It's not a *Yale*, is it?"

"I don't know. It's the key to a safe in my office." *Damn!* I had decided not to tell him that, but it was too late now. It was already out.

I needn't have worried. Ignoring my response, the elderly gentleman had already moved across to a rack on the wall where he kept his stock of blanks and selected a key that looked like mine. He placed one against the other for comparison purposes and then smiled contentedly.

"Yes, that's the ticket," he exclaimed triumphantly. "It'll be £1.50."

"Thanks," I said appreciatively, confirming in that simple expression of gratitude that I was armed with both the willingness and the wherewithal to meet the costs of his labour.

Without further ado the sturdy yeoman bent industriously over his workbench and went busily about his grinding, and in two minutes flat he was straightening his back and proudly examining the fruits of his labour. He squinted lovingly at his handiwork, as he compared the copy key with the original, and seemed well pleased with the likeness. He then gave the copy a couple of cursory caresses with a metal file before rubbing the whole thing over with his dirty rag and handing me the finished article. The taxpayer was the poorer by thirty shillings but I now had a spare key to my safe and could look my security officer in the eye whenever our paths crossed.

As I drove into the office later that morning, the two keys nestling snugly side by side in my wallet, my thoughts turned back to Mr Knox's pebble-dashed assistant, but my grumpy demeanour of earlier that morning had completely disappeared. I had at first been sorely tempted to drive back to Addingham and call in at *Fort Knox*, just for the purpose of showing my furuncled friend that less than half an hour after leaving his premises I had found someone to cut me the key he had refused to copy, but what would have been the point? Even if I had rubbed his unsavoury nose in it, would he have cared? I doubted it. Poor lad. What a day he had had too! He had only been doing his job as he saw it, I suppose, and he must have been just as hacked off with me as I was with him.

In fact, although it was the gulf between us that had struck me when I first met him, and had continued to impress itself on me throughout our confrontation, I could now appreciate how alike the locksmith's assistant and I really were. He had obstinately decided that under no circumstances would I get a key out of him that morning, and I was just as obstinately, and just as irrationally, determined to show that it could be done, despite his refusal to assist me. He had won, but I had won too, so we had both won! Yippee! I could now afford to be magnanimous. Perhaps I had been a tad hasty in cancelling my order for those window locks…

I even felt bad about continued reference to his acne. Surely it was no worse than mine had been, at his age… I made a mental note to reassure him on this issue if ever I should encounter him in happier circumstances.

I didn't go back to the shop later that week, either to complain to Mr Knox about Master Dalmatian's attitude or to reorder my window locks, but I noticed shortly afterwards that *Fort Knox and Co* was no more. The store had closed down. My neighbour told me that old Mr Knox had gone out of business. Competition from Woolworth's, and the high street cobblers, had been something he had been unable to cope with and, finding no way of making his business viable, he had simply folded. Poor old Mr Knox.

Despite myself, I couldn't help wondering whether the locksmith's misfortune might have been the work of his pock-marked apprentice, who had seemed to take a perverse delight in scaring all the customers away, but I couldn't escape an awful feeling that cancellation of my order for window locks might just have been the straw that had broken the camel's back. Or my refusal to go back and ask Mr Knox to cut my key. My thirty shillings' worth of business might have been just enough to keep him afloat until things picked up, but when I had cruelly snatched it from him he had gone under. It didn't bear thinking about. How I wished now that I had just accepted Spottychops's refusal to assist, and gone back to see Mr Knox at the weekend. What was that poor lad to do, now that he was unemployed? He didn't seem to me to have the ability to impress at a job interview, so the workhouse inevitably beckoned. Poor, poor lad.

And, to cap it all, the poor soul was having to contend with all those blackheads too…

Oh dear. We Jaxons carry a lot of guilt with us as we drag ourselves from one new day to the next.

CHAPTER 18 : BASKETCASE

My best, most favourite sport of all
Is one that's known as basketball.
I used to practise day and night
To get my dribbling just right.
I finally realised my dream,
When Oliver picked me for his team,
But then the start of all my folly,
Was trying to be as good as Ollie.
We used to play each week at school,
But sadly, as I broke a rule,
I've been compelled to sit aside
Because I've been disqualified.
When I was shooter on my team,
I thought no one would ever dream,
Because my shooting was sublime,
That I'd been cheating all the time.
I was a star, but not for long:
An umpire spotted something wrong;
I hadn't noticed, as we played,
His watching every move I made.
After the game that wily fox
Made me remove my shoes and socks,
And so at last it was revealed
Exactly why I seemed spring-heeled.
I'd fixed some springs beneath my pumps
So I could make amazing jumps
Above the others in my group,
Then drop the ball into the hoop.
Now I sit sadly in disgrace
While someone else plays in my place;

My punishment brought me to tears,
For I've been banned for ninety years.
"You silly boy," said my old dad,
"You've ruined all the fun you had."
But why I did it's plain to see,
Because I'm only four foot three.

CHAPTER 19 : A LOW-TECH SOLUTION

My granddad keeps on sending me
The most atrocious verse;
Each time I think he's reached the pits
He sends me something worse.

So, in my note to Santa Claus
I asked, as a one-off,
If he could bring me a device
To switch my granddad off.

Then, in my sock, on Christmas Day,
Santa had left a note
To tell me of a special App;
And this is what he wrote:

"I've brought you something good this year,
"An *iPhone Sixty-Nine*,
"Which has a smart deflection mode
"For menace of this kind."

The simple App on this device,
I found, was all it took
To free myself from all the cr*p
That's in my granddad's book.

You click on *Settings*, then on *Tripe*,
And then on *Jaxon Rhyme,*
Then click on *Turn this rubbish off*
For ever and all time!

Then, if he sends more 'poetry',
The message, loud and clear,
Is *Apple* will send someone round
To punch him in the ear.

CHAPTER 20: 200 POUNDS OF UGLY FAT

It was 31st December, the last day of an eventful year, and I had spent it in Manchester. My company had an office there that was situated not far from the airport, and they used to drag me up there several times a year for meetings and the like. I didn't used to mind. It got me out of London, it offered me the chance to see colleagues in the northwest whom I needed to see, and it gave me the chance to catch up on some paperwork uninterrupted, both while in the air and in the lounge at the airport, waiting for my flight to be called.

So I didn't mind having to make those regular trips north. My flights to and from Manchester were booked by my secretary, and the process on this occasion had followed the usual pattern. She knew that the 08h55 departure from London would have me in the Manchester office by about 11h00, and that the flight leaving Manchester at 19h25 would get me back to London by 20h30, so she had booked me on those services.

It had all gone like clockwork on that particular New Year's Eve. I had flown to Manchester that morning, had my meetings, bored lots of people, no doubt upset lots of others, and all the formal parts of the proceedings were over well before 5.00 pm. I had then settled down to deal with some e-mails until shortly after 5.30 pm, when I packed up and headed back to the terminal building for my flight home. Someone dropped me off back at the airport soon after six, right outside the terminal building. As I had no hold luggage and had checked in for the return flight before leaving Heathrow that morning, I could go straight to the departures lounge at Manchester Airport when I reported for the evening's flight. That way I wasted no valuable drinking time. I headed straight for the executive lounge, looking forward to a stiffish gin before my flight south.

When I reached the lounge I became vaguely aware that it seemed strangely empty. The airline lady examined my boarding card, and said, by way of greeting: "Good evening, Mr Jaxon. I see you're booked on the 19h25 flight to Heathrow, but the 18h25 hasn't left yet and you will be able to catch it if you're quick."

"What do you mean by quick?" I asked suspiciously.

"As it's New Year's Eve some of our later flights are leaving a bit early this evening," she explained, "and the 18h25 is about to depart. But I don't think you'll have to run very fast to catch it."

Run? Herbert Jaxon run? She had to be joking. Forty years previously I had been moderately swift over 100 or 200 yards, and I believe my prowess as a high hurdler of note is still a topic of conversation among some of my former schoolmates, but it had been several years since I had actually moved at a pace where, had I been taking part in a walking race, the judges might have been moved to disqualify me for 'lifting'. I decided to let things stay as they were.

"No, that's OK," I said. "I think I'll stay with the one I'm booked on." I was in no mood to test my athleticism, but quite apart from that there was another reason why I decided to ignore her invitation to join the earlier flight. I had arranged a lift to take me home from the airport that evening, and knew that if I reached Heathrow earlier than scheduled I would be kept hanging around in arrivals in London, waiting for my taxi. Far better, I thought, to be hanging around in departures in Manchester, where I could unwind a little, and relax over a drink.

The check-in lady was not pushy. "Suit yourself," she said. "We'll be calling your flight early as well, particularly as you've now checked in and you're the only passenger booked to travel on it."

"What did you just say?" I asked, incredulous. "I'm the only passenger on the flight? Surely that can't be right? You're joking."

"No, that's right," she assured me. "The last shuttle on New Year's Eve is never very full. Everyone wants to get home early. And I've managed to move everyone else who was booked on your flight to the one before. You're the only passenger who's declined the offer."

"OK, thanks," I said, as I took back my boarding card and made my way into the executive club lounge, which was, as the lady had suggested it might be, totally deserted. I think the lights in one half of it had already been switched off. I grabbed some peanuts and poured myself rather a conservative measure of liquid. There was no hurry, I told myself. I had plenty of time before my flight was to be called, so there was no need to attack the refreshments as though prohibition were about to be introduced. I splashed a splosh of tonic water, even added a slice of lemon, just to be sociable, before settling down to look at some of those dailies I had not already read in the departure lounge at Heathrow that morning.

I must confess that it wasn't long before I was beginning to feel rather uneasy about having opted not to switch to the earlier flight when the chance was offered. For one thing, sitting all alone in that vast executive lounge began suddenly to feel a bit eerie, if not surreal, and I began to wonder what the airport and airline staff might be making of my decision. After all, who in his right mind would refuse to take the opportunity to get home a bit earlier on New Year's Eve of all nights? In addition, although it was no real skin off my nose, I began to wonder whether perhaps the crew on the late service might be assuming that everyone would switch to the earlier flight (why wouldn't they?) and might be looking forward to flying an empty aircraft back to London, with no passengers to look after. They might not be best pleased when they heard that one obstinate oik had opted to let his original booking stand, thereby disrupting their plan for a bit of a rest, or even a bit of a knees-up, just prior to the Bank Holiday. If I had been prepared to get a bit of a move on they would have had their wish, and now it really was too late for me to change my booking, because I had allowed another five minutes to elapse and no longer had time to dash down to the gate for the earlier flight, even if the word 'dash' had been in my vocabulary.

I poured myself another glass, an industrial measure this time, and reflected on what kind of reception might be awaiting me when I reached the aircraft. I didn't have to wait long to find out, because at about twenty past six there came an announcement over the public address system.

"Would Mr Jaxon please report to departure gate 143, where his executive jet is waiting to take him to London!"

I blanched. I don't really know what that means, but I am fairly certain I did it none the less. Crumbs, they had called me to the flight by name! Over the years I had flown backwards and forwards between Heathrow and Manchester scores of times, and I had grown accustomed to the anonymity of it all, which I enjoyed. In fact, to my shame the only previous occasion when Manchester Airport had called me to my flight by name had been in order to issue a rebuke. On that occasion I was travelling with a colleague. We had had rather a busy day, and had arranged to hold the last of the day's meetings at the airport, and by the time we reached the departures lounge we had completely lost track of time. If truth is to be told, we had then dallied a bit over the refreshments, before suddenly we had heard over the airwaves:

"This is a third and *final* call for Mr Jaxon and Mrs Eccles, travelling to Heathrow, who are requested to report *immediately* to the departure gate where their flight to London is now closed!"

Oh dear. The ignominy of it all! Would I ever live it down? We would now have to scuttle down to the aircraft, listening to the tut-tutting all around us, and when we got to the gate we would be told off in person by the airline staff as well as having to face the wrath of the passengers on board whom we had thoughtlessly kept waiting. Partially anaesthetised by the refreshments though I may have been, I still shudder at the memory.

But there was no mistaking the tones of the announcement on that 31st December, which were distinctly cordial. Timidly I swallowed the last of my drink and set off for gate 143 at a brisk amble. Everywhere was eerily silent and I passed scarcely a soul on the way. The whole terminal building seemed to be deserted, but as I reached the entrance to the corridor that leads to gates 140-143, a strange sight met my eyes. It was the official who checked boarding cards prior to embarkation. In my experience this individual was usually far too busy checking to see that he had gathered everyone in, so that the flight could depart on time, to engage in conversation, but on this occasion the gentleman strode towards me wearing a big, beaming smile.

"Mr Jaxon?" he asked unnecessarily.

"So I have been told," I faltered. I considered it pointless denying my identity.

"I've never done this before," beamed the official, "but I should like to escort you *personally* to your aircraft!"

He went through the formality of checking my boarding card, and then accompanied me along the pier to the awaiting aeroplane. We resisted the temptation to link arms, but on the way he chatted to me gaily, mainly about the unlikelihood of there ever being a flight to London on which only one passenger was travelling. He said he had worked at the airport for many years and had never known such a situation before. I was a bit embarrassed by it all and didn't say much, although I may have interpolated the odd monosyllabic into the general flow of his exuberance.

When we reached the aircraft it was a similar story; if anything it was a little worse. The Manchester gateman handed me over to the flight crew with a flourish, and the chief steward welcomed me on board like royalty.

"Mr Jaxon," he hyperbolised. "So nice of you to choose to travel with us today! I don't think we've ever before had a flight where we had only one passenger on board! I hope you will find everything to your liking."

"Thank you," I said. "I'm sure I shall," not knowing how far I ought to play along with all this. At the best of times I am the worst of actors, and although acting out the role of VIP was OK to a point, I felt that if I took it too far I might find someone taking me seriously, and then objecting to my exaggerated show of self-importance.

"My name is Dominic," said the steward as he shook my hand warmly, and he went on in fulsome tones: "First I would like to introduce you to my crew. This is Katie, who will be looking after you *personally* on your flight. If there is anything at all you want, just ask Katie and she'll be pleased to give it to you....."

Oh my God, I thought, as I made a right turn into the passenger section and found that all the stewards and stewardesses were lined up to greet me at the entrance. They were all smiling, and everybody laughed as though Dominic might have cracked a joke.

"Hello, Katie," I said, now feeling distinctly uncomfortable.

".....And this is Mandy, and this is Sunita, and this is Cedric, and this is Nicole....." God, there seemed to be hundreds of them, although I realise there could not possibly have been more than five or six. I shook each hand as it was proffered, and played along as best I could.

"Mr Jaxon," said Katie. "Where would you like to sit?"

Instinctively I looked at my boarding card. "The computer's given me 2C," I said. "I'm happy to stick with that." I can be very boring at times.

"Oh, no," said Katie, feigning a hurt look. "You can sit where you like! You have the entire aircraft to choose from!" And she made an expansive gesture with her hands that suggested that the whole aircraft, if not the whole world, was my oyster.

"OK," I said. "Er....."

And I could not decide. I am afraid I am like that in empty car parks too. If there is one space available in a packed car park I will back my car into it without a second thought, but give me a choice of parking spaces and it will take me forever to park. Buying shoes, I am just the same. Why can't you go in and ask for a pair of black lace-ups, size 11, and be given what you ask for? Why do they bring you about fifty million pairs to choose from? And why is the shoe shop assistant always disappointed when you buy the first pair you are shown? Surely it is easier for them if you get on with it and don't muck about? Aren't all black, lace-up, size 11 shoes more or less identical?

"3C will do," I decided eventually.

I was prepared to move seats just to please Katie, but I thought if I jokingly chose something like 68F she might suddenly object to having to decamp to the back of the aircraft, so 3C seemed like a good enough compromise. But, as I have discovered many times, however hard you try you cannot please any of the people any of the time.

Katie was aghast at my choice. Or, at least, she pretended to be.

"3C? But you were already in 2C, and you had the whole aircraft to choose from!"

There was no getting away from it, I had let Katie down. But fortunately, Dominic came to my rescue. He pulled rank.

"No, let's let Mr Jaxon sit where he wants!"

And then to me, as we all moved one row further back: "Would you like something to drink, Mr Jaxon?"

"Yes, I'll have a, er....."

I hesitated again. In the past I had only been offered drinks before push back on long haul flights, or in first class, and I suddenly wondered if I had heard him right. It would be a bit embarrassing if I hadn't, and I were to start ordering alcohol before we were even airborne. They might form the wrong impression of me. Besides, I was already fairly full of refreshment from the lounge, so I was not actually gagging for it. But, on the other hand, I didn't want to risk saying no, in case this was the only drink I was to be offered before we reached... where were we going? I was now feeling so embarrassed that I could no longer remember. I suddenly recalled one awful flight I had made to Warsaw when, just after take-off, the captain had announced over the loudspeaker that he had just noticed a bit of a problem with his landing gear and was going to have to return immediately to Heathrow. The passengers all groaned in unison at the inconvenience of the impending delay – or, as has just occurred to me, some may have been groaning because they were worrying that a bit of a problem with the landing gear might cause a bit of a problem with the process of landing the aircraft. But my own groans at the time stemmed from the fact that, when the captain decided to do his three-point turn, the lady operating the drinks trolley had reached only as far as row 4, and I was sitting in row 5. I realised at once that my considerable thirst could not now be slaked until we had *relanded* and *deplaned*, if they are the correct aeronautical terms.

Why does flying always make me so thirsty? But I digress.

My brain was still not in the right gear, so I couldn't decide what I wanted to drink, but again it was Dominic who rescued me.

"Champagne, perhaps?"

"No, I'll have a gin, please," I said, settling into my seat.

Better not get above my station.... And anyway, I can be very predictable at times.

Dominic didn't argue.

"And would you like some wine to drink with your snack? If it's all right with you, we probably won't be coming round again once we get airborne."

Thank you, God, I thought to myself. I really don't like to be waited on.

"Yes, I'll have some red, please."

Things seemed at last to be settling down, but my torment wasn't quite over because there was to be yet another distraction as a uniformed officer emerged from behind Dominic and extended his hand towards me.

"Good evening, Mr Jaxon," he said. "I'm Captain Biggles," (I don't think that was the name he gave me), "and I will be your captain this evening. And this is Algy," (that probably wasn't the name of his co-pilot either), "my first officer, who will be on the flight deck with me. I don't think we've ever had only one passenger before, have we Algy?"

Algy agreed with his boss, and another hand was thrust into mine. I probably made some inane noises and, these formalities out of the way, the pilots returned to their cockpit and I settled at last into my seat. My drinks arrived in short order and (isn't it always the way?) Katie must have come up with at least three bottles, and she gave me three mini bottles of Bordeaux rouge too. Why is it always feast or famine? I bet that if I had been feeling thirsty they would have lost the key to the drinks cabinet. I suppose I could have refused their generosity but I accepted all of it. It would have been impolite not to do so.

"Well," said Dominic, "I note that you're a frequent flyer's club member, Mr Jaxon, so you have probably seen the safety briefing a million times. If you want me to repeat it for you now I will, but if you're happy I wasn't going to bother."

"No, that's OK," I said. "I've heard it so many times that I could probably recite it by heart, word for word."

"That's good," he responded. "And if there is a problem there will be plenty of us to look after you anyway. So, please fasten your seat belt and have a pleasant flight."

Dominic then told me that this was a special occasion for another reason, in that the captain was expecting to break the record time for a flight between Manchester and Heathrow. I was well into my fourth or fifth livener by now, so I cannot remember exactly what he said, but I think he suggested that the existing best time was in the region of 27 minutes and 15 seconds[25]. Dominic said that the captain believed that he had the best possible chance of setting a new best time, given that he had a particularly light load, with no passengers to speak of, and that flying conditions were also perfect.

With that they left me to it. I strapped myself in, and sucked on my drinks, and we took off, and I unfastened my seat belt, and read my copy of *Private Eye*, and I think Katie brought me some food, and I probably ate it and drank my wine, and they cleared up after me, and they told me to fasten my seat belt, and I did, and we landed, and the adventure was finally over.

As we taxied over to the gate Dominic came over and sat down in the seat across the aisle from me. He asked me politely whether I had enjoyed my flight and I said that I had. I acknowledged that it had been an experience for me, and apologised for not having flown on the earlier service if he and his crew had been looking forward to an easy flight unencumbered by passengers. If that was what he and his crew had been hoping for he was careful not to say so, and he said simply that he hoped to see me again on another of his company's flight very soon.

As he got up to return to the galley I asked him whether the captain had succeeded in setting a new best time for the journey.

"No, he just missed it," said Dominic. "27 minutes and 30 seconds[26], so he was 15 seconds off."

I was pleasantly inebriated at the time, but this news made me feel terrible. Poor old Biggles had probably waited half a career for this opportunity, and he had fluffed it. Flying conditions had been

---

25 Please accept my apologies if you are an aviation expert and I have got all that hopelessly wrong.

26 Once again I apologise if I have got the actual figures wrong.

perfect, as Dominic had told me himself, and the Captain had probably calculated that without having to transport a group of passengers and their luggage he was a sure bet to get his machine from Manchester down to Heathrow faster than anyone had ever managed to do it before. And he had come agonisingly close to seeing his name etched in the annals of history for all time. His planning had no doubt been meticulous, but all that planning had come to nought because he had planned on flying an empty aircraft, and had therefore reckoned without me. I couldn't help thinking that if it hadn't been for that extra 200 pounds of ugly fat the captain was carrying, that a new best time would surely have been set.

Oh dear. If only I hadn't decided not to take that earlier flight…

CHAPTER 21 : PERFECTION

I 'wrote' a 'poem' yesterday,
While I was driving into town,
But didn't have a pen or paper
So I couldn't write it down.

Now most of it has been forgotten,
Which really makes me rather sad,
Because, compared with what I've written,
This effort wasn't quite so bad.

I have my knockers, obviously,
But felt this verse was one to show 'em,
Because, with all due modesty,
I knew I'd written the perfect poem.

You'll simply have to take my word,
Though, at the very least, it's sloppy,
And at the worst it's quite absurd:
I've nothing set down in hard copy.

I can't remember what I said!
The words I used? I've not a clue!
The whole thing's vanished from my head...
But probably, I mentioned you...

Perhaps, if push were come to shove,
And someone asked what it's about,
I'd guess, maybe, I spoke of love,
So you were there, without a doubt!

In fact, I think you'd be quite proud
If you discovered you'd been named,
And, though you wouldn't shout it loud,
I don't think you'd have been ashamed.

I remember using allegory,
And metaphor, and waggish wit,
Litotes and hyperbole,
And all that other clever sh*t:

Enjambement, and consonance…
And anapaestical bravura…
Alliteration, assonance…
And fannying about with the caesura…

I know that Keats, and all that crush
Who used to play the poetry game,
Were up to all that clever gush,
And yesterday I did the same!

My hope was that the reader might
Put down his gin apéritif,
And see things in a different light,
Suspending all his disbelief,

And drink in *ambiance* in its place,
And understand the universe
Was now a wholly better space
Because of my four lines of verse.

I've tried in vain a million times,
While in my study, at my desk,
To woo the muse, and conjure rhymes,
But what comes out's ofttimes grotesque.

Then yesterday, nothing was wrong,
And inspiration simply flowed!
It's odd, I'd written a *perfect* song
While concentrating on the road!

The world is lucky, I would say,
To find me so resilient,
For I persisted yesterday,
And what I 'wrote' was blooming brilliant!

It's such a shame that I'd no pen,
And that the traffic was so bad,
But as I've said, time and again,
There's nothing written on my pad.

Now, I can tell, you're wondering on,
But I assure you that it's true!
My poem was the dog's *couillons*!
It was perfection… just like you!

CHAPTER 22 : BONDAGE

My mum bought me a Premium Bond
Which only cost a quid;
It was the most exciting thing
My mummy ever did.

That was in nineteen-fifty-eight,
Or nineteen-fifty-nine,
When I was just a little kid,
But that bond was all mine!

And every month since then I've checked
To see if I have won;
The checking doesn't take me long,
But brings me untold fun.

Month after month, the word's the same:
I'm told I've had no joy,
But what excitement this all brings
To this old mummy's boy!

It sets me up for next month's draw
To check my bond in vain,
And every month there's nothing new:
No luck this time again!

Persistent failure's what I crave!
As if I ever won
A crummy fifty quid or so
That would destroy the fun!

I don't want any paltry prize,
As such a happenstance
Would simply use up all my luck,
And surely spoil my chance

Of carrying off a million pounds,
To go off on a cruise!
So, every month and every draw,
I pray to God I'll lose!!!!

'Cos every time I lose again
My chance of winning's greater,
I'm *sure* I'll win my million pounds,
One day, sooner or later!

Repeated failure simply means
There's no chance of my using
The fund of luck I'm storing up,
So let's hope I keep losing!

I'm close to being a millionaire!
I'm sure of that so much it
Pervades my every waking thought!
I'm so close I could touch it!

My monthly epinephrine surge
Makes life flash by much quicker,
And all thanks to my Premium Bond
Which only cost a knicker!

CHAPTER 23 : A GOOD WALK SPOILED[27]

Before we go any further, esteemed Reader, I should like to admit to you that I am not very good at golf. Now I come to think of it, I am not very good at most things. In fact, I think I can truthfully say, without fear of contradiction, that there is no activity known to man that I am even remotely good at. But none of that alters the fact that I am no good at golf.

I have never (to my recollection) even broken 100 for a round. I have had a few scores of around 100, or about 30 over par, but even these 'good' rounds I have shot have relied on a number of 'gimmes' from my playing partners. According to something I read on the web, *in golf a 'gimme' is a shot that the other players agree can count automatically without actually being played. When a player has only a very short putt left to play, other players may grant a gimme (i.e. one stroke is counted), but the ball is not actually played. A gimme is a time-saving convention under the tacit assumption that the putt would not have been missed - e.g. when the ball is only a few inches from the hole.*

So, according to convention, in order to expect a gimme from your partner you usually need to be able to propel your ball to within striking distance of the hole. However, I must admit that most of my playing partners have been generous enough to grant me a gimme if I have been able to manoeuvre the ball to within three or four feet of the hole, rather than a few inches. This is because they know that I will probably not sink a three-footer without a gimme. If they make me putt it, they know from experience that I will miss, and that my next putt will likely have to be taken from five

---

27 Golf is a good walk spoiled (Mark Twain, 1835-1910). Or, according to some, somebody else said it.

or six feet away. Most golfers get closer to the hole after every putt, but poor putters like me usually manage to creep increasingly further away. So what becomes all important when someone is playing golf with a rabbit is the time-saving element of the convention rather than what the web calls the *tacit assumption that the putt would not have been missed.*

But although I am no good at it, the game of golf has always fascinated me, partly on account of the incredible complexity of its rules. Surely the rules of golf ought to be no more than about five in number, and all fairly straightforward. (1) Hit the ball with the stick; (2) if the ball doesn't go in the hole, hit the sodding thing again until it does; (3) if the ball goes over the fence, or in the water, tough; (4) count the number of shots you take to get the ball in the hole; (5) the man taking the fewest shots to get it in the hole wins. You would think that ought to be enough, wouldn't you? But you would be wrong. I have learned that the rules of golf occupy countless pages of text, and that they are still being revised. There is even a rule that says you cannot agree to waive the rules! And there is another rule to cover points not covered by the rules! In the light of all that, what a wonderful game golf must be to those who understand it. I don't think the rules of beach volleyball, which is another of my passions, can be nearly so complex. But I am probably wrong about that too.

I once had a quick look at the rules of golf and some of them seemed to me to be both bizarre and counter-intuitive, and I have a feeling that very few people understand all of them. I wonder if that is why, in the major tournaments, there is always a rules official within spitting distance of every player, just so that any issue that is not clear-cut can be resolved as soon as it arises. But I could be wrong. Maybe people understand the rules better than I give them credit for. Perhaps the rules official is there simply to confirm that the players' interpretation of a particular rule is correct. I could understand that. I mean, if a player sought to take advantage of some of the more obscure rules he might be afraid of being labelled a cheat, were it not for the fact that a rules official is on hand to confirm that he can do what he proposes to do.

The fact that I don't understand the rules of golf doesn't prevent me from trying to take advantage of them. Whenever I play a bad shot, which is not uncommon, I am always quick to enquire of those who are knowledgeable in such matters whether there is a rule from which I might gain some kind of benefit (I think that is the word) or relief (maybe it is that one). I am not here to argue vocabulary. Usually there isn't, but sometimes (to my surprise) there is. So my advice to any inadequate golfer is always to check with a rules official before accepting what appears to be the inevitable. Not doing so can be costly.

Whenever possible, I used to play golf in Winter. Winter rules seem to me to offer the best opportunity for the moderate golfer to improve his game, or, at least, to improve his score, which is not quite the same thing but sounds as if it ought to be. In fact, I am surprised that anyone plays golf in the Summer months, because, if you do, I believe you are expected to play the ball from where it lies. Why would anyone do that? When playing under 'Winter rules' I have noticed that my partner will usually allow me to pick up my ball, wherever it lands, and move it to somewhere less inhospitable. That seems to me to be a far more sensible approach. Golf is a game for gentlemen, and there seem to be far more gentlemen playing it in Winter than in Summer.

I am so bad at golf that I am surprised that anyone has ever been prepared to play with me, but in the 1980s I used to play quite regularly with a group of friends. Some of them were quite good and, as is self-evident, if you are quite good you are not in the game nearly as often as those who, like me, are hopeless. The convention seems to be that the person whose ball is furthest from the hole shoots next, and it was therefore usually my shot.

Sometimes the people I used to play with would not get a shot for months.

Ray was a friend of mine and an excellent player, with a handicap of 5. When he played with me he would patiently dispense advice after every one of my poor shots, and would never dream of requiring me to putt out from under twenty or thirty feet. Anything I could land within ten yards of the hole was a gimme for me, but Ray hardly ever seemed to get a shot himself. Where was the fun for him? What a wonderful friend he was.

Surprisingly, I was not the worst player in our group. That honour went to another chum, Arthur by name, whose opponents and playing partner rarely got a shot at all. Even I rarely got a shot when I was playing with Artie. Artie seemed to have mastered the art of always keeping his ball furthest from the hole, so it always appeared to be his shot. But that was really of little consequence, because on the golf course you saw little of Arturo, even if you were notionally playing a round with him. This was because another art Art had mastered was that of the hook, and he had become so enamoured of this weapon that he played it involuntarily every time he picked up a club, with a result that whenever he managed to stay within bounds he played all his golf in the rough to the left of the fairway. With the obvious exception of Ray, who always annoyingly chose to stay on the course, the rest of us, who all seemed to have perfected the slice, preferred to play our golf in the rough to the right of the fairway, so we didn't see much of Arthur during the round. As we all made hesitant progress in the vague direction of the green, Art was left to plough a lonely furrow several bus rides away to our left. In fact, one wag once shook Arthur's hand at the first tee and bade him farewell, promising to see him in the clubhouse after the round, knowing that Arthur was unlikely to be within shouting distance of the rest of us for the next eighteen greens and fairways.

Arthur was the most wayward striker of the ball I have ever seen, and I hold him partly to blame for the fact that my own game is so bad. One afternoon he and I were playing together, just the two of us, at a public course, when, for the first time in my life, I hit what for me was just about the perfect drive at the short sixteenth. The pin was only 180 yards from the tee, and I managed to drop my tee shot on the green, where it rolled forward and stopped a mere eighteen inches from the flag. I was in heaven! I had never before even managed to score a par, even with the help of gimmes, and here I was with a genuine putt for a birdie!!!

"Good shot!" said Arthur grudgingly, as he prepared to take his own tee shot. "What club did you use?"

"A five-iron," I said proudly.

He need not have asked really. I tended to use my five-iron for everything, except maybe for putting, for which I sometimes preferred to use my putter.

Arthur thoughtfully returned the seven-iron he had been intending to use to his golf bag and took out his five-iron, and I permitted myself a supercilious smirk. Surely he didn't think that using the same club as I had chosen was going to see him produce a similar shot? We both knew that, whichever club he used, he was going to hook it over into the bushes on the left. That is where he always ended up, whether at this hole or at any of the others. I watched Arthur as he thoughtfully addressed the ball in the manner he had been taught, keeping his eye on it, and his head still, and his left arm straight, and then, after a preliminary waggle of his own backside, gave the ball a fearful crack up its backside. Judged by Artie's usual standard it wasn't a bad hit. The ball climbed in the air, rising in a fractious arc well over head height, turned abruptly left for no obvious reason, and then disappeared into the bushes about 150 yards away to our left, about 45° away from the direction in which he had been aiming.

"Good sh…" I began, encouragingly.

It was the done thing, but Arthur ignored me.

"Sh*t!" fumed Arthur. "Did you see where it went?"

"Yes, come on, let's go and get it!" I shouted enthusiastically as I galloped after it. I had a putt for a birdie waiting, for Chrissake, and the quicker we could get Arthur's ball on the green the quicker I could attempt my putt!

But we couldn't find his sodding ball!

We found plenty of other golf balls, balls which had been lost at different times by other indifferent golfers (I think one of them may even have been the one Arthur had lost the last time he had played this hole), and I was so impatient to play my next shot that I was prepared to let Arthur claim any one of those as his, and play it from wherever we found it, even offering him a 'free drop' from wherever he fancied but, perversely, he didn't fancy any of that. So, about fifteen minutes later, we were trudging back to the tee for him to play his third shot, after he had declared his first ball well and truly lost.

And, bugger me with a broken bottle if he didn't do the same thing again!

I watched in dismay as Arthur hooked his second tee shot (that is, his third shot) into the same clump of bushes, and we traipsed back to the same spot to begin our search all over again. We found the same cluster of old golf balls as last time, but we couldn't find Arthur's new one – or, for that matter, the one he had lost earlier.

This was getting ridiculous. My birdie putt was not getting any easier while I was scrabbling around looking for Arthur's second lost ball, and I was becoming more and more tense as the minutes ticked by. So much so that I had soon managed to convince myself that the simple tap in for a birdie I had been contemplating was now anything but an easy shot, and I was sure I was going to miss it – if ever it became my turn to take the perishing putt!

But then suddenly our luck changed! Hooray! After some minutes we eventually found Arthur's ball – well, one he thought he recognised – but I didn't argue. It was buried deep in a bit of coarse undergrowth, but Arthur soon had his sand wedge out of the bag, and after he had given the ball two or three meaty wallops he succeeded in moving it about ten or twelve feet, and it was then back near the edge of the fairway. He was now only about 100 yards from the flag, so he took out his seven-iron and gave the ball some more wellie. Oh dear. As hook shots go this next one wasn't a bad example and, ignoring the principle that the shortest way to the hole might be a straight line, the ball veered away in a beautiful curve to our left, and came to rest about forty yards from the green in some lightish rough to the left of the fairway.

"Good shot!" I fumed sarcastically, as I positively danced in frustration. I could see my own ball, still nestling on the green near the flag, but what had once looked like child's play now looked like quite a difficult putt. I was also becoming afraid it might be too dark to play on when next it became my turn for a shot. I must confess that I wasn't very supportive of Artie at that moment, and I called him one or two rude names that might have threatened our friendship.

When we reached Arthur's ball we found it easily enough this time but I noted that it had come to rest in an awkward spot. This particular putting surface was protected by a single bunker, and although Arthur's ball was now less than forty yards from the edge of the green, and only about forty-five from the hole, the wretched spheroid had managed to position itself in such a way that the solitary bunker at this hole was directly between itself and the flag. Oh no, I thought to myself. I can see where this next shot is going to end up. But then I quickly cheered up, as I reminded myself that Arthur had never hit a straight shot in his life. That bunker was perfectly safe, provided that it stayed sitting where it was. Arthur's next shot would obviously be hooked towards the back of the green, well over to our left, I thought smugly. I was then forced to watch in horror as he whacked it again with his sand wedge and (would you bloody believe it?) managed to top it, so that it skidded along the ground and took refuge in the bunker, like a rabbit disappearing into a rabbit hole. Arthur had by now taken about eighty-three shots to cover three-quarters of the distance I had managed with one, and he was now in the sand, while my ball was still lying only a foot and a half from the hole, in the same spot it had been occupying for the past three-quarters of an hour!

Let us cut this short. Suffice it to say that Arthur took about fifteen hundred and sixty at that hole[28], and when I finally got to take my putt I missed it! And I missed the next one coming back as well, so I ended up with a four. I still blame Arthur for the fact that I did not get my first ever birdie at that hole. He had managed to keep me from playing a shot for so long that by the time it was my turn to play I had forgotten what the object of the game was. Needless to say, there were no rules officials on hand for me to consult at once, to enquire whether there was anything in the rules from which I might seek 'benefit' if something like this happens, so I had to reluctantly accept my bogey and forget about it – which I probably will one day.

---

28   1560 shots to reach the green that is – he had needed about seven putts after that.

But for all his lack of prowess Artie was very resourceful, as was evidenced by another incident which took place on another occasion on the same golf course. There were drainage problems at that course, and some of the greens had a tendency to become waterlogged whenever there was rain about. As a result the management had cut a series of drainage channels where the course was worst affected. All those channels ran away from the greens, in some cases for over twenty yards, and from the air these channels must have looked a bit like the spokes of a wheel, with the greens at the hub. One day, when I was playing with our usual group, Artie's ball chanced to drop into one of those channels, and the rest of us were surprised to see him climb down into the ditch and address the ball for his next shot. He seemed to be intending to play the ball from where it was lying.

"Hang on, Art!" called Ray. "That ditch is not a natural hazard. You can pick your ball out of it and have a free drop without penalty."

Ray was obviously doing his best to be helpful but, as we shall discover again later in this chapter, you cannot help some people, however good your intentions.

"That's OK, thanks," called back Arthur from his subterranean refuge, and he promptly ignored the advice proffered. Instead, he proceeded to deliver a venomous swipe to the ball where it had come to rest, and it then careered along the channel towards the green, bouncing off the walls on both sides of the ditch as it sped on its way. Arthur was no fool. He had worked out that all those channels led direct to the greens, and that he consequently had more chance of reaching the green he was aiming at if he stayed in the ditch rather than if he climbed out and took the free drop he was entitled to! It was not quite in the spirit of the game, but then nothing Art did on a golf course ever was.

Arthur did, however, hold a certain distinction which, to my knowledge, has never been achieved by any other golfer. On one occasion he won the hole (and it was a whopping 400 yards par 4 to boot) after he had been granted what, to my knowledge, was the only ever documented instance of a gimme from the tee! I can attest to it because I was the loser of the hole on that occasion, but there was a method in my apparent madness.

We were playing together again, just the two of us, and had reached that particular par 4. On arrival at that hole I had the honour, as I usually had when playing a round with Arthur, and had delivered a perfectly presentable slice, about 160 yards into the light rough on the right of the fairway. Arthur took his tee shot next and hooked his ball out of bounds on the left. Neither of us fancied climbing over that particular fence into that particular field, so the ball was immediately declared lost. Arthur took another ball from his golf bag and gave it the same treatment, unfortunately with the same result. He then rummaged in his bag and found he was out of golf balls – I think he must already have lost about four during that round, even before we reached the hole we were now playing. By now Art was losing his temper as well as his balls, and he spun round angrily and demanded that I give him one of mine. I complied with his request, and he promptly sent it to join its fellows out of bounds to our left. Scarcely pausing for breath he extended his hand in my direction and demanded another golf ball from me. I complied again, and he sent my second ball over the fence to join the other three. I had seldom seen Arthur so angry.

"Give me another ball!" he screamed.

"Whoa! Hang on a minute!" I riposted. "I *concede!* You're in the hole! That's a gimme! You can have it!" He had lost two of his own golf balls, followed quickly by two of mine, so would have been playing his ninth (I think, but haven't checked) off the tee if I had given him another. But I judged that it was infinitely cheaper in the long run to grant him a gimme from the tee rather than have him denude me of balls completely. So he took 9 for that par 4, and went on to win the hole after I took 10. Although I had managed to get my sixth shot to within three inches of the hole, Artie made me putt, and I four-putted from there. Arthur never granted any gimmes. In fact, I think that was the only strength of his game.

But I didn't play golf only with my work colleagues. Sometimes I even used to play with a local clergyman. That vicar was a lovely man, who made his own wine and shared it with his flock after services. He was Church of England, and although he knew I was a Methodist, and the worst Methodist since Vlad the Impaler at that, he didn't seem to hold it against me. He was quite good at golf, and I am surprised he let me play with him, but I suppose he did find he had plenty of time to work on his sermons while I was digging myself out of a bunker or hacking out of the rough. During our rounds of golf, which were often long ones, because I took so many strokes, we would sometimes have quite profound discussions. On more than one occasion I was emboldened to tell him about some of the things in the Bible that didn't make sense to me, and he surprised me, either by straightening out my thinking or by telling me that he had trouble with some of them too. As I said, he was a lovely man, and a credit to his calling.

Sometimes I used also to play golf with another chum, Kevin, who was a keen mathematician. I am surprised he used to let me play with him, too, because Kevin was used to playing with friends who were evenly matched and who could be relied upon to give him a proper game. Being both a generous and competitive soul in equal measure, when playing against me Kevin would be keen to give me shots in order to try and make an interesting match of it, but I am afraid I wasn't even good enough to play under those conditions. The receipt of no amount of shots is ever going to level the playing field if one of the players is regularly in the habit of taking 19 or 20 at the par 3s, with the occasional impressive score of 7 or 8 at the par 5s. Undeterred, however, Kevin would always assume that I must have improved since I last played, and would begin by suggesting that I should receive, say, 2 shots a hole. Then, after the first par 4, where he had taken 5 and I had taken 10, and the next par 4, where he had taken 5 and I had taken 14, he would suggest that I be given 3 shots a hole for the rest of the round. I would then invariably win the next hole, by taking only 7 to his 5 at the third par 4. This would prompt him to revise the scoring system again, and offer me only 1 shot a hole thereafter. But the system would break down again at the par 3 fourth, where I would take about 11 to his 4, prompting him to suggest that 3 shots a hole might be a better offer. And so it would go on, with the number of shots I was to be given changing hole by hole. Although there was no doubt at the end of each round who had won the match, it would have taken a mathematician of the calibre of Archimedes, or even Euclid himself, to calculate Kevin's precise winning margin.

As I said, the rules of golf fascinate me, but they were rarely a problem for Kevin and me. Despite my lack of expertise we played in a relaxed manner, and if I occasionally infringed against the letter of the law (for example, by grounding my club in the sand) Kevin was not quick to penalise me. However, we used sometimes to play at his golf club in a rural part of the country, where some of the other players we saw on the course were less sporting. I think some of them might have benefited if a rules official had accompanied them on every round. Let us take one particular round as a for instance.

Perhaps I ought first to describe the shape of Kevin's home course, so try to imagine a giant butterfly, its wings a few acres in dimension, pinned down on a pleasant and carefully manicured slab of the gently undulating Wiltshire countryside. Now imagine, if you will, that the edges of its wings are the perimeter fences and out of bounds markers on a golf course and you will have a rough idea of the shape of the course. The clubhouse was situated where the butterfly's head would be, and, when you emerged from the clubhouse, the first tee was located to your left. The front nine holes then unfurled counter-clockwise on your left, occupying the space encompassed by the butterfly's left wing, and the ninth green was situated outside the clubhouse and more or less alongside the first tee. Playing each successive hole seemed to take the golfer back and forth across the butterfly's left wing, so that the golfer successfully completing the front nine would therefore have covered most of the territory enclosed within that wing, while tracing a somewhat circular perambulation.

Have you got that? Perhaps I haven't described it very well, but if you have understood, you will be able to understand that the back nine holes were spread out in more or less the same pattern on the butterfly's right wing, because the course was pretty symmetrical. So the tenth tee was situated a short walk away to the right of the clubhouse, with the eighteenth green more or less alongside it.

One other thing you need to be aware of is that when you came out of the clubhouse there was a rather large lake directly in front of you. You had to skirt that lake both when walking to the first tee on your left, and again when walking to the tenth tee to the right of the clubhouse. And the lake actually came into play when you were making your approach shots to both the ninth and the eighteenth greens. Put simply, if you hit either of those approach shots too hard there was a danger of your ball ending up in the water. As you will see, the lake was quite an important feature of the course, and it has quite an important part to play in the plot of the remainder of this chapter.

So, how are we doing, Reader? Have you got a rough picture of what I am driving at? Let us recap. You emerge from the clubhouse and turn left. The first tee is situated near the bottom of the clubhouse steps, alongside the ninth green, and when you whack the ball up the first fairway the lake is on your right. The second hole takes you on a dog-leg to your left, and then the next seven holes require you to follow a zig-zagging pathway, all encompassed within the outline of the butterfly's left wing, in a more or less anti-clockwise direction, so that when you finally drive up the ninth fairway you are heading back towards the clubhouse, and must be careful not to hit your ball over the green and into the lake. I am sorry if that is not a perfect description, but I am afraid it is the best I can do.

Once your ball is safely in the ninth hole you proceed to the tenth tee via a path that runs in front of the clubhouse and round to the right of the lake, which is now on your left. You now play the back nine holes which, more or less, are laid out in the same way as the front nine, but this time all within the outline of the butterfly's right wing, this time in a clockwise direction. Once again, you have to be careful not to overshoot the eighteenth green, or you will end up in the water. OK?

One day, Kevin and I were playing a round on that course and had just putted out on the ninth. I think it is probably a fair bet to assume that Kevin was in the lead but I do not know what the exact score was, although Pythagoras would probably have been able to tell you. We retrieved our balls from the ninth hole and, keeping the lake to our left, proceeded along the path that ran in front of the clubhouse in the direction of the tenth tee. To do this, of course, we were obliged to skirt the eighteenth green, and as we did so we saw a golf ball land on it and bounce towards the eighteenth hole. As golf shots go this was not a bad one, for the ball rolled up towards the hole and stopped about twelve or fourteen feet short of its target.

"Hmmm," I observed unnecessarily, "someone has a putt for a birdie."

I must confess that I liked to talk like that, because it made me sound as if I knew what I was talking about, even though Kevin and I had no way of knowing how many strokes the golfer had played in order to get to where he had landed. Have you noticed that those who are no good at golf frequently talk a good game? I am afraid that I'm one of those people.

The person who had struck that shot was out of our field of vision, because the eighteenth fairway sloped away from the raised green down a slight incline, and trees around the tenth tee obscured most of the eighteenth fairway from the clubhouse. As we headed towards the tenth Kevin and I therefore watched the eighteenth green with interest, not only for a sight of the player who had hit that decent shot but also in anticipation of seeing another golf ball sail onto the green. We assumed that the invisible golfer would be playing with someone else, and I for one was interested to see how close his playing partner could land his approach shot, bearing in mind that the person playing second could well have been closer to the green when pitching on.

We didn't have to wait long, for suddenly over the edge of the green fizzed a second golf ball, undoubtedly as determined to reach the hole as the first one but, alas, this second one had been hit with just a little too much oomph. In fact, it was going like a train and, had it been on line for the hole, it might have hit the pin and rebounded back a considerable distance. But it was not headed for the pin. In fact, there was nowhere that ball was going but out over the back of the green and into the lake. Oh dear.

There comes a time in every man's life when he is obliged to make a decision. In fact, that time has come to me rather too frequently for my liking but on that fateful day, had I been thinking about it, I would have realised that another such time had arrived. The choices available to Kevin and me were simple. Were we simply to stand there, uninterfering, and watch the inevitable happen, allowing this second golfer's ball to drop into the lake with a plop? Should we then compound its owner's frustration by passing on to him the sad news that: "Your ball is in the lake," as soon as he hove into view? Or ought we to act, and change the course of history?

Hmmm. Tricky one, that.

Tricky, for me, that is, but not, apparently for Kevin.

For the record, Kevin opted to watch history unfold, while I decided, to my eternal shame, to change its course.

Spontaneously, and without properly considering what I was about, I sprang forward and arrested the flight of the golf ball that was hurrying to its doom in the lake. To put no finer point on it, I caught it in my hand! As soon as I felt it in my palm I experience that uneasy feeling you get when you know you have done something you might regret later. I could see from his expression that Kevin was mortified by what I had done, and it didn't take long for the enormity of my misdeed to hit me. I began to feel uncomfortable even standing on the hallowed turf of the eighteenth green when I had no business to be there. My place was the tenth tee, and there was probably a rule of golf that said trespassing onto the green of a hole you were not actually in the course of playing entailed the incurring of something in the region of a thirty-four stroke penalty and the insertion of a sand-wedge into the anus.

Oh Christ! I had actually interfered with someone else's ball! And not unintentionally, after finding it in the rough and then playing it by accident, in the mistaken belief that it was my own. That would have been embarrassing enough, but no! I had deliberately intercepted someone else's golf ball while it was still in motion! Was there a more heinous crime on the statute book of golf? Probably not. My mind was by now racing, and I conjectured that for an offence as severe as the one I had just stupidly committed, the rules of golf probably called for the extreme punishment to be carried out, not with a sand wedge, but with a red hot poker.

Overcome by panic, and horror and alarm, and dread and more panic, I did what I always do in such panicky circumstances: I panicked. Trying to think quickly, I wracked my inadequate brain in search of a plausible way out of this mess of my own creation, but found no obvious solution. In less than twenty seconds, two enthusiastic and perspiring sportsmen would heave into view, eager to discover the fortune of their respective approach shots, over which they would both still be entertaining hopeful aspirations. However, while one golfer would be delighted to find that he had a putt for a birdie, the other would undoubtedly be furious to learn not only that his ball was theoretically in the lake but also that some nerd had molested it before it got there, thereby obviating the possibility that it might have pulled up of its own volition before it reached the water. Oh dear! In that light even my act of charity, designed to save the owner the cost of a golf ball, could be seen only as treachery of the highest order. Despite having acted with the best of intentions, I could now see that I had cost the owner of the ball at least two strokes, plus a drop from an uninviting position and a difficult pitch back onto the green, from which he might even incur further penalties. Was that worth the out of pocket expense of a couple of quid or so, the cost of a golf ball, that I had saved him? The point was at best moot.

Now that my best course of action was probably to clutch at a straw, I decided to clutch at a straw. Stop worrying, I told myself. The likeliest outcome, I tried to convince myself, was that the two golfers would stride onto the green and recognise my act of charity for what it was. The first golfer would see that he had a putt for a birdie and immediately commiserate with his friend. With the latter's ball invisible, he would assume that it was in the lake and that his friend now had a difficult drop followed by a chip from an awkward position. He would be aware, too, that his partner was out of pocket to the tune of at least two penalty strokes plus the cost of the golf ball. His friend would be feeling particularly downcast when he realised that all this was painfully true. But a glimmer of happiness would be waiting to tinge his sadness. He would discover this only when, greeted by me with a friendly call of: "Your ball is in the lake," he would be delighted to discover, also from me, that his ball was not *physically* in the water, but was actually in my hand! He would therefore take his two shot penalty like a man and thank me eternally for the fact that his misery was not to be compounded by his also being out of pocket by a couple of quid. In fact, he would be everlastingly grateful to me for allowing him to re-use a ball that was technically lost for good.

Hmmm. Was that likely, I wondered? I would soon find out, because at that moment the two golfers bounded eagerly onto the eighteenth green. Although neither player had been able to see where their respective balls had finished up, it was clear from their demeanour that each had more than an inkling of how they had fared, for there was a definite spring in the stride of one of them, as the pair clambered onto the green to inspect the damage.

Golfer number one clearly knew he had played a good shot. He had probably been able to sense it as soon as he had made contact with his six-iron, and he was delighted to find confirmation that his ball rested no more than fourteen feet from the hole. By the time she drew level with me, however, his companion's stride was quite the opposite of springy, and she was looking apprehensive and down in the mouth; her eyes were no longer on the pin but on the water. Her shoulders drooped, and it was evident from her bearing that she was aware she had over-hit her eight-iron, and knew by now that her ball had probably met with a watery grave.

If you have been paying attention, perceptive Reader, you will have picked up from the pronouns in the preceding paragraph that the protagonists of the eighteenth green were of opposite biological persuasions. One was a man, and the other was… well, the other was not. I should think that they were both in their early forties and, from what followed, I would guess that they were probably married, possibly to each other. I should also imagine that they were both keen golfers, who had no need of rules officials to help them out on tricky occasions. Rather than carrying their clubs in a bag, in the manner favoured by Kevin and me, they were each towing golf carts behind them.

Dressed in a fawn sweater and brown slacks, the man was tall and energetic, and I would imagine that he enjoyed his golf. His faced creased in a warm smile when he saw where his ball had landed, and, noting that he had a putt for a birdie, he was quick to switch on a sympathetic frown and commiserate with his playing partner, whose ball was nowhere to be seen.

"Oh, dear, is your ball in the lake, darling? What a pity," he murmured. Then he quickly turned his back on her to size up his birdie putt.

His wife was also tall, and she looked equally fit and energetic. Clad in a tight-fitting grey v-necked sweater over a white polo-neck, and figure-hugging grey slacks, she looked more like an advertisement for golf clothing than a golfer. Her distressed expression suggested that she could have done without her partner's patronising commiserations, and she glared darkly at him from under a frown of anger as he turned away to enjoy the spot where his own golf ball had landed.

"Thanks, Pancho," she snarled, sarcastically.

Both golfers ignored me at first, and I wondered for a wild moment whether I might get away with stealing quietly away, but it was not to be. The woman seemed suddenly to become aware that I was there, and span round to face me. In that moment she looked into my eyes and I into hers, and we might have read each other's thoughts. She couldn't see her ball on the green, and assumed it must be in the lake, but if I had been passing at that moment I might possibly have seen its approach. Could I confirm her worst fears? She didn't pose the question, but I surmised that that was possibly what she might have been wondering.

It was time to test my theory. Mustering as much courage as I could, I called out: "I'm afraid your ball is in the water."

I then opened my hand and showed it to her, not daring actually to admit what I had done, but instead allowing her to work out for herself that I had prevented it from actually dropping in the drink. At the sound of my voice the man she called Pancho looked round at me too, and the lady smiled when she saw the ball in my hand. It seemed I might get away with it after all!

The lady was about ten feet away from me when I spoke to her. Without waiting for her reply, I tossed the ball underarm in her direction, in the hope that she might catch it. OK, Reader, I *know* what you're thinking. She was a woman, and there is no woman on Earth who could catch a golf ball if you threw it to her. You could throw her golf balls from ten feet away all day and she would not catch any of them. *Well, I'm glad* you *said that, Reader; and I'm certainly glad that I didn't say it, but I'm not going to argue with you.* Suffice it to say, therefore, that, knowing everything you have just said was true, and that you have probably never said a truer word in your life, I had decided to make the catch as easy as possible for her by sending it towards her slowly and underarm, so that it climbed high in the air and described a gentle inverted parabola before (hopefully) nestling in her fist at a convenient height on a level with her waist.

It was *not* a difficult catch. I had seen to that, for Chrissake. Indeed, it was the *easiest* of catches. It was the kind of catch that any Yorkshire cricketer would no doubt have averred that his granny could have caught in her pinny. But the lady on the eighteenth green made no effort to catch it. As soon as the ball's trajectory showed signs of approaching her pectoral area she pirouetted on her axis, pulling her natural hazards out of its path, so that the ball floated past her and fell to earth, where it rolled forward. In fact, it rolled towards the hole. I hadn't realised it when I threw her the catch but when I released the ball she had been standing more or less directly between me and the pin, so her evasive action simply allowed the ball to head on its way towards the flag. The ball stopped rolling about ten or twelve feet from the hole.

"Thanks," said the lady, and cast another beautiful smile in my direction, before turning on her heels and rejoining her ball. Looking lovingly at it, she then began sizing up *her* birdie putt.

I was aghast! Surely the lady was not proposing to play the ball from where it had landed after I threw it? Surely her partner would not let her get away with that? Surely there was a rule of golf that said......? Where was that bloody rules official when you needed him?

I quickly scampered after my chum, Kevin, who was hurriedly disappearing in the direction of the tenth tee, but not before the lady's male companion had had time to shoot me the dirtiest look I have ever seen. When I was satisfied that the couple were convinced I wasn't going to look back, I snuck a discreet peek at them over my left shoulder, all the time pedalling desperately towards the tenth tee. Pancho still had his putter in his clenched fist as, hands on hips, he remonstrated angrily with his partner. For her part the lady was studiously avoiding his gaze and, head down, bottom out, was busily engaged in lining up her putt. I hurried on towards the tenth with their conversation ringing in my ears. Oh dear. I had certainly spoiled their afternoon walk, and no mistake.

"*Don't* think you're going to be playing it from there, Judy!" came the male voice. "You'll have to go over *there* and drop it." And he pointed towards somewhere over in Cumbria.

She ignored his remark. Straightening up, she spoke.

"Come on, Pancho, it's your shot. Get on with it," was her irritable rejoinder, as she crouched once again over her own ball.

"Listen, Judith, if you think I am going to let you putt from there you have another think coming! Your ball is in the water!" And he moved menacingly towards her.

"No it isn't," she replied sweetly. "It's right here. See? Look."

"Oh, come off it!" Although the sound of his voice was fading as I beetled off at a brisk six miles an hour, I could tell that he was becoming rather cross. "You know your approach went in the lake. That guy told you so!"

"Did he? Well, he was wrong, wasn't he? This is my ball, right here. See?" I detected a note of triumph in her voice.

"Yes, but it would be in the lake if that *f*cking* clown hadn't stopped it!"

"Would it? Yes, I suppose it might. But we'll never know, will we? It might have gone in the lake, or it might have bounced off something and ended up here, where I found it."

"Bounced off something? *Bounced off something???* You saw what it 'bounced off'! It 'bounced off' that *f*cking* idiot who stopped it from going in the lake! You're in the water! You'll have to go back over there and take a drop! And you're **not** playing it from **there!**"

"I think it's your shot," she simpered amiably, completely ignoring his outburst.

Oh dear, thought the f*cking clown he was referring to, quickening my pace still more as their voices, one raised and the other sickeningly calm, faded gently into the distance. I don't like to take sides in disputes that don't concern me, but I have to admit that my sympathies were entirely with Mr Punch on this one, although I feared that those pesky laws of golf might actually be on Mrs Judy's side. What concerned me more, however, was that Pancho seemed to be on the point of slipping into character and hitting his partner over the head with his stick. When would the policeman arrive? I was so appalled as I scampered away that I half expected to see the crocodile crawl out of the lake in search of the sausages.

While all this was happening Kevin had been busily putting (putting, that is, with a long u, not putting, with short u) as much distance between himself and the eighteenth green as possible, and, firmly if silently, making the point that he had had no part to play in this nightmare. He appeared to want to erase the whole sorry episode from his memory banks as quickly as he could, and he seems to have succeeded. When I mentioned the incident to him recently he had only a vague recollection of it, even though I still flush with embarrassment whenever I think of it.

The consensus among the experts I consulted after the incident was that the lady was perfectly entitled to play her shot from where her golf ball had landed after I threw it to her. If anything, this discovery made me feel even worse. I didn't dare look in the *Wiltshire Foghorn* for days afterwards, for fear of reading that a woman's dead body had been found on a golf course. I knew that such an outcome would inevitably lead to my being called as a murder-trial witness at Swindon Crown Court, and being forced shamefacedly to admit that I had indeed interfered with Judith's ball while it was still in motion, after Pancho, trying to avoid the hangman's noose, had offered this evidence as a plea in mitigation. Would I escape the noose myself after such an admission? Pancho's goose would be well and truly cooked, because all the expert witnesses (policemen, forensic scientists, doctors, golf rules officials) would give damning evidence against him, but I am sure the judge would have much more sympathy for the accused than he would for me. Pancho had only murdered someone, after all, whereas I had actually interfered with another golfer's golf ball!

I don't know exactly what it was that made me give up the game of golf when I did, but I have not played for half a century. Perhaps the incident on the eighteenth in Wiltshire all those years ago had something to do with my decision to retire from the game, but nowadays it is much more likely to be beach volleyball that I turn to when in search of relaxation, although, strange to say, the rules of that particular sport do not interest me in the slightest.

CHAPTER 24 : A LOVE AFFAIR

My girlfriend works in groceries,
A job I think must please her;
She is the filler who's in charge
Of topping up the freezer.
Whenever frozen peas run short,
Fishfingers or fruit pies,
She dashes out, from round the back,
Replenishing supplies.
She always wears a happy smile,
I've never seen her stroppy,
But our affair's not going well:
The sea of love runs choppy.
In fact, I think it's worse than that,
Our union might be fated;
I have a feeling that my love
Goes unreciprocated.
For if I try to catch her eye,
To check that she adores me,
She hardly seems to notice me,
In fact, she just ignores me.
My only chance to catch a glimpse
Of that delightful creature,
Is when the frozen stuff runs low:
That's when I try to reach her.
I'd like to sweep her off her feet
And shower her with presents,
But she just won't acknowledge me,
Despite my constant presence.
I try to pop in every day,
And hope to catch her working,
But have to dodge the manager,
Who doesn't like me lurking.

He often tells me to clear off,
Sometimes, six times a day,
But I've devised a strategy
To keep him out the way.
I just keep buying frozen food,
Which makes her stock run low,
So *Sweetie* has to top it up,
Which brings her back on show,
And gives me yet another chance
To tell her that I need her,
Although this risks another clash
With her accursed leader.
But why the hell should he complain?
I'm buying his *patatas*!
And frozen edamame beans!
And frozen chipolatas!
So why's he got a down on me?
He must surely be knowing
That when I buy his frozen food
It keeps his business going?
But things cannot go on like this –
I have to plight my troth,
Though this might irk my enemy,
And risk the bounder's wrath.
I bravely snuck in there today,
Intending to confront her,
And lay in wait all afternoon,
Like any big game hunter,
But *Loveheart* was invisible,
I saw not hide nor hair,
And when the frozen fish ran low
Another girl was there
Usurping my beloved's role
To top up calamari!

I was so shocked I fleetingly
Considered harikari!
But rapidly recovering
My erstwhile cool composure,
Instead I ambushed *Icecream Maid,*
In her ice-cold enclosure.
Not wasting time with chat-up lines,
Like asking what her name was,
I arrowed swiftly to the point
And asked her what her game was!
What business was that fridge of hers?
She knew I had her measure,
When I asked what the hell she'd done
With my heart's only treasure!
At first the poppet looked perplexed…
She said this was *her* shift…
But all at once the penny dropped,
And then she caught my drift.
My angel, this new girl explained,
Restocking iced mallotus,
Had run off with an Eskimo,
And handed in her notice.
She'd gone away late yesterday,
But no one knew quite whereto;
Though all supposed that she, by now,
Was tucked up in his igloo.
I am distraught! What can I do?
I cannot be consoled!
Cuckolded by an Innuit!
It makes my blood run cold!
And, what is worse, I've forty tons
Of fast defrosting peas!
Where can I offload all that veg?
Make me an offer!!! *Please!!!*

CHAPTER 25 :
SELF-DECEPTION

I thought of you the other day;
Something I almost never do,
For ever since you went away
I simply started life anew,
And never, ever think of you.

Fond memories of you are gone,
And I've not thought of you for years,
For when you left life just moved on;
I soon erased the lingering fears,
And endless nights of bitter tears.

Perhaps I may have felt bereft,
But tried hard not to let it show,
When I came home, and found you'd left…
I may have missed you once, although
That was so very long ago.

You're never in my thoughts no more,
Not now I've learned to live again,
And of the love I felt before
There are no traces that remain,
Despite the ever aching pain.

I never wonder what you do,
Or where you go, or what you eat,
Or whether there is someone new,
To bring you comfort when you meet,
For you to love, for you to cheat.

Since you've been gone I've lived alone
And no one ever comes to call
But I prefer life on my own;
I'm never sad, that I recall…
I swear I don't miss you at all…

I see no one, from day to day;
I live the life of a recluse;
If someone comes, they're turned away,
I don't need love, or any excuse
For friendship. What would be the use?

How long is it since you departed,
And dealt me that upsetting blow?
Not that I care, I'm not downhearted,
And I don't count the days… although,
It's twelve-four-five, if you must know.

Twelve hundred days you've been forgotten;
How many years is that, that I
Have set aside our misbegotten
Love affair, and ceased to cry?
Or ceased to even wonder why?

I found some things you'd left behind –
Not things that you would worry about,
But odds and ends of every kind,
So if you want them back, just shout;
I'm not about to throw them out.

I keep your picture by my bed,
Perhaps a curious thing to do,
But never look at it… Instead,
I've put aside all thoughts of you
And count my blessings that we're through.

So, if you're wondering if you're missed,
And, if you are, to what extent –
No… Sadly, you just don't exist…
My time with you was all misspent…
In fact, I'm rather glad you went…

If that's a hurtful thing to say,
You've got to understand, Marie,
I bless the day you went away,
As now I'm free to think of me…
Your leaving merely set me free…

THE
WATERSHED

CHAPTER 26 :
THE WATERSHED

So…

Now we've arrived at the watershed,
All little tots should be tucked up in bed;
Now's when the oldies will come out to play,
Nattering, and frittering their lives away;
Chattering of corn plasters, backache, and dung,
Dreaming of moments when they were still young,
Living their lives with their foot on the throttle,
Long before happiness came in a bottle…

So…

Everyone who's under seventy-one:
Please close the book, as your race is now run.
Better to veil this abstruse vale of sorrow,
Saving your energies all for tomorrow,
Rather than sample, and then misconstrue,
All that will follow, which isn't for you.
Stick to the rules, please, if you're underage,
Don't take the risk… And do **NOT** turn the page…

CHAPTER 27 : A VISIT TO THE ZOO[29]

I took my grandson to the zoo
To see the polar bear,
The zebra, rhino, and big cats,
The kangaroo, and hognose bats,
The chimpanzee, and Timor rats,
Orangutan (and any gnats,
Or other gubbins there.)

But barely had we entered in,
And spied the bongo brindled,
When we began to realise,
That we were in for a surprise:
We just couldn't believe our eyes,
As all the labels were just lies!
I knew we'd just been swindled!

Whoever did that labelling
Behaved without propriety!
The info they put out was duff!
The keepers hadn't got enough
Wild animals, so had to bluff;
Apart from goats, they had no stuff,
So there was no variety.

The 'rhino' was a farmyard goat
Whose flanks were padded out
With puffa jacket, overblown;
With no bit of his horn his own,

---

29 No children or animals were discommoded during the excretion of this
doggerel. But those of a nervous disposition should exercise caution before
perusing.

A large, inverted megaphone,
That looked just like a traffic cone,
Was sellotaped to his snout!

The 'tiger' was another goat
Who really looked quite funny;
Someone had used a stencil set,
Unsupervised by any vet,
To paint stripes on his back, and yet
When we were there the paint was wet
So all his stripes were runny!

The 'lion' was a sorry sight –
A pile of old detritus!
Someone had found an old fur coat,
Applied a coat of creosote,
Then wound it round the creature's throat,
So he looked like an elderly goat
With chronic tonsillitis!

The 'orca', painted black and white,
Was making not a sound;
A putrefying mess that stank,
All four legs severed at the flank,
He lay in his aquarium tank –
He'd been thrown in, and promptly sank –
That goat had clearly drowned!

The next enclosure made us think
Someone was having a laugh:
Had no one thought it might be wrong
For some great thug, who's superstrong,
To stretch a goat's neck six feet long,
And keep it straight with a metal prong –
Then call it a 'giraffe'?

The 'Bactrian'? A humble goat,
Two cushions on his back!
Both were stuck on with chewing gum,
They mustn't be too cumbersome,
For on weekends, as a rule of thumb,
They take one off so he'll become
The 'dromedary' they lack!

The 'kangaroo' has springs attached
To his rear bovid hooves;
And from his waist there hangs a sack,
Which, loosely knotted round his back,
Contains his offspring, in a pack,
Who scrape along the gravel track,
And fall out when he moves.

The 'elephant'? Guess what! A goat!
Force-fed with tons of pasta!
He's streaked with blood, still dripping red,
Where holes atop his skull have bled
When horns were ripped from off his head,
And glued beneath his cheeks instead –
As tusks they're a disaster!

And when we saw the creature's 'trunk'
It gave us quite a fright;
A ten-foot rubber garden hose,
Complete with metal sprinkler rose
(Why that's left on, God only knows!)
Is stapled to the bovid's nose –
It's such a sorry sight.

The 'gorilla' (yet another goat)
Was stood up on two legs!
But what they'd done, I now suspect,
To fabricate this strange effect,

That makes the creature stand erect,
Is shoved a broomstick down his neck,
Affixed in place with pegs!

The canteen, where we went for lunch,
Struck quite a chilling note:
We had a choice of goat with fries,
Or Bagot goat and kidney pies,
'Goat fricassée', or 'goat surprise',
Or goat in vegetarian guise,
Or sweet and sour goat.

And through a window at the back,
As we were repositioning,
The sight we saw gave us a shock,
For there were several goats in stock,
With surgeons working round the clock;
This clearly was the assembly block
For goats who were transitioning.

Dismembered goats were stacked on shelves,
Some body parts still trembling;
We saw some legs, and heads, and feet,
And entrails, some with lungs complete,
And backsides, plus what they excrete,
And various other chunks of meat,
Awaiting reassembling.

We won't go near that place again –
The SAS should bomb it!
With just repackaged goats to see,
It disappointed him and me
And wasn't worth the entrance fee.
We simply couldn't face our tea,
But both went home to vomit.

CHAPTER 28 : A THONG FOR EUROPE

It all happened one glorious summer in the mid-1980s, while I was on holiday in France with Patience, my wife, and our two daughters. Sara was nine-ish, and Veronica was four-ish, if I have estimated correctly. What I remember is that it was another searingly hot day – they were all hot days that summer – and we were all on the beach. Patience was sunbathing. I was sprawled under an enormous parasol, trying to read my book and doze at the same time. The girls were building sandcastles, and splashing in and out of the Atlantic Ocean.

The beach was crowded. Under normal circumstances this might have been enough to challenge my habitual good humour, but we were into our second week and I suppose I'd grown used to it. By arriving early we had initially managed to lay claim to about three square yards of yellow sand for our exclusive use but, as the beach had filled up, new arrivals had simply parked themselves ever closer to everyone else, and the space between my family and our neighbours had been gobbled up by Gallic latecomers, who had thereby become for us a succession of new neighbours. Pretty soon we were no more than two or three feet from the sunbathers next door to us. I was married to the sunbather next to me on my right, but the sunbather next to me on my left was a complete stranger whom I could have reached out and touched if that simple act had not, on account of what she was wearing, been more than enough for her to have me arrested.

Goodness me, I had never seen so much lack of clothing. Er... I mean... Oh, you know what I mean.

At the point at which this episode begins we had just entered that blissful period after lunch when, full of Pastis 51, obscure French cheeses and an industrial measure of Beaujolais-Villages, I was, simultaneously, reading a book, drifting peacefully in and out of slumber, and ogling my fellow sun worshippers from behind sinister dark lenses. Officially I was also keeping a weather eye on the children but, initially at least, that did not seem to be too arduous an imposition.

Suddenly my peace was interrupted and I was shaken awake by my eldest, who told me that some little French kid had just pinched her sister's plastic bucket. A tearful and bucketless Veronica seemed to confirm this version of the story. The last thing I was looking to do at that moment was leave the cover of my parasol and venture into the furnace that was burning all around my private patch of shade, just to go in search of a careless child's plaything, but my suggestion that the girls manage without their bucket for a while and play with something else merely drew a stern rebuke from Patience and a hard stare from Sara. So, with no other option, and already feeling a smidgen grumpy at having been so rudely disturbed, I climbed angrily to my feet and went off in search of *le voleur*.

With Sara's help I soon tracked him down. The miscreant turned out to be a four-year-old, snot-nosed guttersnipe of the French persuasion, an urchin undoubtedly as malevolent as he was mischievous, wreaking of garlic and onions, and with a streak of vicious nastiness in him as wide as *La Manche*. He held the evidence in his hands, so he couldn't deny responsibility for the theft. I once had a smattering of French and could still remember a *soupçon* of it (well, let's put it this way: I'm never going to die of thirst in France) so I opened negotiations by quietly asking the little scoundrel to return the bucket to its rightful owner. He ignored my request completely, merely staring defiantly into my eyes, his indifference seeming to imply that possession was nine-tenths of the law in any language. I tried to reason with him for a bit to no avail, so I retrieved the bucket by force and gave it back to Veronica. My adversary did not put up much of a fight. Mind you, as well as giving away about fourteen stones in weight he was also conceding around four feet in height and more than thirty years in animal cunning, so his decision not to mess with *Monsieur le Biftek* was probably a wise one. *Mission accomplie!* Don't truck with me, *Monsieur le Frog!*

Sacré bleu! No sooner had I settled back down, and was once more snugly supine on my inadequate towelling, than the same thing happened again! Sara was back to say that Veronica was once again in tears, and that her plastic bucket was once again in the hands of *le criminel*. Grumpily, I climbed back to my feet, strode over to the little robber and, this time with a lot less ceremony, snatched the bucket out of his thieving little fingers and returned it to its owner. I said nothing at all to him this time, my judgement being that it would have done me no good had I opened my mouth. Besides, I had probably already used up all my polite French the first time. Congratulating myself on a second job well done, I settled down under my parasol once more.

Vains dieux! Within no more than five minutes the same thing had happened again! And again! Three or four times in all *le petit* perisher waited until I had cleared off and then calmly strode back up to Veronica and stole her bucket, and in the end this particular English gentleman was becoming just a tad tetchy. I finally decided that enough was enough, so on the last occasion I retrieved the bucket and then pulled the young terrorist in for questioning and had a stern word with him. The little *voyou* was no more than about two foot-six to my six-foot-four, and he listened in sullen and insolent silence while I told him in no uncertain terms that I considered him to be the worst recidivist known to the French penal system since *Barbe Bleue*. I issued no formal caution before questioning him, but I left him in no doubt that if he didn't mend his ways pretty damn soon I would probably be fitting him up for various other crimes, including the Brighton trunk murders. For now, I told him I would be going forthwith in search of *un gendarme* who would happily go round to his house that very evening and fill his *bouche* up with *béton.* In the interests of balanced justice I then rounded on Veronica and told her that unless she took better care of her sodding bucket in future I would be confiscating it for the rest of the holiday. I then bawled out Sara and told her that if she didn't do a better job of protecting her younger sister's interests she would be spending the night locked in a dark, damp cellar, with no supper, but with all manner of spiders and other creepy-crawlies for company!

That little lot appeared to do the trick! With all three children now in tears and seeming suitably chastened I felt justifiably satisfied with my parenting skills as I stonked proudly back to my postage-stamp-sized portion of a beach, lay down, and closed my eyes contentedly. I was so pleased with myself that I may even have brazenly left my head sticking out of the shade a little bit, in order to top up my sunburn. All was well with the world once more, and I felt able at last to go back to enjoying my holiday.

Vérole de moine! I had been rewarded with no more than two minutes' peace before, once again, my share of the sun was blotted out as a dark shadow fell across my physiognomy, and a concerned voice sought my attention. Assuming that Sara was back to report another crime, and now exasperated beyond the limits of patience, I half leaped to my feet intending to take dramatic action, this time resolving that there would be no more Mr Nice Guy! Did they still use *Madame Guillotine* in France? I didn't care if they did!

Oh dear. *Pas une bonne idée.*

As soon as I looked up I found that this time my attention was being sought not by four-foot-eight inches of a ten-year-old Sara but by five-foot-six inches of a mature and rounded French woman, who was quite obviously the mother of *le gamin sodding*. By the time I had shaken myself awake she was already in mid-flow, and she was glaring at me as if she meant business. Although she was dressed for the beach, I assumed from her tone and her bearing that she was ready to go to war. Oh dear. My confidence of twenty seconds earlier suddenly drained away through the soles of my feet.

It is odd but, fearful as I was of her wrath, while the lady was speaking I found myself strangely distracted, and she had been rabbiting on for almost half a minute before I began to take in what she was saying. I had been expecting her to berate me for having spoken so sharply to her son, but, surprisingly, that seemed to be the furthest thing from her mind. She had indeed heard me chiding the youngster, but she had also witnessed the latest of his crimes and she was keen to apologise on his behalf, which she then proceeded to do, abjectly, profusely, profoundly, sincerely and from the bottom of her heart. Well, would you blinking believe it!

As soon as I had picked up that the lady's overtures were friendly I quickly recovered some of my composure, and I was, of course, most generous in my acceptance of her apology. I told her not to worry about it, that these things happened, that boys will be boys etc, and she was very grateful to me for adopting this mature attitude. I shrugged and assured her that we men of the world were accustomed to taking these minor setbacks in our stride, and she told me how humble it made her feel to have run up against someone of such a forgiving disposition. *L'entente cordiale* was never so well burnished as it was over the next few minutes. Our conversation went on and on, and on and on, and the verbal excesses tumbled from my lips as I strained every sinew to keep it going. I cannot remember much of what I said, but I genuinely believe that my old French master, *Monsieur Varicelle*, would have been rightly proud of me. Vocabulary I had not used for years was dragged out of obscure corners of my memory and pressed into use; obscure past participles were dusted off and forced into agreement with obstinate preceding direct objects as though there were no tomorrow; and imperfect subjunctives were summoned up and told to report for duty as though I had been born with a string of onions around my neck. And, as I have said, all this twaddle passed through my mind and out of my lips without ever once touching the sides, and I have no idea to this day what I was banging on about for so long, although I do recall that *la belle femme* kept her end up magnificently well.

But that is only part of the story. If truth be told, that is also the least interesting part.

Something you may recall, esteemed Reader, is that when the woman had first approached me I had been lying on the ground, but as she started to address me I had begun angrily to rise to my knees, which had put my eyes roughly on a level with a point approximately four and five-eighths inches above her navel. I was soon aware, of course, that chivalry and good manners called for me to clamber entirely to my feet, but the proximity of other sunbathers had obliged the lady to stand far closer to me than would have been considered polite in, say, the checkout queue at *Tesco's*, and I was fearful that the simple act of standing up might actually cause me to rub up against her, which, in the peculiar circumstances of the moment, I felt would never do. This was because, despite my initial confusion, I couldn't fail to notice that the Amazon was thoracically equipped with substantial weaponry, principally in the form of two huge, nude, gelatinous hemispheroids of hormonal provenance, each one of which threatened either to batter my temples to a pulp every time they jiggled or else to have one of my eyes out each time the lady inhaled. Our negotiations were therefore of necessity carried out in this most unusual and uncomfortable of poses, with the two of us no more than four or five inches apart – she on her feet, looking down on me over her nose, and me on my knees, doing my best to peer up into her face, in spite of the diabolical distractions on each side of my head, and forced all the while by her striking proximity to inhale the sweet fumes of her suntan lotion.

Although this was a French beach in the height of summer it would be wholly dishonest of me to suggest to you that the lady was completely unclothed. However, as I have already hinted, throughout the whole of our discourse I remained strangely and totally unfocused, and this was because what had first grasped my attention far more insistently than the sincerity of the lady's apology was the fact that she was wearing nothing but the tiniest, most minuscule and narrowest thong I had ever seen. In fact, in the act of rising to my knees I had felt compelled to examine it closely in order to correct my first impression, which was that the thing might not be a thong at all, but rather a length of dental floss, or even a tattoo of a piece of dental floss, applied direct to the lady's skin by some dusky needle merchant in the back streets of Marseilles. In the circumstances I didn't stop to wonder why anyone would have wanted a tattooed likeness of a length of dental floss snaking around their hips and down under their crotch, but with the benefit of hindsight I put that down to my initial shock.

The lady herself was about thirty-five, and she looked as if she had been lying in the sun all her life. She was olive-skinned and dark-haired, and her white teeth flashed as she spoke at fifty to the dozen. While making her point I think she must have used every irregular verb in the book, but it all washed painlessly over me. As we conversed I tried desperately to stare unwaveringly into her hazel eyes, and failed miserably. Indeed, I fear that I may have addressed much of what I said direct to the thong. The thong, under which she appeared to have trapped a colony of tiny spiders when putting it on, concealed nothing at all, apart from a strip of the lady's skin a fraction of a millimetre wide, and as she burbled on about how mischievous her son was, and how magnanimous I had been to put up with him, little did she realise that my mind was racing wildly over dangerous terrain. As I knelt there in my uncomfortable pose, apparently listening intently, I was wondering insanely whether she removed the thong for bathing, and whether there would be any point in doing so, and, if she did, whether there might be left behind a strip of white flesh about the width of a razor blade amid all that sun-bronzed magnificence.

So there we stood, or knelt, as was our wont, for upwards of several minutes – well, if truth be told, for as long as I could drag it out – ostensibly discussing sociological profundity as manifested by contemporary juvenile delinquency in the France of the 1980s: she, a picture of sun-tanned athleticism, healthy and gleaming all over from the combined effects of an expensive sun-oil and the mid-day Vendée sun; and me, white-limbed, pot-bellied, tongue-tied, gasping for air, and with my eyeballs standing out on stalks.

Suddenly I became aware that Patience, now wide awake and propped up on an elbow, was eyeing us ominously.

Well, that's about it, really. Sorry.

CHAPTER 29 : COVID JAB

Health warning: contains lamppostist[30] 'humour'.

I had my Covid jab last week;
I didn't make a fuss;
I had it done in Ippardly:
I went there on the bus.

I'm rather picky about my jab,
Because I have been told
That some jabs carry side effects
Much worse than any cold.

I've heard that someone in Crouch End
Developed kennel cough,
While someone else, in Gerrards Cross,
Had both his legs fall off.

A third chap, on the Isle of Mull,
Was something to be seen:
His pelvic floor turned inside out,
And all his toes turned green!

Another guy, when he'd been jabbed,
Discovered very soon he
Was writing silly verse (like this):
He'd gone completely loony!

And so I'm careful what I pump
Inside my precious body:
When sniffing coke, or shooting speed,
I won't touch anything shoddy.

---

30   See *Secondhand Worms*, p56.

I asked for *Astra Thingummybob*;
The pharmacist looked glum;
"They don't make that top sh*t no more,"
She told me, "which is dumb,

"Because I think it was the best,
"But, on account of Brexit,
"The Europeans vetoed it,
"Which just hastened our exit."

"All right, I'll have the *Oojah*, then,"
I offered: "That's OK."
She countered she was out of stock:
Sold out the previous day!

"Oh dear," I said, "what have you got?
"I don't want something risky,
"That's not tested on animals,
"Or might dilute my whisky."

She rummaged round, in all her drawers,
Then said: "Can you believe it?
"I've only got the other one,
"So it's: 'take it, or leave it'!"

"I'll have it if I must," I said,
"But just before I do,
"Do you know something I should know,
"Between just me and you?"

"This is the country singer's batch,"
Explained the good clinician;
"She helped to fund the shooting match,
"That brought it to fruition."

"That's good enough for me!" I said,
And offered her my thumb,
But, when my back was turned, she pumped
An armful in my bum.

I went home, after thanking her,
And paying my respects;
And, apart from gynecomastia,
I've had no ill effects.

CHAPTER 30 : A TRAP
FOR THE UNWARY

The Memsa'ib and I once decided to take a holiday at the coast, somewhere down in Devon, so we rented a cottage for a couple of weeks in the sun. They were happy times, but my family's cheerful enjoyment of that hedonistic idyll need not concern us overmuch, which is extremely fortunate for the episode that follows is the only incident of that blissful holiday that sticks in my memory.

My dear wife, Patience, has a good friend, rejoicing in the name of Gloria Leluia, who lived near us at the time. You need to be aware of that because Gloria had somehow contrived to be down in the Southwest at the same time as we were. Gloria had a sister and brother-in-law living somewhere out on the moors, and she was staying with those very same relatives. Whether or not Patience and Gloria had contrived for our holidays to run concurrently I was never informed, but I think it had always been their intention that we should get together at some stage during that fortnight. However it came about, the opportunity arose one particularly hot day when Gloria's sister invited Patience and me over for an al fresco luncheon. I had never met our hosts, Shirley and Steve, and I think Patience had met Shirley only once or twice, but that is of no matter. As soon as we arrived after our short drive up from the coast it was obvious that we were all going to get along like a house on fire.

The weather was delightfully warm, and the pre-prandial alcohol was soon flowing freely, so by the time we were ushered to the excessively large, wooden refectory table, which had been set up outside in the garden under a generous awning to protect us from the burning sun, I for one was feeling well and truly at one with the world. All told there were six of us at refection, if I've not miscounted, for in addition to Gloria, Patience and me, our hosts had invited a much younger lady of their acquaintance to join us. This lady was a teacher, a neighbour of our hosts, who had lived in Devon all her life. Five of the company thus assembled were of a similar vintage, all by now just the wrong side of sixty years young, while the sixth was this nubile and, if truth be told, rather attractive minx of around thirty, who delighted in the name of Sonia.

Have you noticed, perspicacious Reader, that when it comes to luncheon parties the world seems to divide itself into two categories of human being? First, there are those who are good at throwing and organising such dos; and then there are those dreary souls whose only function is to hang around at the far end of the hive with the other drones until everything has been readied, and then turn up and wait for their nosebags to be filled. I might as well come clean and confess to you now that I am unashamedly a member of the latter club, so as soon as my offer of 'help' had been rejected by our genial hosts I was hastily instructed by Patience, seconded by Gloria and thirded by Shirley, to keep out of the way, and I was quickly dispatched by Steve to a distant corner of the refectory table with a generous refill to my gin and tonic. Patience, on the other hand, was soon found some useful occupation or other, either washing tomatoes or slicing cucumbers, or it may have been the other way round, so that she could join in the conversation being enjoyed by our hostess and her sister, who were both engaged in a similar destruction of vegetables. Most of the actual cooking seemed to be done by the man of the house, our genial host, and he was to be spotted busily scuttling between kitchen and garden in his shorts, with lashings of dead meat in tow, although he was still finding time to quaff affectionately at the necks of countless bottles of European beer. He was also, bless him, finding time to ensure that my glass of gin was never less than half full.

Unwanted, unneeded and unloved, I simply sidled off and did as I was told. All around me there was hustle and bustle, but I was content merely to sit quietly waiting to be fed, while occasionally amusing myself by using my table napkin to try and swat one of the numerous fat flies that chose unwisely to land from time to time beside me on the refectory table, within splatting distance of my weapon. It was a harmless enough pastime, requiring no real effort or expertise, but it became strangely addictive after a while and had soon become the focus of all my attention. Indeed, with everyone else engaged in one way or another in the stocking of the communal trough, my far end of the table might have been destined to become rather a lonely location had not the lovely Sonia suddenly spotted my splendid isolation and, joyfully abandoning the catering chore she had been allotted, sidled seductively over in my direction and sat down beside me to keep me company.

That table was long and inviting, and would, I reckon, have comfortably seated thirteen or fourteen patrons, one and a half at each end and five and a half along each of its long sides. When I was summarily banished to it I was able to identify without difficulty which end belonged to the head of the household, the end where mine host was clearly planning to sit himself, so, knowing my place, I dutifully took myself off to the opposite end and plonked myself down there. When Sonia joined me she sat down on the long side of the table, on my immediate right. Out of politeness, when Sonia arrived at my elbow I abandoned my attack on the insect population of Devon in order to give her my full attention. For a short while we were the only two at table and, from what I can recall of it, she and I enjoyed a pleasant enough chat until the others were ready to join us at the trough.

I cannot remember what Sonia and I discussed. Patience assures me that I am pretty boring at the best of times so I would assume that Sonia did most of the talking, while I probably just made gormless and monosyllabic interjections. I have to confess that this is the type of discussion I most enjoy, since it involves no intellectual contribution from me, nor any real obligation to keep abreast of what is being discussed. As far as I have been able to ascertain, in such exchanges, as long as you have a voluble and indefatigable nattering companion, and can come up with an endless supply of 'ohs' and 'uh-huhs', you can keep this kind of thing going for hours on end without ever once having to engage any of the old grey matter.

Please don't misunderstand me. I am not for one moment suggesting that talking to young Sonia was in any way uninvigorating. It was just that she was one of those people in conversation with whom it is virtually impossible to get a word in edgeways, and provided I gave the impression of listening dutifully she seemed perfectly content to do the lion's share of the gum-bashing. But the sun, and the alcohol, and my general feeling of wellbeing were all conspiring to ensure that everything she said was going in one ear and straight out the other, if it ever managed to find its way in in the first place, and there is no doubt that if she had been moved later to ask questions about her discourse I would have scored a healthy no marks out of ten, perhaps fewer.

Eventually, after what seemed like a pleasant age, the food was deemed sufficiently dead for human consumption and the other four diners assembled at the manger. Our host duly took his rightful place at the head of the table, at the end farthest away from the one at which I was sitting, from where he could both direct operations and carve the enormous joints of posthumous animal he had lovingly prepared earlier. His wife settled her pretty bottom on the seat beside him to his left, with her sister on her left, while Patience sat down on our host's right, directly opposite our hostess. There was thus a rather heavy presence at the opposite end of the table from where I was ensconced, and that presence was shortly to become 16%[31] heavier, for the beautiful Sonia, who had been content to sit beside me and chew the fat while we were the only

---

31 Approx.

two at table, now abandoned me and shuffled her lower cheeks up alongside Gloria, so that she was able to join in whatever girlie yak had arrived from the kitchen.

As I have said it was a very big table, and I suppose I should by rights have abandoned my chair at the opposite end from the action and moved to sit in the one next to Patience, so that if I had wished to interject the odd erudite comment of my own it would have been less of an effort. I must confess, however, that the thought never entered my head, and I seem to have unconsciously decided that my position at the furthermost end from the 'colloquy' best befitted my mood. I will also confess to you, astute Reader, and how you manage to keep getting these things out of me is a complete mystery to me, that there are times when I quite like eating at big tables like this one, where I can spread myself out and ignore the company altogether, so as to give my full attention to the serious business in hand. I was therefore quite content to stay where I was and splash about at the shallow end, letting the others do the talking, so that I could concentrate on Steve's excellent cuisine, washed down with his excellent claret.

A pleasant forty-five minutes simply evaporated amid joyful company, with the delightful food and drink in front of me soon finding its way inside me, and with spirited but untaxing conversation taking place just out of earshot. It was simply wonderful! I wasn't altogether excluded from what was going on elsewhere, but demands on me were mercifully small. Patience would occasionally ask me if I was 'all right', as she frequently does, and either our host or his wife would occasionally call down to me to see whether I 'needed anything passing', or whether my glass required replenishing. Even beautiful Sonia, bless her, would occasionally point her head vaguely in my direction before saying something, God knows what, because I wasn't listening, just so as not to leave me out. As I said, it was a very pleasant interlude, and

I spent it simply enjoying the fare on offer, and assuring everyone that I was OK, thank you.

All that was suddenly to change without warning. I unexpectedly became aware that Sonia, who, throughout the meal, had been seated well away to my right, at about three o'clock on the dial, had detached herself from the conversation that was still bubbling along to her own right and slid noiselessly along her side of the table in my direction. There was an empty chair beside me (the one she herself had vacated earlier) and she now unobtrusively settled her delightful *derrière* into it before leaning conspiratorially towards me. She seemed to be about to speak, but then checked herself and took a furtive glance to her right before opening her mouth, as if she feared she might be overheard.

She needn't have worried. Our four luncheon companions were deep in conversation and appeared not to have noticed that Sonia was no longer among them. Satisfied that she had me all to herself, Sonia leaned her delicate body forward once more, turned her pretty head sideways to face me, raised her sizzling eyes lecherously to meet mine, and dropped her voice to the barest whisper.

There was a heavy pause, but when she eventually spoke the air between us crackled with electricity. Slowly and deliberately she asked: "Would you like to have sex with me?"

I looked up in alarm, quickly sobered up, and nearly fell off my chair in astonishment. It was now my turn to glance furtively toward the distant company opposite. But all was well. Everyone was still eating and talking, laughing and joking, and no one appeared to have overheard Sonia's question.

Suddenly I was wide awake and my addled brain was trying to think straight. I opened my mouth to reply but my throat was dry and no words came. Sonia was now staring expectantly into my face. There was a mischievous smile about her lips, which didn't move, but her sparkling eyes said it all: I had not misheard. She really had posed that question, and she was now eagerly awaiting my response.

I no longer trusted myself to speak, so the question remained hanging for some little time. It was agony.

Finally, after what seemed like an age, the penny dropped for Sonia: I had been struck dumb by her offer. Finding me temporarily deprived of the power of speech, she realised she was going to have to repeat her question.

"I said would you like to have secs – you know, *seconds* – with me?" she repeated innocently, now dropping her gaze and carefully avoiding my eyes as she lifted a dish of potatoes. Did I not detect the hint of an even more mischievous smile about her lips as she prepared to serve me a generous helping?

"Er..... Yes..... Er….. Thanks," I stammered, as she repeated the process with the chicken and salad vegetables. When she had finished she laid down the dish and the spoon, lowered her head and looked directly up into my eyes, as if daring me to say something else.

"Er….. Thanks," I repeated sheepishly. "Er……"

Oh well. I would like to have made a clever rejoinder but couldn't think of one, so I held my tongue.

I have since concluded, astute Reader, that this cautionary tale bears ample witness to the truth of an old axiom, namely that there are times when it is preferable to be as paralytic as a penguin rather than *compos mentis*. I mean, imagine the trouble I would have been in if I had actually had the capacity to think, and therefore to answer truthfully, within a reasonable timeframe, when that question was first put.

It doesn't bear thinking about.

CHAPTER 31 : BENDER

I have just been on a bender with my girlfriend, who's
     transgender,
Which was quite the daftest thing I ever did,
For I bet her I was able to imbibe her under the table,
And then quickly found that I'd lost twenty quid.

Thinking I was on a winner, I soon felt like a beginner,
And can see now what a bloody fool I am,
For assuming little girlies, with their bobby socks, and curlies,
Would be rat-a*sed after one small *Babycham*.

Might as well just give up betting, if I'm going to start forgetting,
That my sweetheart used to drink with all the blokes,
And that when she was a navvy she'd sink fourteen pints of
     heavy,
Washing it down with six or seven rum and cokes.

Though I quite deserve your scorning, I just hope you'll heed my
     warning:
If you gamble like a prat, you'll surely lose;
Be they sister, be they brother, be they switched from one to
     t'other,
Alcoholics never lose their taste for booze.

CHAPTER 32 : SPOONS

It had been a good trip, so I am still not sure why I was feeling so grumpy that day. I love Rome, but as I joined the queue of passengers at Fiumicino Airport boarding the return flight to London that Friday evening I was feeling anything but cheerful. My boss, Leo Lionheart, had been excellent company, our Italian hosts had bent over backwards to accommodate and entertain us, and the wine had flowed freely throughout our visit. Perhaps that was at least part of the trouble: I had certainly been nursing a bit of a hangover all day.

I also thought I might be starting a cold. My head had been aching a bit when I woke up and now it was really beginning to thump. I had taken a few gin and tonics in the departures lounge as a medicinal precaution, but they had done little to lift the air of gloom that surrounded me. West Bromwich Albion weren't exactly trying to raise my spirits either. They had managed to lose an important mid-week league game while I had been away, and I certainly wasn't looking forward to Saturday's fixture. As if all that weren't bad enough, it certainly hadn't helped my mood that morning, when the maid at my hotel had managed to slam shut the door of my bathroom without noticing that three or four of my fingers were propping it open. On reflection, perhaps I had more than enough to be feeling grumpy about.

Another thing to upset me was the seat I had been allocated by the airline for the flight home. It was 5B. That bloody B was the bit that bugged me. Not only did the B indicate that I had neither the window seat (5A) nor the aisle seat (5C), and was instead to be squashed in the middle of the row, between two other passengers, but it also indicated that the flight was likely to be fairly full, because I suspected it was the carrier's usual practice to leave the middle seats of each row up front unoccupied if possible, thereby affording their premium customers a bit more elbow room. I shouldn't really have been complaining, because there was plenty of room in business class, even when the cabin was fairly full, but a full flight also meant slower service, and, coupled with that, the middle seat in a row always left a corpulent person like me feeling slightly uncomfortable, and therefore slightly aggrieved.

Leo, who had been allocated seat 5C, might have read my thoughts. "Do you want the aisle seat?" he offered generously, as we stowed our hand baggage in the overhead lockers. "With your long legs you'll be able to stretch out a bit more in the aisle."

"Are you sure you don't mind?" I asked him. Giving up an aisle seat in exchange for one in the middle was an act of munificence I had never previously experienced in all my years of airline travel, and I wasn't sure that Leo, who was a less frequent flyer than I was, understood the true implications of his offer.

"No, that's quite all right," he responded cheerfully, plonking himself down in the middle seat. "You sit down there on the end. I'm fed up with looking at your ugly mug anyway, and I'll probably get a nice little dolly bird sitting in the window seat, who I can chat up all the way to Heathrow!"

The window seat was as yet unoccupied.

"You'll be lucky," I told him confidently, as I lowered myself into the aisle seat and gratefully stretched out my legs in front of me. "You'll probably get some oily, fat Italian businessman sitting next to you, wreaking of BO, and breathing garlic fumes over you all the way to London."

"No, no, no," countered Leo with a smile. "I'm sure it'll be a little dolly bird!"

"I bet you a fiver it's the smelly businessman," I said, and then bit my tongue. Although confident that my money was safe, I didn't want to talk Leo into having second thoughts about switching seats.

"Done," he chuckled happily. "But you're chucking your money away."

I was fairly sure that I was on a winner this time, but I didn't really care if I lost. Leo and I would occasionally spice up our discussions with a wager of the odd £5 here and there, but there was an unwritten agreement between us that the loser wouldn't have to pay up. If we had been keeping a tally, one of us probably already owed the other £15 or so, simply from bets placed over the past four days while we had been away, but no one was counting. In the circumstances you may wonder why we bothered to limit our wagers to a fiver. We might as well have been betting in millions.

"How are you feeling now? Any better?"

"Pretty rough," I told him, as I lay back and closed my eyes. "Wake me up when we get to Heathrow. On second thoughts, wake me up when they bring the booze round."

Leo smiled again. "Don't get too comfortable yet," he counselled. "You'll have to get out to let my dolly bird in when she gets here. She won't want to step over you."

Unlike me, Leo was an extremely nice guy. Also unlike me, he wasn't a forensic document examiner by trade, and he hadn't worked for the company for donkey's years, but had arrived recently following an external recruitment campaign. I was still a bit miffed that I hadn't been offered his job myself, but as I hadn't applied when they advertised it I suppose my disgruntlement on this score was a bit illogical. That was another of the differences between Leo and me; he was logical and I wasn't. He was prepared to apply for a job he wanted, but I couldn't be a*sed. Because I knew I was the right person for the job, I expected the job to fall into my lap, but I realise now that that simply doesn't happen in real life. Jobs simply aren't offered to the people capable of doing them, and whereas Leo knew that, I didn't. Leo was absolutely right though. You don't want the company to be run by people who know what they're doing, do you? Far better to have it run by people without a clue, but who have a wide range of irrelevant experience gained elsewhere. Only then will the company avoid becoming stale. Only then will it flourish and move forward. Hey ho.

Leo too leaned back in his seat and closed his eyes, while I picked up the *Daily Telegraph* and turned to the crossword puzzle on the back page. During air journeys my preferred form of in-flight entertainment was to try to complete the *Telegraph* crossword before we landed. I was successful only occasionally, but I could usually complete most of it and that was good enough for me. I am very much a percentage man. I think I read somewhere that sumo wrestlers are considered to be a success if they can win more than half their contests during a season. If that is true, I am in wholehearted agreement with that philosophy. I suppose I am a *rikishi manqué*, if truth be told.

The cabin was filling up fast and already the aisle beside me was as crowded as a tube train in rush hour. As they struggled past in search of seats towards the rear of the cabin, my fellow passengers were constantly jostling my shoulder, and this steady buffeting was doing nothing to improve my humour. I tried to shut it all out by concentrating on my puzzle, and had been poring over clue 5 across[32] for a few minutes when I suddenly became aware that my nostrils were being assailed by a subtle and far from unpleasant

---

32 How many legs has a dog got? Four letters. First one an F; third one a U. Hmmm? Eight? No, too many letters. Pity.

aroma. Raising my eyes from the page I noted that the sweet odour was emanating from the person of another passenger, a young lady of about thirty, who had made her way along the aisle and stopped at my right elbow. She was dragging behind her one of those suitcases on wheels which business class passengers always seem to think they can get away with calling 'hand luggage', but which cantankerous old blokes like me firmly believe should be checked into the aircraft's hold. At row 5 she consulted her boarding pass, and then turned away from me and bent gently at the waist to push the retractable handle of her overnight valise back into its casing. In so doing she bent slightly at the knees and succeeded, inadvertently and no more than momentarily, in thrusting a delicate and finely crafted buttock full square into the jaxonian physiognomy. The contact between fundament and face was faint and fleeting, but nevertheless it was sufficiently forceful to be noticeable to both of us.

"Oh, I'm so sorry!" exclaimed the lady, hurriedly straightening up and wheeling round to face me. "I didn't mean to be so clumsy, but it's so crowded in here."

I instinctively looked up into her eyes, and was confronted by what can only be described as a vision of loveliness. A woman with finely chiselled features, green eyes, black hair and unblemished skin, shot me the most apologetic of smiles. She was tall, slim, and immaculately dressed, and I could see that her awkwardness had stemmed in part from the fact that as well as trying to manage her suitcase she was carrying a handbag and an armful of newspapers and glossy magazines.

"That's quite all right," I assured her charitably. "No harm done."

Our conversation was over before it began, and the perfumed one turned away to address the problem of her case. I use the word 'problem' advisedly, because it was definitely a problem. The lady had opened the locker above my head, clipping my brow as she did so with the stiff hem of her jacket, which boaked out in front of her when she raised her arm, and found that there was not enough space to accommodate her over-sized valise. What to do now? She was obviously embarrassed by the fact that she was blocking the corridor, and impeding the progress of passengers who were still trying to board the aircraft, but she stood helplessly rooted to the spot, gazing whimsically up and down the aisle, while sending out the distinct and unmistakeable signals of a damsel in distress.

However, if the sweet scented one thought she might look to any of her fellow Friday night passengers for help, she clearly had another think coming. No one, apart from those who were trying to push past her, was taking any notice of her at all. *Good*, I thought to myself grumpily! Next time you decide to bring a cabin trunk on board an aircraft and try to pass it off as a handbag you might think twice! And, ignoring both her and her quandary, I settled down to consider clue 16 down.[33]

My concentration was abruptly disturbed by a commotion at my left elbow. Leo had suddenly become aware of the lady and her plight, and, quickly sizing up the situation, had jumped to his feet, eager to offer her his assistance. With hindsight I suppose that, to the lovely one, the chivalry he was so keen to display, even from his imprisonment in seat 5B, must have contrasted very favourably with the indifference to her predicament being shown by the unhelpful slob sprawled out in seat 5C.

"Are you in here?" burbled Leo, indicating the vacant window seat beside him. "Can I help you with your case?"

---

33 What's the French for *eau de cologne*? Three words:3,2,7? Third letter a U, sixth one a C.

"Yes, I'm in 5A," simpered the fragrance on a stick, consulting her boarding pass once again for confirmation, and switching on a look of total pulchritudinous vulnerability. "And my silly bag won't seem to fit in the overhead locker."

So great was his eagerness to assist that Leo would evidently have careened over me like a steamroller if I had not recognised undiluted testosterone when it was unleashed and leaped sharply to my feet and out of his way. To the lady's unalloyed delight, Leo opened one or two of the overhead lockers on the opposite side of the aisle and, finding one that still had some free space inside, attempted to swing her case up into it with a swift clean and jerk. But he was only 5½ feet high, the case was heavier than he had imagined, and the logistics defeated him. The effort left him panting and spit-speckled and, with his usually immaculate coiffure now tousled, he sagged at the haunches as he put the case down again. Fortunately he had the innate breeding to resist the temptation to fondle his groin with his hand, but I believe he suspected inguinal rupture.

"Do you want me to do it?" I offered moodily, now that I seemed to have no choice. I was quite used to geriatric ladies in supermarkets using my 6 feet plus to lift packets of *Daz* or *Horlicks* down from the top shelf for them.

"No, no, I'll do it," grunted Leo with determination. And this time, with the aid of a knee to get it started, he succeeded in hoisting the heavy article up into the overhead locker, almost decapitating me, the beautiful lady and three other passengers as he did so. Having succeeded in his objective, he stood briefly motionless, flushed and dishevelled, his chest heaving, but looking rather pleased with himself.

"Thank you, _so_ much," purred the vision of loveliness. "I can't tell you how grateful I am."

"That's quite all right," beamed her benefactor big-heartedly, grinning from ear to ear. And he then shepherded her lovingly towards her seat by the window, like a surprised cinema usherette who has been unexpectedly called upon to minister to royalty.

"Excuse me," said the lady to me as she gently brushed past, and once again I caught a whiff of her fragrance. I don't really like the smell of perfume, but this one had a certain exciting *frisson* about it. It seemed both understated and expensive and, all right I will admit it, it was a far cry from the pungent fumes of kakidrosis I had so boldly predicted would by now be billowing from the window seat.

Once the lady was comfortably seated, little Leo quickly followed, and I was at last able to sit down again myself. "I am so pleased to have been able to help," he told her, unctuously and unnecessarily.

The lady paused in the act of stashing her magazines in the seat pocket in front of her, and shot him a wonderful smile, of the type I imagine Helen of Troy might have conjured up in order to instil a sense of urgency into any ship's captain who might have been dawdling in Troy harbour, but she said nothing. Leo turned surreptitiously towards me and gave me a sly wink. Then, in case I had not quite got his message, he rammed an elbow painfully into my ribcage, and his breath was hot in my ear as he whispered: "You owe me a fiver!" Whereupon he settled back in his seat, chuckling contentedly, and looking for all the world like a satisfied garden gnome. I ignored him and turned tetchily back to my crossword puzzle. Recognising that I was not going to react to his taunting, Leo turned back to address the exquisite creature on his left.

"How long were you in Rome?" he asked her cheerily.

The lovely lady glanced up from her magazine. She seemed surprised to discover that their conversation was not yet over, but she responded politely to his inquiry nevertheless. I noticed that she had removed her jacket and hung it on the hook in front of her, revealing that she had on a starched, white blouse underneath. I couldn't help noticing, too, that about two of the top buttons of her blouse were undone, and I couldn't help noticing that Leo couldn't help noticing it either, because his question seemed to have been directed more towards the lady's *décolleté* than to her ear. I could now see her legs too, and fancied I also noticed a hint of a multi-coloured decoration just above her right ankle. It looked like a climbing plant, clambering upwards God knows where, but I could not determine whether it was a tattoo or a pattern on her stocking. Feeling I had already noticed more than enough I quickly buried my nose back in my crossword.

"Only overnight," she said. "I was there for an antiques fair," and her eyes dropped back to her magazine. But if she thought my chum had run out of questions, she was wrong.

"That's interesting. Are you in the antiques business then?"

Gosh, I thought to myself without looking up, Leo must be psychic.

"Yes. I have a shop near the King's Road."

"What do you sell?" he enquired, presumably seriously. I wondered whether she would be able to resist the temptation to say: "Antiques." I don't think I would have, but she was obviously far better brought up than I was.

"All sorts of things," she replied. "But my main interest is in jewellery."

"Oh, what kind of jewellery?" Leo persisted. He had won his fiver, there was no question about that, but by continuing to 'chat up his dolly bird' he seemed to be trying to ensure that I could not use semantics to avoid paying up. Perhaps he thought the rules of our little game required him to keep it going all the way to London in order for him to claim his winnings.

The intricacies of antique jewellery occupied them for some minutes, and the fact that Leo seemed to know nothing at all about the subject didn't deter him from pestering her with all sorts of inane queries. It therefore came as something of a relief when one of the lovely one's replies was drowned out by an announcement from the aircraft's address system.

"This is your captain speaking. My name's Hilary Benson and I have the pleasure of welcoming you aboard this British Airways flight number BA 559 to London Heathrow. With me on the flight deck today is my first officer..." Etc.

It was a male voice speaking, and Leo looked at me and smiled when he heard the Christian name. I didn't respond, but the lady picked up on his reaction and her eyes grew wide.

"Hilary!" she whispered. "What kind of a name is that to give your son?"

Obviously more politically correct than she was, Leo turned pinkish and smiled, but he said nothing. Later, however, after we had successfully taken off he seemed to have decided to pursue her theme. I have no idea why he chose to do this, since he was clearly uncomfortable with the subject. Perhaps he wanted to keep the conversation going and could think of no other way of doing so.

"What's wrong with Hilary?" he asked. "Tony Benn called his son Hilary."

She turned up her nose in mock disgust. "Oh, I don't think I could trust a man called Hilary," she grimaced, shaking her head slowly.

"I hope he knows what he's doing up there." And she nodded towards the flight deck.

It was idle banter, and Leo must have recognised it as such, but it was the kind of banter that made him uneasy. Didn't our employer send us on courses to encourage us *not* to engage in this type of loose chatter? It was bound to offend someone, and although there was no one within earshot who was likely to be offended by it, Leo took seriously matters of this kind. He would clearly have preferred not to reply at all, but he must have felt that politeness called for a response of some kind, so he simply shook his head strangely and made a funny sort of whinnying noise that could have meant anything.

"By the way, I'm Kate," she cut in abruptly. "And you are.....?"

"*LEO*!" boomed Leo proudly, and manfully, in a tone that seemed also to proclaim that there were no Hilarys in *his* family! No male ones anyway. "Pleased to meet you."

The drinks trolley arrived and Kate accepted a gin and tonic while Leo contented himself with a tomato juice. In the aisle seat I was served last, as was the convention, and I too chose gin. I am afraid I can be very predictable at times. Kate had by now folded away her magazine and seemed happy enough to continue her conversation with Leo. He had well and truly won his fiver, and I thought I might even pay up this time. He certainly deserved it.

"What were you doing in Rome?" she asked, popping open her can of tonic water and drowning her gin with it, so that the ice cubes cracked and fizzed in her glass.

"We were organising a conference," he replied. Then he added importantly: "We're forgery experts, "and an Italian company had brought us in to help them set up a conference."

"Couldn't they do that themselves?"

"No, not really," he replied. "They're novices at this game, compared to us. We in the UK are the world's leaders."

Kate was asking Leo all the same questions that he had asked me only a month or so beforehand, when the Italian company had first invited us to their conference, but Leo now answered her in a matter-of-fact manner that suggested he had been a forgery expert all his life and had been born into a long line of forensic scientists. The truth was that he knew next to nothing about document examination, but had used his position of pre-eminence in the company's hierarchy in order to gatecrash this trip, and had even used his *lack* of familiarity with forgery techniques in order to justify it (he was new to the company, which meant he felt he needed to come along for the experience). Yet here he was, trying to pass himself off as an expert! If he hadn't insisted on accompanying me I would have taken along one of my *real* experts and he or she could have done the business in Rome while I checked on the wines. As it was, on this trip *I* had had to do all the work myself, while Leo watched.

But Kate was clearly impressed. "And what's *your* speciality?" she asked him.

"Well, nothing really," Leo replied modestly. "I'm just the man in charge of it all." He did not tell her that he had been 'in charge of it all' only for a couple of months, or that he had next to no qualifications that fitted him for the position, or that he knew roughly as much about document examination as a Parisian *cul de jatte* knows about funambulism. But, then again, had he done so, I suppose it might have ruined his chosen chat up line.

"You must be very important," she cooed admiringly.

He shot a quick glance in my direction, to make sure I wasn't listening, before averring modestly: "Well yes. But modesty forbids..."

Actually, he probably didn't really say that exactly, but he must have said something equally toe-curling because what he did say almost had me reaching for my in-flight sick bag. I really was trying not to listen. I hate eavesdropping at the best of times, but I couldn't help it and this hogwash was truly awful. I lay back and closed my eyes and tried to blot out the conversation that was being conducted on my left. It was difficult though, because every few minutes Leo looked round to see if I was awake, and gave me a sharp jab in the ribs with his elbow if he thought I was. On one occasion Kate seemed to notice him steal a glance in my direction and even remarked on it.

"Your friend doesn't look very happy," she opined, peering over my neighbour's tummy to look at me.

"Oh, he's OK," Leo diagnosed. "He's just grumpy because he's having a bit of a bad day. He's just starting a cold, his team's just lost an important football match, and he managed to shut his fingers in his hotel room door this morning..."

"Ouch!" she said sympathetically.

"..... *And*," (he paused for effect) "….. he's just lost a bet!"

My boss must have been quite proud of his little joke, because he favoured me with a very superior look, as a little grin played across his features. I continued to feign sleep, and didn't react. He therefore turned his back on me and continued to chat to the lady. I tried again not to listen, but it was difficult at times, and some of his remarks seemed to me to be slightly over familiar. Perhaps he was merely trying to establish that his bet was well and truly won, but I shuddered a little when I heard him ask: "What's that on your leg? I can't make out whether it's a pattern on your stocking, or a tattoo."

"It's a tattoo," she replied, adding that it was supposed to be the image of some kind of climbing plant. I am afraid I forget which. Ivy perhaps?

"It's very nice," he avowed approvingly, and then he wanted to know all sorts of details about how she had chosen the design, where she had had it done, and so forth. Crumbs Leo, I thought, do you think you ought to be asking all this? We are talking about this lady's leg, for Chrissake. But she did not seem to mind, and was happy enough to answer all his questions. The conversation in my left ear droned on and on and on, and I think I probably did manage to doze for a bit because I didn't hear much more until the next thing I recall, which was Leo giving my shoulder a little shake.

"Excuse me, Herbert, can you let the lady out?"

He nodded conspiratorially, and with what I assume he considered to be appropriate decorum, towards the front of the aircraft, where the toilet was, flashing me an unspoken signal, suggesting the lovely lady might need a wee – or perhaps something else. I am sorry, but Leo's unspoken signal was not sufficiently precise for me to be able to interpret it word for word.

I clambered to my feet and backed into the aisle. In so doing I noticed that a stewardess with a food trolley was making progress towards us, and judged that she would be alongside Row 5 in a minute or two. Kate would have to be quick if she wanted some nosh, otherwise the food would be past our row before she got back. The sweet-scented lady flashed me another of those beautiful smiles as she passed in front of me, and was then obliged to interrupt the trolley-dolly as she struggled around her *en route* for the loo. When she had gone Leo lost no time in exhibiting what I considered to be an unhealthy strain of triumphalism.

"Isn't she *gorgeous*?" he enthused. "So much for your oily, old, smelly, fat Italian businessman! You owe me a fiver! Come on! I take cash or all major credit cards!"

"She's pretty boring though, isn't she?" I said grudgingly. "You said a dolly bird. I wouldn't call her a dolly bird. She must be at least forty!"

"Ho, ho, ho," mocked Leo, rocking gently from side to side with hollow laughter. "Who's a bad sport, then? She's *gorgeous*! Come on, I want my fiver. You can pay up now!"

"All right," I said grouchily, like the old curmudgeon I am, but then I added crudely: "How about double or quits? I bet you a tenner that I can get her back to my place quicker than you can!"

Leo pinkened, and gave a little embarrassed laugh. I suppose he knew me well enough to expect an attempt at humour of some kind, even in my present delicate state of health, but I am not sure he was expecting it to take quite this offensive form, and I don't think he was particularly amused by it. I should make clear that it *was* no more than an attempt at humour, and that when I made my bet I had absolutely no intention of trying to win it. It was just one of those stupid things that stupid people say, perhaps for effect. Leo had been needling me and I had reacted. I knew he didn't like sexist or *lamppostist*[34] comments, so that is probably why I spitefully hit him with one. I regretted making the remark as soon as it was out, but it was too late to worry about that now. Sorry.

---

34 See *Secondhand Worms*, p56.

We relapsed into silence, and that was how Kate found us when she returned to her seat. She arrived just ahead of the stewardess with the meal, and I cannot remember any conversation between us while we were being served. Kate chose red wine with her food, while Leo opted for white. I quite like airline food as a rule, but I was still feeling pretty rough and therefore passed over the offer of fodder, but, in order to be sociable, I accepted a bottle of red wine.

Once the nosebags were firmly strapped in place, Leo lost no time in resuming his conversation with his gorgeous neighbour. I listened with half an ear and noted that he was now telling her about his wife and children, but I noticed that she didn't reveal any personal details about herself. I tried to blot it all out by concentrating on my crossword and I think I was pretty successful. The fact that my head was now aching and I felt I was beginning to run a temperature may actually have helped. In my present condition, even the noise of the aircraft's engines provided a welcome bonus, as it blotted out much of the verbal effluent being discharged on my left.

Some short while later it was Leo's turn to visit the little boys' room, and he leaped to his feet with a spring in his stride and a satisfied look on his face. I moved aside to let him pass into the aisle, and there was a twinkle in his eye as he gave me another violent jab in the ribs as he passed. He was really enjoying himself, and he skipped contentedly along towards the front of the aircraft. In fact, if I hadn't known that the popular song *Skip to my Lou* had been around for hundreds of years, I might have sworn that it had been especially written for Leo that evening, to commemorate his joyful progress towards the dunny in the sky.

When he had gone I resumed my seat and continued to stare at my crossword puzzle. I said nothing to Kate, and didn't even look at her, but I could sense that from time to time she was glancing in my direction. Then, as I looked up and stared straight ahead, deep in thought over a clue, she spoke.

"Hello," was all she said, and she said it very softly.

"Hello," I replied, looking across and nodding politely.

"I'm Kate."

"Hello, Kate," I said, and I returned to my newspaper.

There was a pause, then: "And who might you be?"

I looked at her again. I allowed a longish pause to develop, then I said: "My name's Hilary."

I don't know why I said that. It wasn't a particularly funny remark, but it had a strange effect on Kate. She was in the act of sipping from her glass as I spoke, and my unexpected response seemed to cause her to choke. I can only assume that some of her wine must have entered her nostrils from the back. Can it do that?

"Oh dear," I said. "Are you OK?"

She nodded wordlessly as, still coughing, she dabbed first her nose then her eyes with her serviette. Then she chortled noisily. I think that, like me, she must have been attacking the complimentary drinks in the departures lounge before boarding, because there was more than a gin a tonic and a small bottle of *Bordeaux* fuelling that explosion of titters.

"No you're not!" she spluttered when at last she found her voice. "You're Herbert Jaxon. You're an expert in forensic document examination, and you've just been to Rome to attend a forgery conference with your Italian counterparts."

"Crumbs," I said. "How can you tell all that just by looking at me?"

She laughed again, exposing a pinkish tongue and a mouthful of perfectly white teeth. After her long chat with Leo I was amazed at her good humour. I would have thought that by now she would have been bored knickerless and looking forward to seeing the back of the pair of us, but she seemed up for some more punishment and willing to laugh at anything I said. In fact, if I had been a comedian at the London Palladium I couldn't have asked for a more appreciative audience.

Seriously, I am convinced that people ought not to laugh at my 'jokes'. Usually they don't, but when they do it only encourages me to become sillier. Even though I was feeling unwell I found that as soon as I had Kate laughing I was looking for new ways to amuse her. She was a complete stranger; I didn't know her at all, and had no idea what her tastes in humour were, yet I felt I had to keep it going. Silly, isn't it?

"Are you a police officer?" I asked, prolonging the banter. "I've heard they can tell things just by looking at people."

"No," she chuckled. "I've been talking to your boss. He's told me all about you."

"My boss?" I responded, frowning, and feigning puzzlement. "How do you know my boss?"

She nodded towards the vacant seat between us, and then towards the throne room, adding: "I was talking to him while you were asleep."

"Oh, my *boss*!" I said, simulating dawning realisation. "That guy's not my boss. He likes to tell people that sometimes, but it's not true."

"Who is he then?" she asked, appearing a little puzzled.

I hesitated for a second, then, leaning across the vacant seat between us so as to bring my mouth close to her ear, and, dropping my voice to a conspiratorial whisper, I confided: "Well, er.... I don't know if I can tell you this really, but he's a resident at the secure unit where I work. I'm one of the keepers there, and I was sent over to Rome to collect him after he went walkabout, and Interpol picked him up for us."

Kate roared with laughter. "You're *awful*!" she said, but she continued to snicker. She was right. I *am* awful. But I had had a bit too much to drink and was beginning to warm to all this. Oh dear.

I remained straight-faced: "It's true!" I insisted. "He's harmless enough provided you don't provoke him, but there are certain things that set him off."

"Oh yes?" she said. "What sets him off?"

"Lots of things, really. Horses, tomato juice, footballs, *quattro stagioni* pizzas, corsets, tattoos...." I stared at her, but she didn't rise to my bait, and there was another short pause, so I added: "He hasn't asked you if you've got any tattoos, has he?"

She remained smiling, but said nothing. She didn't seem particularly keen for me to pursue this line so I feel I ought probably to have stopped it there, but I think the gin took over and I was now in full flow. So, I am ashamed to say, I added: "He's got a thing about tattoos, so if he asks you to take your clothes off, *don't* do it, OK?"

I knew I had gone too far, but fortunately she laughed politely again before saying: "That's no way to talk about your boss! And behind his back, too!"

"He isn't my boss," I protested.

"You're lying!" she protested back, as if there might have been some doubt about it!

"I'm not!" I retorted, with what I hoped was a hurt expression.

"Yes you are!" she shot back. "They don't call them 'keepers' in secure hospitals!" And she smirked in the self-satisfied knowledge that she had caught me out.

"They do in the one I work at," I replied reasonably.

"Which one's that?" she challenged.

"Whipsnade," I replied.

For some inexplicable reason my response caused her to dissolve into another fit of uncontrollable giggles, so much so that I was afraid she might wet herself, and I was glad she had already 'been'. I couldn't help laughing myself as this particular thought crossed my mind, and when my boss chose this moment to arrive back from his errand he found an air of unrestrained jollity in Row 5, which he immediately picked up on.

"Hello," he said, smiling. "What's the joke?"

"Oh nothing," I said, "I was just telling Kate about the lunatic asylum where we work!"

"Yes, it's a madhouse!" concurred Leo, and then wondered why this innocent remark provoked a fresh fit of hysterical laughter from his neighbour in the window seat. He waited for a bit before joining in heartily, which only seemed to add to the fun.

Mental illness is, of course, no laughing matter, but that didn't seem to occur either to Kate or to me at that moment, now that we both had a couple of drinks inside us. But that, of course, is no excuse. I wish now I hadn't said it.

Back in his seat Leo sought once again to pick up his conversation with Kate and he made a quarter-turn towards her, so that his back made clear to me that this was private. Even though it was now quite obvious that I was awake, he had no intention of allowing me to share in any three-way conversation with his latest conquest. I didn't care, and was happy to go back to my crossword. My five-minute chat with the lady had briefly illuminated a dull flight, but I was already regretting it and was glad that it was now at an end. However, as will be seen, I had reckoned without the lady in question.

"Where is your shop?" I heard Leo ask her.

"It's in Chelsea. Do you know...?" And she mentioned the name of a store that was presumably to be found in the same street.

"No," he said.

"Do you know ...?" And she mentioned a street, presumably nearby.

"No," he said again.

"Well, it's quite near there," she concluded. She obviously had no confidence in Leo's grasp of the relevant geography, and was unwilling to spend the rest of the journey trying to give him directions when he was clearly unfamiliar with the area. So instead she called across to me: "How's your crossword going, Herbert?"

I looked up. I hadn't expected to be included in their conversation but didn't wish to be impolite, so I said: "Not too bad, thanks, but

I'm stuck on 13 across. What's got six legs and a bra? Peter, Paul and … ? Four letters. Begins with an M."

Leo smiled benignly. "I forgot. You've met Herbert, haven't you?" he said.

"Oh yes, we had a nice little chat while you were away." I acknowledged that this was true with a faint nod, as Kate continued to address me: "So, Herbert, you're another forgery expert, like Leo, are you?"

"No," I replied. "We've left all the experts at home, working. Somebody's got to mind the shop. Leo and I don't do any work. We're just in charge. We were in Rome just to sample the wines."

"Don't believe him," said Leo. "Our expertise is famous throughout the world and we're always being asked to give advice on document examination in other countries."

"So you do a lot of travelling, do you?"

I think the question was directed at me, but Leo replied for both of us. "*I* don't, I'm fairly new to this game, but Herbert does. He's hardly ever at home!"

"Oh," said Kate. "And what does *Mrs* Jaxon think about that?"

"I haven't really thought about it," I replied. "I don't see my old mum very often so I haven't really asked her."

"You're not married then?"

"No."

"You *liar!!!!!*" broke in Leo excitedly. He had been hanging on every word of the conversation taking place across his chest, and now clearly felt I might be trying to steal some unfair advantage in the secret war being waged between us. He was not about to let me get away with anything as underhand as claiming that I might be 'available', so he petulantly turned to Kate and advised her: "He's been married for over twenty years, and his eldest daughter's just gone up to university this Autumn!"

"Oh, that's right," I said hurriedly. "I forgot about that. Sorry."

Leo laughed and Kate smiled, but she didn't respond. I don't know whether she had been amused more by my rather obvious untruth or by Leo's even more obvious determination to expose me. The discussion seemed in danger of flagging, but then Leo informed me: "Kate's in antiques. She has an antiques shop in Chelsea."

"That's nice," I said. "What do you sell in there? Not antiques?"

She ignored my sarcasm, which, in any event had not been directed at her. "Yes. Why? Are you interested in antiques?"

"No, not really," I replied honestly. "My wife is though. She bought some antique silver spoons just the other day."

"Oh yes?" said Kate. "What are they?"

I didn't think she was particularly interested; I assumed she was just being polite.

"I don't know – just spoons, I suppose. I can't read the hallmarks."

"What do you mean, you can't read them? I don't understand."

"Well I can see them clearly enough, but I can't find them in the book."

"That's strange," she agreed. "Where are you looking?"

"On the back of the handles," I replied. "At the opposite end from the end you use to stir your tea."

"No, I don't mean that, I meant which book? You should try having a look in *A Dictionary of Marks*."

"That's the one I'm using," I replied. "But I can't find them in there."

Leo puffed out his cheeks, and seemed about to blow the whistle on what he thought was another obvious untruth from me. How could I possibly be familiar with a specialist publication on the subject of antiques? But Kate's reply was too quick for him.

"What?" she exclaimed. "They're not in the *Dictionary*?"

"Well, if they are, I can't find them," I said defensively.

Leo was following this discourse in astonishment, his face swinging back and forth between Kate and me, like a tennis umpire at Wimbledon during a rally, and his eyes had opened wide in amazement as he witnessed what he assumed was a piece of bare-faced effrontery on my part. Surely I didn't expect to get away with professing some kind of knowledge in the matter of antique silver? Not in the presence of one who was an obvious expert on the subject?

"They *must* be in the *Dictionary*," went on Kate. "You're sure we're talking about the same book?"

"I assume so," I said nonchalantly. "You mean the one by MacDonald-Taylor?"

"Yes, of course," she averred, and Leo's eyes seemed to pop out of his head when it appeared that I even knew which book she was talking about. "They must be in there somewhere. Perhaps they're just too faded, or scratched, for you to be able to read them."

"No, they're not. They're very clear. I can make out every symbol, and every letter and number. I just can't find them in the book."

"That's very strange," she said frowning. Then another thought occurred to her: "I take it you're using a loupe?"

"Of course I'm using a loupe," I replied testily.

"What's a loupe?" cut in Leo innocently.

She looked at him incredulously. "Don't you know what a loupe is? But I thought you said you were a forgery expert....."

"Of course Leo knows what a loupe is," I broke in quickly. "He's a *forgery* expert, remember?" Then, rubbing it in, I told Leo: "A loupe's a kind of magnifying glass used by antique dealers, *and* by forgery experts, like you and me..."

She smiled. Leo smiled too, even though the joke was on him. You win some, you lose some, he seemed to be saying. I told you he was a lovely man. I didn't smile though. I realised I had gone too far and embarrassed my colleague unnecessarily, so I pressed on quickly: "Like I said, the marks are quite clear but I just can't find them in the book."

"Perhaps they're not antiques," said Kate with a grin.

"Perhaps they're not," I agreed. "Perhaps I've been done. It wouldn't be the first time. But my wife was definitely told they were antiques, and she paid antiques money for them."

"Do you want me to look at them for you?" said Kate suddenly, catching me completely off guard. She must have noticed my look of surprise, because she went on, slightly embarrassed: "Look, I don't usually make offers like this to complete strangers, but do you want to bring them in, so that I can have a look? Where do you live?"

"Buckinghamshire," I stammered.

This was suddenly all happening far too fast for me, and I could hardly think straight. I had no idea what Kate's game was, or what she was up to. I have noticed before that silly mickey-takers, like me, are frequently thrown out of their stride when roles are suddenly reversed. But I was still able to take a strange comfort from the fact that things were happening too fast for Leo, too. His eyes remained as big as dinner plates, and his mouth had dropped open in surprise at this new turn of events.

"That's not too far away," she said airily, "and you must come up to town occasionally, don't you?"

I nodded. "Yes," I stammered again, trying to keep the tremor from my voice.

She looked out of the aircraft window and seemed to hesitate for a moment, as though reflecting carefully before doing something she might regret later, but then, picking up her handbag from the floor and burrowing inside, she said: "Look. Believe me. I *don't* make a habit of giving my telephone number out to strange men, but..."

She had pulled a notebook and a pen out from her bag, and she wrote something on the top page. As she did so I noticed that Leo peered intently over his nose as he tried to make out what she had written. When she was finished she tore out the page and handed it to me across Leo's paunch. "That's my number. Just give me a call first to make sure I'm there, then you can bring them in."

As the page passed under his nose and across his chest Leo made a move to take it from her, presumably to hand it on to me, but she checked herself and pulled it back. She then folded the paper, not once but twice, ensuring there was no way that he could read what was written without unfolding it, before asking him: "Give that to Herbert, will you?"

Wordlessly he took the page from her hand and passed it to me.

"Thanks," I said, making sure that I accidently dug my elbow painfully into his ribcage as I took it from him. Then to Kate: "Where did you say the shop was?"

"In Chelsea," and she gave me a street and number, but I am afraid I can no longer remember what it was. "Do you want me to write it down?"

"No thanks, I'll find it. This really is very good of you," I told her, as the power of speech began slowly to return, and I placed the paper in the top pocket of my shirt without unfolding it. "Are you around tomorrow?" And I gave her a meaningful look that I hoped she would read some meaning into, but I must confess that it was more for Leo's benefit than hers. I must also confess that I clumsily caught him in the ribs again with my elbow as I said it.

But I got more from my question than I had anticipated. Kate stared back at me, unblinking, and I felt a certain tension building. There was something about those eyes that gripped me, and even offered me a glimpse of what had so captivated Leo. My throat was suddenly dry.

"No, I'm not there tomorrow," she said slowly, steadily returning my gaze. "What are *you* doing *next* Saturday, tomorrow week?"

"I don't know," I said.

The tension between us was now electric, and was slowly intensifying. She wouldn't drop her eyes. This had gone too far. I was already way out of my depth, and looking for a means of escape, but could initially find no satisfactory retreat.

Kate was still staring at me intently, waiting for a reply, so I eventually sought refuge in a weak joke, and asked: "You don't happen to know off hand who West Brom are playing that day, do you?"

She smiled, and dropped her eyes. Leo laughed. The tension was broken, and I suddenly felt a bit of a heel. It was bad enough that I had been making fun of Leo, but I was afraid Kate might now think I had been mocking her as well. But if she did, she didn't show it. Picking up her magazine and settling down to read, she said simply: "Just give me a call when you're ready, to let me know when you're coming in."

"I'll do that," I said, picking up my crossword. "Thanks very much."

Well, would you bloody believe it? That was a turn up for the books, and no mistake.

I think the remainder of the flight was fairly uneventful. I didn't speak to the lady again (although I believe she and Leo continued to exchange pleasantries) until we landed at Heathrow, when she offered me a word of thanks for lifting her luggage down from the overhead locker. I was the first of the three of us to leave the aircraft, and once I was off I waited at the pier for Leo to catch me up. However, he was slow to emerge from the plane and I realised that he had been waiting for Kate. Thus it was that the three of us walked to the immigration hall together. I was well in front of the other two, who were deep in friendly conversation behind me the whole way.

The queue at the British Desk at Terminal 1 was fairly long, and barely moving. As I recall, it was nearly always like that. The three of us tagged on the end of it.

When we reached the baggage carousel it was time for us to say our goodbyes, for Leo and I had hold luggage to collect whereas Kate had nothing but her hand luggage. I stood aside, a little way apart from them, and watched them shake hands as they bade each other farewell. Kate then called over to me:

"It was nice meeting you, Herbert. I won't say goodbye because I'm seeing you again, aren't I, when you bring the spoons in?"

"Yes," I said, nodding. "I'll see you when I come in." And then I shot a stern look at Leo: I didn't want him to miss the significance of the slightest nuance.

"Don't forget to ring me first though," she counselled. She made as if to turn and be on her way, and then stopped again. "Wait," she said, letting go of the handle of her case. "Give me back that paper I gave you."

I pulled it from my pocket and returned it to her, and Leo's eyes widened again as he took in this new development. He shot glances from Kate to me and back again in quick succession. What, he seemed to be wondering, is happening now? I was wondering precisely the same thing, but I tried to give the impression that this kind of occurrence was all in a day's work for a man of the world like Herbert Jaxon. The lady extracted her pen again and, unfolding the page, used her case as a makeshift desktop as she hastily scribbled another line on the paper. She then thought for a moment and added something else, which took much longer to write. Leo and I waited with bated breath as she carefully replaced the cap on her pen and put it back in her handbag before folding the paper twice as before and handing it back to me.

"I never, *ever* do this," she said with a smile, "but I've given you another number there. It's my flat. Try that one if I'm not at the other one. Goodbye." And with that she flashed both of us another beautiful smile, turned on her heels, and was gone. I replaced the folded piece of paper in my shirt pocket without opening it, and we both watched her in silence as she walked to the door of the baggage hall and disappeared in the direction of the taxi rank. Our four eyes followed her every step of the way.

"Well!" was all Leo could say when she had gone. I think Kate had quite taken his breath away.

"You owe me a tenner," I replied nonchalantly, and turned back towards the carousel to await my luggage.

As we collected our bags and made our way outside towards the taxis I deliberately did not mention our antiquarian friend again. I think Leo was expecting me to bring her up, and I am sure he would have raised the subject himself if I had let him, but all my discussion was about our trip to Rome. I did most of the talking, and Leo said very little. Finally, however, as we were about to say our goodbyes he could contain his curiosity no longer.

"How did you know about that book she was talking about?"

"*Which* book *who* was talking about?" I asked him.

"The antiques book Kate was talking about, of course! I was sure you were making it all up and that you were about to come a cropper."

"No, I think that *Dictionary* she mentioned really is the bible," I told him.

"How did you know that?"

"Patience told me."

"Very impressive that you even knew who'd written it," he said admiringly.

"Patience has got it," I replied. "I was looking at it only the other day."

He laughed. "And I thought you were making it all up."

"Would I do that?"

Leo's taxi had pulled up alongside us, and the driver was hauling his luggage into the boot. Then Leo spoke again.

"So.... Are you going to look her up, then?" he asked.

"Look *who* up?" I responded innocently.

"Kate, of course!" he snorted. "Who do you *think* I'm talking about, moron?"

I frowned, and wrinkled my nose, as though considering my options, then: "No, I don't think I will."

And, so saying, I removed the folded sheet from my shirt pocket and, without opening it, tore it into scores of little pieces and carelessly dropped the debris into a waste bin near the kerb. I think they have now removed all those bins for security reasons, but they were definitely still around in those days.

"Hang on, what are you doing?" screamed Leo in alarm. "I wanted to see what she'd written. It was obviously more than just a telephone number!" And for a moment I thought he was going to turn the bin upside down and rummage through the contents, like a vagrant searching for dog ends. But he stopped short of doing that, and just gazed wistfully at the bin.

"'Bye, Leo," I said, as he climbed into his taxi. "Don't forget that tenner you owe me."

We both laughed. It had been a good trip.

CHAPTER 33 : POTTYMOUTH

J'avais autr' fois une p'tite copine,
Qui m' racontait des blagues affreuses,
Vilaines, grossières, peu sibyllines,
Vulgaires, obscènes, et toutes honteuses.

En m'écrivant elle me passait
Souvent quelqu' chose de dégoûtant,
Pour me faire rire, si elle pouvait… !
Ce qu'elle me manque, en ce moment… !

CHAPTER 34 : THE BEGINNING

No more joy, no more pain,
No more sun, no more rain,
No more filling my face, no more slimmin';
No more lager, or shorts,
No more soft single malts,
No more wine, no more song, no more women.

> *Goodbye, Gudrun; cheerio, Chérie;*
> *Adiós, querida Isabela;*
> *Mush mush, Mimi; farewell, Fifi;*
> *Arrivederci, Bella.*

No more crimes to confess,
No more chasing success,
No more worries, or fears for tomorrow;
No more trying to impress,
No more failure or stress,
Nor more gut-wrenching doubt, no more sorrow.

> *Pip pip, Pierrette; night night, Nanette,*
> *Liselotte, Auf Wiedersehen;*
> *God speed, Gisette; bye bye, Babette,*
> *You'll none of you see me again.*

No more scoff, no more booze,
No more wooing the muse,
No more time, no more rhyme, no more resonance,
No more rant, no more curse,
No more desultory verse,
No more poetic licence, or assonance.

Take care, dear Claire; adeus, Estér;
Proshchay, dorogaya Katerina;
Ciao ciao, Chiara; ta-ra, Sara;
Hasta luego, dulce Catalina.

No more grief or despair
No more tugging my hair,
No more tight or impossible deadlines;
No more dreading my mail,
No more chasing my tail,
No more trying to keep out of the headlines.

Salut, Chantelle; merci, Marcelle;
Take care, ma chère Marie;
Farewell, Estelle; that's it, Noelle!
You'll not see more of me.

No more cold, no more heat
No more rain, no more sleet,
No more thunderstorms, wrapped up with macs on;
No more fug, no more fog,
No more gin, no more grog,
No more glee, no more me, no more Jaxon.

Adieu, Adèle; so long, Solange;
Und Tschüss, meine liebe Laure,
Vale, Avril; toodle-loo, Lulu;
You'll never see me no more.

No more time to reflect,
No more scorn, or respect,
No more lies, no more spin, no more spinning;
For it's time to slow down,
But you'll not see me frown,
Though it feels like the end is beginning...

www.ingramcontent.com/pod-product-compliance
Lightning Source LLC
Chambersburg PA
CBHW020817260626

47169CB00003B/707